Turning Point

Book Three
The Blackout Series

A novel by

Bobby Akart

Copyright Information

Other Works by Amazon Top 50 Author, Bobby Akart

The Doomsday Series

Apocalypse
Haven
Anarchy
Minutemen
Civil War

The Yellowstone Series

Hellfire
Inferno
Fallout
Survival

The Lone Star Series

Axis of Evil
Beyond Borders
Lines in the Sand
Texas Strong
Fifth Column
Suicide Six

The Pandemic Series

Beginnings
The Innocents
Level 6
Quietus

The Blackout Series

36 Hours

Zero Hour

Turning Point

Shiloh Ranch

Hornet's Nest

Devil's Homecoming

The Boston Brahmin Series

The Loyal Nine

Cyber Attack

Martial Law

False Flag

The Mechanics

Choose Freedom

Patriot's Farewell

Seeds of Liberty (Companion Guide)

The Prepping for Tomorrow Series

Cyber Warfare

EMP: Electromagnetic Pulse

Economic Collapse

DEDICATIONS

To the love of my life, thank you for making the sacrifices necessary
so I may pursue this dream.

To the *Princesses of the Palace*, my little marauders in training, you have
no idea how much happiness you bring to your mommy and me.

To my fellow preppers—never be ashamed of adopting
a preparedness lifestyle.

ACKNOWLEDGEMENTS

Writing a book that is both informative and entertaining requires a tremendous team effort. Writing is the easy part. For their efforts in making The Blackout Series a reality, I would like to thank Hristo Argirov Kovatliev for his incredible cover art, Pauline Nolet for making my important work reader-friendly, Stef Mcdaid for making this manuscript decipherable on so many formats, and The Team—whose advice, friendship and attention to detail is priceless.

The Blackout Series could not have been written without the tireless counsel and direction from those individuals who shall remain nameless at the Space Weather Prediction Center in Boulder, Colorado and at the Atacama Large Millimeter Array (ALMA) in Chile. Thank you for providing me a portal into your observations and data.

Lastly, a huge thank you to Dr. Tamitha Skov, a friend and social media icon, who is a research scientist at The Aerospace Corporation in Southern California. With her PHD in Geophysics and Space Plasma Physics, she has become a vital resource for amateur astronomers and aurora watchers around the world. Without her insight, The Blackout Series could not have been written. Visit her website at http://www.SpaceWeatherWoman.com.

Thank you!

ABOUT THE AUTHOR

Bobby Akart

Author Bobby Akart has been ranked by Amazon as #55 in its Top 100 list of most popular, bestselling authors. He has achieved recognition as the #1 bestselling Horror Author, #2 bestselling Science Fiction Author, #3 bestselling Religion & Spirituality Author, #6 bestselling Action & Adventure Author, and #7 bestselling Historical Author.

He has written over twenty-six international bestsellers, in nearly fifty fiction and nonfiction genres, including the chart-busting Yellowstone series, the reader-favorite Lone Star series, the critically acclaimed Boston Brahmin series, the bestselling Blackout series, the frighteningly realistic Pandemic series, his highly cited nonfiction Prepping for Tomorrow series, and his latest project—the Doomsday series, seen by many as the horrifying future of our nation if we can't find a way to come together.

His novel *Yellowstone: Fallout* reached the Top 50 on the Amazon bestsellers list and earned him two Kindle All-Star awards for most pages read in a month and most pages read as an author. The Yellowstone series vaulted him to the #1 best selling horror author on Amazon, and the #2 best selling science fiction author.

Bobby has provided his readers a diverse range of topics that are both informative and entertaining. His attention to detail and impeccable research have allowed him to capture the imaginations of his readers through his fictional works and bring them valuable knowledge through his nonfiction books.

About the Blackout Series

WHAT WOULD YOU DO
if a voice was screaming in your head - *GET READY* . . .
for a catastrophic event of epic proportions . . .
with no idea where to start . . .
or how, or when?

This is a true story, it just hasn't happened yet.

The characters depicted in The Blackout Series are fictional. The events, however, are based upon fact.

This is not the story of preppers with stockpiles of food, weapons, and a hidden bunker. This is the story of Colton Ryman, his stay-at-home wife, Madison, and their teenage daughter, Alex. In 36 Hours, the Ryman family and the rest of the world will be thrust into the darkness of a post-apocalyptic world.

A catastrophic solar flare, an EMP—a threat from above to America's soft underbelly below—is hurtling toward the Earth.

The Rymans have never heard of preppers and have no concept of what prepping entails. But they're learning, while they run out of time. Their faith will be tested, their freedom will be threatened, but their family will survive.

An EMP, naturally generated from our sun in the form of a solar flare, has happened before, and it will happen again, in only 36 Hours.

This is a story about how our sun, the planet's source of life, can also devastate our modern world. It's a story about panic, chaos, and the final straws that shattered an already thin veneer of civility. It is a warning to us all ...

never underestimate the depravity of man.

What would you do when the clock strikes zero?
Midnight is forever.

Note: This book does not contain strong language. It is intended to entertain and inform audiences of all ages, including teen and young adults. Although some scenes depict the realistic threat our nation faces from a devastating solar flare, and the societal collapse which will result in the aftermath, it does not contain graphic scenes typical of other books in the post-apocalyptic genre.

Previously in The Blackout Series

The Characters

The Rymans:

Colton – Colton Ryman was in his late thirties. Born and raised in Texas, he was a direct descendant of the Ryman family which built the world renowned Ryman Auditorium music hall in downtown Nashville. His family migrated to Texas from Tennessee with Davy Crockett in the 1800s. The Rymans became prominent in the oil and cattle business and as a result, Colton inherited his skill for negotiating. After college, he landed a position with United Talent, the top agency for the country-western music industry. He eventually became managing partner of the Nashville office. He is married to Madison and they have one child, Alex.

Madison – Madison, in her mid-thirties, is a devout Christian born and raised in Nashville. She grew up a debutante but quickly set her sights on a career in filmmaking. But one fateful day, she was introduced to Colton Ryman and the two fell in love. They had their only child, Alex, which prompted Madison to give up her career in favor of a life raising their daughter and loving her husband—two full time jobs.

Alex – Fifteen-year old Alex, the only child of Colton and Madison Ryman, was a sophomore at Davidson Academy. Despite inheriting her mother's beauty, Alex was not interested in the normal pursuits of teenaged girls which included becoming the prey of teenaged boys. Her interests were golf and science. It was during her favorite class, Astronomy, in which the teacher encouraged his students to become *solar sleuths* that Alex learned of the potential damage the sun could cause.

Supporting Characters of Importance:

Dr. Andrea Stanford – Director of the Joint Alma Observatory (JAO) Science Team at the Atacama Large Millimeter Array (ALMA) in the high-mountain desert of Peru. She is a graduate of the Harvard-Smithsonian Center for Astrophysics in Cambridge, Massachusetts. Her long-time assistant is Jose Cortez.

Members of the Harding Place Association (HPA) – In 36 Hours, book one of The Blackout Series, Shane Wren and his wife Christie Wren make their first appearance. They have two daughters and live just to the north of the Rymans. Shane Wren is the President of the HPA. In Zero Hour, two other members of the HPA are important players in the saga. Gene Andrews, a former director of compliance with the Internal Revenue Service, and Adam Holder, a former banker, make their appearance. Jimmy Holder, Adam's stepson, is a key player in the story as well.

Primary Scene Locations

Ryman Residence – located on Harding Place in Nashville. It is located approximately two miles east of historic Belle Meade Country Club and just to the west of Lynnwood Boulevard. It is a two-story brick home similar to the one depicted on the cover of Zero Hour.

Harding Place Neighborhood – The portion of the Harding Place Neighborhood depicted in The Blackout Series is bordered by Belle Meade Boulevard to the west, Abbot-Martin Road to the north,

Hillsboro Pike to the east, and Tyne Boulevard to the south. Generally, this area is southwest of downtown Nashville in an area known for its historic homes—Belle Meade.

ALMA – the largest telescope on the planet—the Atacama Large Millimeter Array, or ALMA. It's located at an altitude of over sixteen thousand feet in Atacama, Chile.

Previously in The Blackout Series

Book One: 36 HOURS

The Blackout Series begins thirty-six hours before a devastating coronal mass ejection strikes the Earth. Dr. Andrea Stanford and her team at ALMA identified the largest solar flare on record—an X-58—hurtling toward the Earth.

This solar flare was many times larger than the Carrington Event of 1859, widely considered the strongest solar event of modern times. Alarm bells were rung by Dr. Stanford and soon eyes at NASA and the Space Weather Prediction Center, SWPC, in Boulder, Colorado, were maintaining a close eye on Active Region 3222—AR3222.

AR3222 was a huge dark coronal hole which has formed on the solar disk. It had grown to encompass the entire northern hemisphere of the sun. As the story begins, AR3222 had only fired off a few minor solar flares, but as the hole in the sun rotated out of view, Dr. Stanford knew it would be back.

That same evening, Colton Ryman was in Dallas, Texas on business. One of his country music clients was being considered for a spot on the upcoming Super Bowl halftime show. Colton participated in a dog-and-pony show hosted by Jerry Jones, owner of the Dallas Cowboys which included tours of the Cowboys stadium and a concert in downtown Dallas.

Via news reports and text message conversations with Madison, Colton became aware of the unusual solar activity. At first, he brushed off the threat, but as time passed he became more and more convinced.

Madison and Alex were in Nashville going about their normal routine. Alex was the first to ring the alarm that the threat they faced from a major solar storm was real. She tried to raise the level of awareness in her mother, but Madison initially brushed it off as the overactive imagination of a teenage girl.

By noon the next day, all of the Rymans were beginning to see the signs of a potential catastrophic event. While the rest of the country went about its normal routine, Colton, Madison, and Alex made their decision—*Get Ready!*

The initial reports of the solar event were widely downplayed by the media. Even the President refused to raise the alarms for fear of frightening the public unnecessarily. But the Rymans were convinced the threat of a catastrophic solar flare was real, and the three sprang into action.

Colton, unable to catch a flight back to Nashville from Dallas, rented a Corvette and began to race home. Madison, using a valuable resource in the form of a book titled *EMP: Electromagnetic Pulse*, studied the *preppers checklist* included in the back of the book which enabled her to apply a common sense approach to getting prepared in a hurry.

Madison pulled Alex out of school and they immediately hit the Kroger grocery store for food and supplies. It was during this shopping expedition that news of the solar flare broke. Society began to collapse rapidly.

After forcing her way out of the grocery store parking lot using her Suburban's bumper to shove a KIA out of the way, Madison and Alex made their way to an ATM. The lines were long, but Madison waited until she could withdraw the cash. However, she let down her guard and was assaulted by a man who tried to steal her money. While the rest of the bank customers stood by and watched, Alex sprang into action with her trusty sand wedge. She beat the man repeatedly until he crawled away—saving her Mom, and the cash.

Meanwhile, Colton's race home—doing over one hundred miles

an hour in the rented Corvette—was almost red flagged when he was stopped by an Arkansas State Trooper. While he was waiting for the trooper's deliberation of what to do with Colton, a gunfight ensued between two vehicles in the southbound lane of the interstate. Having bigger fish to fry, the state trooper left Colton alone, who promptly hauled his cookies toward Memphis.

Madison, despite being battered and bruised, elected to make another *run* with Alex. They added to their newly acquired preps but encountered a group of three thugs on the way home. Frightened for their safety, Madison once again used her trusty Suburban bumper to pin one of the attackers against the car in front of her. This brought an abrupt end to the assault.

As Colton drove home, he listened to the scientific experts on the radio broadcasts talking about the potential impact an EMP would have on electronics and vehicles. He learned pre-1970 model cars were more likely to survive the massive pulse of energy associated with an EMP. This knowledge served him well when he stopped at a gas station in eastern Arkansas.

Colton was confronted by three men who took a liking to the shiny red Corvette. Not wanting any trouble, Colton made the deal of a lifetime. He traded the new Vette for a 1969 Jeep Wagoneer. The good ole boys thought they'd gotten the better of the city slicker, but it was they who were hoodooed. Colton took off with his new, old truck and sufficient gas to make it to the house.

Madison's and Alex's exciting day was not over. After dark, a knocking on the door startled them both. It was their friendly neighbors, Shane and Christie Wren. Madison attempted to keep her conversation with them brief, and her newly acquired preps hidden, but the simple mistake of turning on a light revealed her bruised face to the Wrens. The couple immediately suspected Colton of being a wife abuser despite Madison's explanation to the contrary.

After Madison sent the nosy Wrens on their way, she and Alex settled in to watch CNN's coverage of Times Square and the Countdown to Impact Clock. Thousands of people had gathered in New York to witness the apocalypse's arrival. The drama was high as the scene in Times Square was reminiscent of a New Year's Eve countdown without the revelry and deprivation.

The girls anxiously waited as they were unsure of Colton's whereabouts. Then they heard the kitchen door unlock, and Colton entered—reuniting the family. They began to move into the living room when Alex exclaimed, "Hey, look! The clock stopped at zero and nothing happened."

The CNN cameras panned the mass of humanity as a spontaneous eruption of joy and relief filled the packed crowd. The trio of news anchors couldn't contain themselves as they exchanged hugs and handshakes. Jubilation accompanied pandemonium in Times Square, the so-called Center of the Universe, as the bright neon lights from the McDonald's logo to the Bank of America sign continued their dazzling display. Then—

CRACKLE! SIZZLE! SNAP—SNAP—SNAP!

Darkness. Blackout. It was — *Zero Hour.*

Book Two: ZERO HOUR

The central theme of The Blackout Series is to provide the reader a glimpse into a post-apocalyptic world. Book One, 36 Hours took a non-prepping family through a fast-paced learning curve. In the period of a day, they had to accept the reality that a catastrophic event was headed their way and accept the threat as real. Once the decision to *GET READY* was made, then the Rymans scrambled around to prepare the best they could with limited time and resources.

Book two, Zero Hour, focuses on the post-apocalyptic world in the immediate hours and days following the collapse event.

Zero Hour picks up the Ryman's plight immediate after the collapse of the nation's power grid and critical infrastructure. First, they accept the challenges which lie ahead and then they apply common sense to establishing a plan.

First order of business was security. Colton recalls a story from his grandfather who reminds him to never underestimate the *depravity of man*. While they accept their fate, and attempt to set up a routine, there are neighbors who have other ideas about what's best for the Rymans.

Under the pretense of banding together to help the neighbors survive, the self-appointed leaders run a survival operation of their own. Using the intel willingly provided by unsuspecting residents, the three leaders of the Harding Place Association loot empty, unguarded homes and keep the contents for themselves.

When a rift forms between the Rymans and some of their neighbors, things turn ugly. There are confrontations and arguments. One of the leaders attempts a raid on the Ryman home at night with plans to steal the generator and some supplies. A gunfight ensues which wounds several of the attacking marauders. One of the three HPA leaders later dies due to lack of sufficient medical care.

There are also undercover operations including one involving Alex and a teenage boy. Alex recognizes the family's weakness in not having sufficient weapons to defend themselves and this boy's stepfather has an arsenal ripe for the pickins. Alex befriends the boy, procures weapons and ammunition, and everything is going smoothly until she finds the stepfather abusing her teenage friend. In self-defense, Alex shoots and kills the man, who happened to be one of the HPA leaders.

The death of the other two leaders has a noticeable effect on Shane Wren, the ringleader of the HPA who is the cause of the rift between the Rymans and the other neighbors. We're left in the dark as to whether the death of his cohorts resulted in the turnaround, or simply the knowledge that the Rymans are capable of defending themselves with deadly force, if necessary.

As a new threat emerges, the HPA and the Rymans come together to repel the vicious group of looters as they make their way deeper into the neighborhood. It was, however, too little too late for the majority of the neighbors in the HPA. Many, because they were out of food, and scared, opted to leave their homes and walk to one of the many FEMA camps and shelters established in the area.

The Rymans debated and considered their options. Madison

stepped up and set the tone for the next part of their journey by making a large meal and announcing that it was time to go. The family gathered their most valued belongings to help them survive. It was time to go.

Here are the final paragraphs from ZERO HOUR:

Madison shed several tears as she closed the kitchen door behind them. Colton opened the garage door, revealing the trophy received for the most cleverly negotiated deal in his career—the Jeep Wagoneer. This old truck was their lifeline now. It was their means to a new life far away from the post-apocalyptic madness of the big city.

Colton eased the truck out of the garage and worked his way down the driveway until he had to veer through the front yard to avoid the Suburban. As he wheeled his way around the landscaping, all three of them looked toward the west where fire danced above the tall oak trees. Reminiscent of a scene from *Gone with the Wind*, the magnificent antebellum homes of Belle Meade were in flames.

Madison began to sob now. "Will we ever be able to return?"

"What about our things?" asked Alex.

"Having somewhere to live is home. Having someone to love is family. All we need is right here in this front seat—our family." With that, Colton drove onto the road and led the Ryman family on a new adventure and to a new home.

They'd reached their turning point—a point of no return.

The saga continues in… TURNING POINT

EPIGRAPH

Anything that can go wrong, will go wrong and probably at the worst
possible moment.
~ Murphy's Law
*****

I am not a product of my circumstances. I am a product of my
decisions.
~ Stephen Covey
*****

It is in your moments of decision that your destiny is shaped.
~ Tony Robbins
*****

May your choices reflect your hopes, not your fears.
~ Nelson Mandela
*****

Ya' lives by da' sun and ya' dies by da' sun.
~ Old Man Percy
*****

Because you never know when the day before
is the day before.
Prepare for tomorrow!

Turning Point

Book Three
The Blackout Series

PROLOGUE

November 1976
McNairy County
Adamsville, Tennessee

Not many people knew the real story of Buford Pusser, the long-time sheriff of McNairy County in southwest Tennessee. Even fewer knew the story of his daughter, Betty Jean Pusser.

This is the tale of one of the darkest days in the history of the tiny town of Adamsville, Tennessee. The town, and all of McNairy County, had seen its share of crime and punishment—administered by a man some called a hero, and others called part of the problem, Sheriff Buford Pusser.

The city's worst day began quietly enough when a used-car salesman discovered one of his cars missing, an anonymous-looking black Ford. The theft was strange, because the boxy '62 Fairlane was about the least valuable car on the lot, so ordinary it seemed invisible—like an undercover police car or a getaway car.

It was the morning after Election Day in 1976 and the peanut farmer from Plains, Georgia, had defeated that Yankee Gerald Ford, much to the delight of democrats across the south. The car salesman's head was swollen from too much 'shine and celebration, but he managed to open his dealership on time nonetheless.

The day ended quietly, too, with a series of muted popping noises, much like the sound of a newspaper rolled loosely into a fly swatter and slapped on a tabletop. Few people heard those nine innocuous pops, and those who did never spoke of them. Yet those sounds would destroy a family, alter countless lives, transform a town, and

1

create a monster. Little would remain the same in Adamsville, Tennessee, or the surrounding counties, in their wake.

Between those two events that fateful day, Clarence and Wanda Tindle lived as they always had, taking no special precautions, exhibiting few outward fears. Adamsville was a quiet town now, following Sheriff Pusser's tumultuous time in office. Clarence went to the law office he'd occupied for nearly twenty years, where he'd served McNairy County as a criminal defense lawyer. Wanda, as always, worked much of the day on her one great obsession— exposing McNairy County's legendary corruption, in her capacity as the editor of the *Independent Appeal* newspaper. On the surface, they were above reproach and widely respected in McNairy County.

During that last day, Clarence also found time to walk his German shepherd, joke with his law partner—a staunch Republican—about the election, get his thick shock of graying hair cut at the local barbershop, and gas up his new Buick Estate station wagon in preparation for a trip Friday to Memphis.

Wanda spent the better part of that Wednesday shopping for clothes for her increasingly round five-foot frame, buying one of those newfangled microcassette voice recorders, and planning a United Daughters of the Confederacy convention she was chairing in December. At one time or another during the day, she told people she had contacted the FBI about the harassment they'd been receiving from a private investigator who'd been digging around in the death of the illustrious former sheriff since his accident in 1974.

Sheriff Pusser was a legend in McNairy County. As the sheriff of this small rural county along the Mississippi-Tennessee state line, he'd become a one-man army fighting gambling, prostitution, and moonshining operations, which had run rampant during his term in the late sixties.

His life gave rise to several books and movies, and one very large conspiracy. You see, Buford Pusser died in August 1974 after his Corvette careened off Highway 64 at a high rate of speed, and he was ejected from the car before it caught fire.

Moments later, his daughter, thirteen-year old Betty Jean, came upon the scene while on her way home with friends. She found her pa holding on to life, and with his last, dying breath Pusser whispered in Betty Jean's ear, "They finally got me."

Although an autopsy was not performed, the state trooper working the accident, who later became the sheriff of McNairy County, took a sample of Pusser's blood. The hospital released the results stating his blood-alcohol level was in excess of the legal limit. That state trooper was Clarence Tindle's younger brother.

As the rumors ran rampant throughout the county, accusations were leveled at Trooper Tindle. The Tindles fought back with a hit piece exposé on Pusser's dealings while sheriff, using Wanda Tindle's position at the newspaper as a bully pulpit.

Pusser's mother hired a small-time private detective, who quickly developed a working theory that the Tindles had the motive and opportunity to sabotage Pusser's Corvette, resulting in his death. Clarence was tied to the crime figures who Pusser tried to put away. Wanda relentlessly pursued corruption charges against Pusser. And former Trooper Tindle, the sole investigating officer, declared his intentions to become sheriff. The private detective was paid handsomely for this theory—to the tune of over one hundred thousand dollars.

The war of words continued for over a year, during which time the hostilities finally simmered down—until Election Day, 1976. Trooper Tindle became Sheriff Tindle on that date to much fanfare throughout the county.

This enraged Buford Pusser's mother, who was convinced the Tindle family was responsible for her beloved son's death. She exploded in anger in front of her orphaned grandchild, now fifteen-year-old Betty Jean, who took it to heart.

On that fateful Wednesday night, Clarence and his brother, newly elected Sheriff Tindle, shared a drink in celebration of his victory. Wanda went upstairs to draw a bath and soak her weary bones.

While Wanda relaxed with a glass of wine, she thought she heard a faint knock, but then the boys started laughing, so she disregarded it. It was probably several minutes later, nobody would know for sure, when she heard, faintly, the first popping noise.

She then thought she heard a vague sound of movement in the living room, followed by more *pop—pop—pop* sounds. There went Clarence again, swatting flies with a newspaper. They were both drunk and probably couldn't hit the broadside of a barn with their best effort. She laughed to herself as she finished off the glass, allowing the warm wine to soak into her bloodstream.

It was several minutes later when the bathroom door creaked open and frail, impish Betty Jean Pusser walked in, carrying a .22-caliber Ruger with a black tube silencer sitting fat and obscene on the lip of the barrel. Wanda attempted to cover her naked body with her arms as young Betty Jean pointed the gun at Wanda's head. Betty Jean wasn't shaking from nervousness. Her eyes were dark, lifeless. She only allowed herself a slight smile as she gently pulled the trigger.

Wanda Tindle never heard those last four quiet pops. Consciousness, dreams, and fear were all obliterated before the sound of that first silenced shot stopped echoing off the tiled bathroom walls.

And the day ended as quietly as it had begun, with a nondescript Ford Fairlane disappearing down a deserted street to a faraway rock quarry and its final resting place at the bottom of a murky lake.

Everyone's life contains a seminal event, a turning point that shapes who they are and how they interact with their fellow man. Betty Jean Pusser's turning point came that day at the age of fifteen.

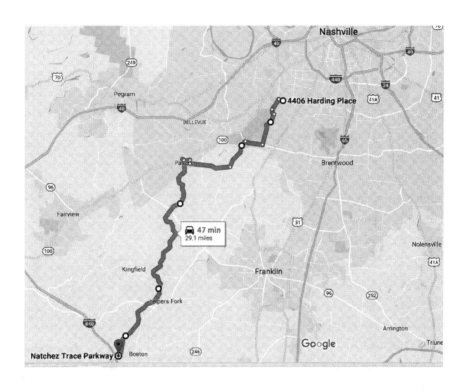

CHAPTER 1

DAY FIFTEEN
6:15 a.m., September 23
Chickering Road
Belle Meade, Tennessee

The Jeep Wagoneer's headlights caught a cardboard sign nailed to a telephone pole—a handwritten sign—*The End is Nigh*. Darkness swallowed it and Colton was left with the sense he was on the road to eternal damnation. His family had taken God's most precious gift, the lives of his fellow men. He wasn't sure if asking forgiveness would be sufficient to avoid the fate in store for them.

The high beams of the Wagoneer clawed the grass along the side of the tree-lined road, plowing a furrow through the dewy landscape so neon green in color it looked unnatural. The lawns of Belle Meade, which were once pristinely maintained by efficient gardeners, had become overgrown and unruly.

Everything Colton knew, or thought he knew, about Nashville and Belle Meade had been erased by the end of the world as he knew it. Two weeks after the devastating solar storm that caused the collapse of the nation's power grid, his family had gone from days filled with work, social activity for Madison, and school for Alex, to a post-apocalyptic dystopia where death had become commonplace.

The Rymans' worldly goods were crammed into the Wagoneer— memories of the past and the tools to survive an unknown future. Colton reached for Madison, who'd remained quiet since their departure from Harding Place. He gave his devoted wife's hand a squeeze to gain a reaction from her. Madison turned her face to look at Colton, managed a smile, and wiped away the last of her tears.

"Are we there yet?" She laughed, letting out some emotion. They'd been on the road for only fifteen minutes.

"I wish," chimed in Alex from the backseat. Alex had been remarkable as the world of a teenage girl crashed around her. She was very mature and logical for her age. Daily activities for Alex revolved around her school and love for golf, which had both been ripped from her life.

She'd also killed a man. After an initial period of shock, Alex had become incredibly at peace with the shooting, which was clearly in self-defense. Colton wasn't sure whether he should be proud of her acceptance of taking another man's life, or concerned that his daughter might be harboring feelings that needed to be released.

In any event, there wasn't time to explore the mind's inner workings. A lot had happened in the last fourteen days and he needed to focus on the task at hand—safety and a new home for the Ryman family.

Colton rolled down the window of the 1969 Jeep Wagoneer using the hand crank. Fresh morning air filled the truck as the sun slowly began to rise to their left. Another hand-printed sign came into view, this one riddled with bullet holes—REPENT. FINAL WARNING.

The Rymans had reached a turning point and were forced to make a decision. The neighborhood had collapsed around them. Fires were burning out of control to their west. Gangs were infiltrating the streets and homes to their north. Families were abandoning their residences in droves, seeking the utopian comfort and security of the FEMA camps established throughout metro Nashville. The Rymans, however, chose the potential safety of the countryside over a certain life of gunfights and scavenging in the city.

"It's really quiet, isn't it?" replied Colton, attempting to make small talk as they drove into a future where nothing was sure and anything was possible. "It's been a while since we took a road trip. Kinda nice without traffic."

Neither Madison nor Alex provided a response. Colton continued to ease his way along Chickering Drive as the Rymans headed southwest out of town—destination Shiloh, Tennessee, on the banks of the Tennessee River.

The concept of hitting the open road was almost romantic in its scope. We liked to think of everything going crazy in the world being left behind as we head out into the presumed serenity of the farms and desolate countryside.

But just like life, a winding road contained unknown perils and troubles. You never knew where the bend in the road might take you.

As he wheeled the Wagoneer through several abandoned cars, a downed tree limb blocked their progress. Colton approached slowly, scanning the sides of the road for indications of trouble. The sun was rising and the morning light allowed him better visibility. There didn't appear to be any other signs of life, so Colton slipped his gun into his paddle holster and shut off the engine.

"Wait here. I've got this," said Colton to Madison and Alex. He exited the Wagoneer and stopped, stunned by his surroundings.

This stretch of road was relatively uninhabited. Once outside the car, the silence was shattered. Surprised by the sheer magnitude of the sounds, Colton stood and listened.

A choir, a community, no, a nation of frogs sang from the darkness still engulfing the woods surrounding him. Wide and deep, the croaking critters chirped and chortled from every direction. Croaks both rough and guttural filled the air, buoyed by a mixture of higher tones from other frog species.

Big croaks. Big doggone frogs, Colton thought.

Then, in unison, as if directed by a conductor, they stopped.

Silence.

Intuitively, Colton immediately crouched down next to the Wagoneer. He considered leaving, but Colton hesitated to start the engine for fear of being discovered. He peered over the driver's door and held a finger up to his lips. He mouthed the words to his girls—
be quiet!

A crack of a tree branch and the sounds of heavy steps coming from the woods to his left caught his attention. He scrambled to the front of the Wagoneer, keeping the hood of the large truck between him and the potential threat.

Already? Really? We've only been gone half an hour!

Colton pulled his sidearm and released the safety. He trained the weapon on a clearing in the woods from which the sounds emanated. He was ready as the sounds grew louder. *Heavy steps. Not attempting to hide their approach.* Colton was sweating, slightly obstructing his vision.

Bursting into the clearing from the woods, two chestnut and black quarter horses trotted towards him and then abruptly turned down the shoulder of the road toward the south. Off they went in a slow gallop, rounding the curve as they took life's hurdles in stride.

Colton's body relaxed and he leaned toward the hood of the Wagoneer, intentionally bumping his head on the hood to restart his heart, which had momentarily taken a break during the stressful arrival of the horses.

He stood and began to laugh nervously. Madison rolled down the passenger window.

"Hey, Colt, do I need to get you another pair of pants?" she asked, laughing. Unconsciously, Colton reached behind and felt the seat of his jeans, just in case.

"Very funny," he replied. Colton holstered his weapon and efficiently removed the obstructing tree limb from their path.

As he did, Colton thought about the fact that any game plan always looked good on paper, but rarely did it turn out that way. Murphy's Law, *whoever Murphy was*, stated that anything that could go wrong, would go wrong and probably at the worst possible moment.

Colton reached for the handle of the truck just as the conductor struck up the Croakin' Frog Jamboree.

Big croaks.

CHAPTER 2

DAY FIFTEEN
6:45 a.m., September 23
Chickering Road
Forest Hills, Tennessee

Alex leaned against the door and stared out the window toward Harpeth Hills Golf Course on her right. She'd miss golf. Obviously, there wasn't room in the Wagoneer to bring her clubs. She wasn't even sure if there was a course near Shiloh—not that it mattered.

She'd miss some of her friends, although she'd learned early on in high school that many were conniving backstabbers. The night the lights went out, Daddy had warned her and Mom about the depravity of man. Alex didn't find the need to remind him that she'd learned about the depravity of her fellow teenagers years ago.

Alex would miss Disney movies and her favorite reality television shows—*Survivor* and *Big Brother*. She'd miss chocolate and Facebook. But that was about it. Seeing Harpeth Hills devoid of golfers was a grim reminder of a life without her favorite pastime.

As the sun rose, so did the walkers. No, not the walkers referenced on *The Walking Dead*, one of her favorite shows. Alex never could figure out why the characters on *The Walking Dead* didn't call them zombies. That was what they were, and that was also what these people looked like as well.

Her dad slowed as refugees began to appear on both sides of the road. Once in a while, one would approach the truck, holding out their hands, looking for some type of mercy. The family had talked about this the night before. There would come a time when they'd be able to help others in need. First, they had to protect themselves.

Alex studied the walkers. There appeared to be two types of post-apocalyptic refugees—those who were marginally prepared and those who were not. The way they were dressed was one indicator. The way their skin hung on their degenerating bodies was another. Those who'd gone longer without food appeared drunk, at times staggering toward the truck as they turned to look at the odd sight of a moving vehicle.

Alex began to imagine every man, woman, and child leaving Nashville, fleeing the apocalyptic carnage of the city in search of shelter, food, and safety. As the heavily populated areas of South Nashville succumbed to anarchy and out-of-control fires, neighbors became survivors, but eventually, survivors sought other options besides their homes and became refugees.

Either the sound of their approaching vehicle or the rising sun caused the refugees to awaken. Faces of women and children peered through the windows of abandoned cars. Whole families living in lean-to shelters made up of cardboard boxes and tarps poked their heads out to take a look. Harpeth Hills golf course had become a tent city.

"Are we refugees, Daddy?" asked Alex as she continued to wonder at the masses of people who'd congregated here.

"I guess so," he replied. "In a way, anyone who's displaced from their home due to a catastrophe would be considered a refugee."

"Like after Hurricane Katrina?" asked Alex.

"Exactly, although many of those people were more like evacuees because they had homes to return to," responded Madison. She turned to look at Alex in the backseat. "I think a refugee is someone that's permanently displaced."

"Like us," said Alex, who began to get emotional at the thought of never being able to return home.

"Not necessarily, Allie-Cat," said Colton. "We had to leave for our safety, just like the evacuees from Katrina. When they returned to their homes, they didn't know what to expect. We're in the same situation."

"That's right, honey," said Madison. "We'll return home one day when things return to normal."

Alex pondered this thought for a moment, doubting that her mother was certain of her own words. They'd taken the steps to leave the doors to the house unlocked but closed. Madison had left all of the cupboard doors open and the closet doors ajar. They had even created the appearance that their home had already been looted. With a little luck, any thieves would move through quickly, realize there was nothing of survival value, and go on to the next home. Her daddy thought this would increase their chances of having something to return to if their home wasn't consumed by the fires.

"Honey, most people are creatures of habit," Madison continued. "They'll only move if something forces them to. Some people, like these folks on the side of the road, left before us. They didn't have any place to go. They just needed to get away from what was happening all around them."

Alex continued to stare at the makeshift tent city as Colton continued the conversation. "It's like your mom said, humans are habitual. We're also creatures of comfort. In most emergencies, people will not want to leave their homes. Kinda like us. Something has to dislodge them, and when it does, it may be too late.

"When the power grid went down and the water stopped working, a lot of folks, even our neighbors, thought the government would get things up and running again. They didn't accept reality right away and used up their resources like food and water."

"I know," said Alex. "Jimmy Holder told me that some of the neighbors were drinking water out of their water heaters and then their toilets. It was gross."

"They were desperate," said Colton. "When those options ran out, they left the city, looking for water, food, shelter and safety."

"Why did they stop here, at a golf course?" asked Alex.

Colton wheeled the Wagoneer through several abandoned cars and turned right onto Old Hickory Boulevard. "We're fortunate to have transportation," he replied. "All of these people got the heck out of Dodge, searching for places to hunt and fish. They'll stay here until something dislodges them again, and then they'll strike out for points farther away from the city."

"They seem to be getting along," observed Alex. The sun was in full view and the day was under way for the refugees. Many stood talking to one another, pointing at the Wagoneer as it eased down the road.

Colton continued. "As time progresses and things get more dangerous, they'll begin to weigh their options. Just like at home, these folks will band together and take the approach that there is strength in numbers."

"Will they become marauders too?"

"Maybe," said Madison. "As we've learned, desperate people will do desperate things. People who've walked this far will realize there aren't enough fish in the pond around here, or notice that it's getting too crowded and dangerous. They'll begin to think the grass is greener somewhere else, causing them to migrate towards the farms or towards a river."

"Unfortunately, they might loot along the way," added Colton. "As this group of refugees walks out of the metropolitan area toward the farms and small towns, they'll branch off the main highway onto small side roads or gravel driveways. Mile after mile after mile, they'll approach the scattered houses and barns off in the distance, searching for food, water, and shelter. They might find them empty or heavily defended. The owners might say *stop*, or *I'll shoot*. Others will simply shoot and ask questions later. That's the risk you run in wandering aimlessly into the countryside."

Alex sat quietly, staring at the sullen faces and starving children as they drove past. The sun was rising and, with it, her apprehension. The vague picture she'd conjured up in her mind last night of farms full of crops and fields teeming with cattle had been replaced with thoughts of locust-like refugees spreading far and wide, creating a bleak and plundered world ravaged by the hungry walkers—dotted with burned-down homes and broken-down vehicles.

She quietly said a prayer thanking God for her parents, and their 1969 Jeep Wagoneer, before she drifted off to sleep.

CHAPTER 3

DAY FIFTEEN
7:15 a.m., September 23
Old Hickory Boulevard
Bellevue, Tennessee

Madison continued to study the map as they cleared the last cluster of homes along Old Hickory Boulevard. They'd need to take a left up ahead on Vaughn Road, which provided them a direct shot to the Natchez Trace Parkway.

When she'd plotted their route toward Shiloh over the past couple of days, she decided on the Natchez Trace Parkway because it was a relatively direct route and they wouldn't encounter many small towns. What she didn't envision were the temporary towns springing up outside the city. Seeing the number of refugees camped out on the golf course surprised her.

The false alarm caused by the horses and the appearance of the refugees were cause for her to reconsider if this was the right thing to do. Madison knew there would be challenges to face, but the rising sun shed light on the realities of what the Rymans might face along the way.

Madison recalled the words written in the prepping books she'd purchased just before the solar storm hit. *Bugging out* was the terminology used by the preppers. At the time she was reading about the concept, Madison was unaware that Colton had successfully traded a shiny new, but now worthless, Corvette for this partially rusted out hunk of junk.

During those thirty-six hours, Madison first had to come to grips with the threat their family faced if the predictions and possibilities were true. Admittedly, the thought of having to bug out hadn't crossed her mind. Any plan involving leaving their home was murky and, as a result, shoved to the rear of the preparedness planning line. The way she looked at it, the notion of bugging out was simple—grab your stuff and go.

Bugging out was considered a last resort for Madison. Like so many others, she never imagined the threats would escalate to the point her family would be forced out of their home. The rose-colored glasses got ripped away from so many people at once. Tensions were bound to boil over. Somehow, their beautiful city and their once quiet neighborhood had become a field of battle. Decades of pressure and stress had pushed ordinary Americans to the brink, and all it took was one catastrophic event to push them over the edge. Now in hindsight, Madison was amazed her family had lasted in their home as long as they did.

As Colton slowly approached the intersection of Vaughan Road, Madison realized her biggest regret was not having a specific place to bug out to. Jake Allen's ranch in Shiloh seemed like the perfect location, but nobody knew they were coming. Plus, the Rymans only assumed they'd be welcomed in.

Madison leaned forward to focus her view on the upcoming intersection. Ahead were numerous tents set up within the baseball fields, and more than a dozen stalled vehicles along the road slowed their progress. Edwin Warner Park had become a temporary town of its own.

"Turn left here, honey," said Madison. The intersection appeared to be blocked ahead, but Colton improvised by navigating the Wagoneer onto the shoulder and past the grassy baseball diamonds of Heriges Memorial Field.

After the solar storm, their world got much smaller. Their boundaries were limited by the distance they could walk or ride a bike. While the Wagoneer expanded their world, the Rymans quickly learned that the roads were not passable in many instances, like this one.

Madison's mind wandered back to the bug-out process. Madison had learned that the art of prepping was not an exact science. For one thing, predicting when and where a catastrophic event would occur was anyone's guess. From what she'd read in the EMP book, solar storms were more predictable than something like a nuclear-EMP attack by North Korea, Iran, or one of the other countries that didn't like the United States very much.

Timing a bug-out, she determined, was critical to its success. In a perfect world, they'd have a destination, Colton would've been home, and the family would've left hours before the solar storm hit. If nothing happened, then they had a night or two away from home as a family getaway. They could always go back after the threat passed.

If you bugged out too late, which she now realized they had, you'd face masses of people with the same idea. The whole concept of sheltering-in-place might make sense in a bad storm, but in a catastrophic event like this once-in-a-lifetime solar storm, Madison realized that societal collapse occurred much faster than anyone could imagine. She'd seen the signs before, and after, the power grid went down.

The Wagoneer bounced through the field as Colton ran through ruts in the dirt and hopped over potholes in the ground. This jarred Alex, who let out a grumble, as most teenagers awoken from their slumber might do. Colton continued through the fields, looking for an entry point back onto the road.

"Maddie, I don't like the looks of this," said Colton as several people started toward them. "We're attracting too much attention." Having one of the few operating vehicles in town was another reason to bug out before everything collapsed, thought Madison.

"What if we turn around and find another way?" asked Madison, but as she glanced in the side-view mirror, she answered her own question. People were gathered behind them and walking behind the truck. Soon, they would be surrounded.

They began to hear shouts as suddenly people began running toward them from the parked cars on Vaughn Road. Two men had reached their tailgate and began to tug at the tarp that covered the extra gasoline and the generator.

"Colton, we've got to do something," urged Madison. Colton pressed the gas and swerved to the left, abandoning the attempt to regain access to the road, instead heading towards the open fields surrounding the baseball diamonds.

"I'm gonna try to make it to the asphalt driveway that circles around the pavilions over there," said Colton as the rear end of the Wagoneer swayed in the dust, kicking up dirt and gravel on their pursuers. The truck hit the asphalt road at an angle, causing it to catch and sway back and forth. But Colton gained the much-needed traction to speed up and put distance between them and the chasing mob of at least three dozen people.

Alex, fully awake again, shouted, "There, Daddy, to the left of those power poles. There's an opening by those big rocks."

Colton picked up speed and burst onto the field again, bouncing the truck up and down until he finally slowed his pace. Madison glanced back and saw that the pursuers had given up the chase.

"We're good, Colton," she said, bracing her hands against the dashboard. "You can slow down now."

Colton reacted slowly to her suggestion, his hands gripping the wheel to the point his knuckles were white.

Madison reached over and rubbed his shoulder. "Honey, we're good."

Colton let the air out of his lungs and shook his head, acknowledging that the threat was over. He found his way through the large rocks and onto Vaughn Road.

"Colt, do you wanna pull over somewhere and catch your breath? Maybe grab a bottle of water?" asked Madison. She could tell Colton was shaken by the incident.

"Nah, but thanks, guys," he replied. "Let's keep rollin'. Somehow, I think the farther we get away from the city, the better it'll be."

Madison leaned over and kissed her husband on the cheek. She rubbed his neck and shoulders for a while to help him release some tension and to remind him that she loved him. She studied the face of the man she'd loved for so many years.

They were more at risk than she realized. Their operating vehicle stocked full of food and supplies was one of the most prized possessions on earth right now. People would stop at nothing to take away these things. Madison was prepared to make the tough choices. She vowed that she would protect, and defend, the most prized possession in her mind—her family—whatever it took.

CHAPTER 4

DAY FIFTEEN
7:35 a.m., September 23
Loveless Motel and Café
Highway 100
Bellevue, Tennessee

Colton carefully approached the intersection with Highway 100. The NHC Assisted Living Center to their right had been looted. He took a double take to confirm there were two dead bodies decomposing in their hospital gowns, lying facedown at a side entrance. He immediately began to speak, attempting to draw the girls' attention away from the morbid sight like a good dad would do when traveling on the interstate to avoid their laying eyes on a dead critter in the road.

"We'll take a left here at the church and it should be a quarter mile or so past the Loveless Café," said Colton. He looked both ways out of habit and turned to the west and the entrance to the Natchez Trace Parkway. They passed a family of four walking down the road, pushing shopping carts with all of their worldly belongings.

Colton slowed the truck as the Loveless Café came into view. For nearly seventy years, the Loveless Motel and Café had been a fixture in southwest Nashville, known for its refuge as a cozy home away from home and its Southern comfort food.

In the 1950s, Highway 100 was the primary route between Nashville and Memphis two hundred miles to the west. Lon and Annie Loveless began a small business serving the travelers meals through the front door of their home, usually at picnic tables adorned with red-and-white tablecloths in their front yard.

As their business grew, the couple elected to expand their private home into the Loveless Motel and Café. Lon ran the motel and was responsible for smoking the meats while Annie whipped up batches of her homemade preserves and made-from-scratch biscuits.

Over time, the Loveless Café became world famous and had been featured on *The Today Show*, *Martha Stewart*, and *The Ellen DeGeneres Show*. For seventy years, it remained true to its origins, serving travelers across the rural South who enjoyed the backroads leading to hidden treasures as opposed to the interstates, which zipped them from city to city.

It was the sight of the current visitors to the Loveless Café that forced Colton to bring the Wagoneer to an abrupt stop, throwing Alex forward in her seat, and she slammed into the back of Madison's.

"Daddy!" she immediately protested.

"Sorry, look," he said. Colton pulled off the shoulder under a canopy of oak trees and shut off the motor. Thus far, they hadn't been noticed.

The parking lot in front of the Loveless Café was filled with military vehicles and construction trucks. A dozen uniformed National Guardsmen were huddled under a tent, drinking coffee.

Beyond the motel, several soldiers were setting up pylons at the exit off the Natchez Trace Parkway. Farther down, a military Humvee was parked sideways across the road, blocking access. The entrance to the Natchez Trace was not blocked, but Colton would have to drive past the entire contingent to get there. He recalled the provisions of the martial law order signed by the President, which provided for the confiscation of operating vehicles and all weapons.

"Should we go for it?" asked Madison. "We're not bothering anyone. We could just explain that—"

"I don't trust this at all, Maddie," replied Colton, cutting her off in mid-sentence. "It's a different world now. Although this looks like an official military exercise, it could be designed to entrap people like us. It's not worth the risk."

Madison began to unfold the map as Colton continued to study the activity in the parking area. The majority of the soldiers appeared to be preoccupied, focused more on their coffee and playful banter than what was going on around them. The Wagoneer was not well hidden and could have easily been spotted if they were paying attention.

Colton leaned over to study the map with Madison as they sought an alternative entrance to the Natchez Trace when someone tapped on the rear passenger window. Alex shrieked and Colton immediately fumbled for his weapon. His clumsy hands tried to find the grip and knocked it onto the floorboard of the Wagoneer. As he frantically reached down, another knock came, this time at his window.

"Hey, mister," said a young boy's voice. "Y'all gonna get busted by them po-pos."

Colton looked up into the young boy's face with his nose just inches from the truck's window. He was maybe ten or eleven years old and wore a Tennessee Titans jersey bearing the number 29 of star running back DeMarco Murray. He didn't see a weapon, or anyone else, so he slowly opened the window with his left hand while he finally found his gun with his right.

"How's it goin'?" asked Colton harmlessly.

"All right, I guess," said the boy matter-of-factly. "You know, if they was payin' attention, they'd be on you like white on rice."

Colton turned his attention to the National Guard personnel, who were beginning to make their way out of the tent and were now gathering around their vehicles. He needed to make a decision. He returned his attention to the young boy.

"We need to get on the Natchez Trace and head south, but it looks like they're gonna block the road."

"Yup, they is," said the boy. "They come in last night and took over the Loveless. I went over there to get sumptin' to eat, and they run me off. I heard 'em say they was gonna close off the roads."

Colton's mind raced. If they were gonna drive past the military in full view, they needed to do so now before they loaded up into their vehicles. There wasn't another entrance to the Natchez Trace for many miles and it would require them to backtrack another fifteen miles or so.

The youngster interrupted his thoughts. "You can go through our yard if'n you want."

"What, what do you mean?" asked Colton.

"Well, my pa had a trail cut through dem woods which comes out on the Trace. He used it for his four-wheeler when he went fishin' over there at Haselton's pond. Your truck will fit."

Colton studied the activity at the Loveless one last time. It was worth a try.

"Are you sure your father won't mind?" asked Colton.

The boy became morose and lowered his head. There was a moment of awkward silence before he spoke again.

"He dead. They kilt him a week ago at the Loveless. He worked there as a cook and was watching over things for the owners when a bunch of white men come and kilt him. There wasn't nuthin' to steal, but they kilt him anyway."

Colton didn't know what to say as he became overcome with emotion. Alex began to sniffle, as did Madison. This young man had lost his father barely a week ago to a senseless murder. Yet, here he was willing to help a *white man* protect his family from possible arrest.

"What's your name, young man?" asked Colton.

"LaRon."

"Are you alone, LaRon?"

"Nah, I've got my ma. We're makin' out okay 'cause Pa brung da food over to our place. I dug holes and hid it on the property so as nobody could find it. Plus, I still walk over to the pond and fish."

"Colton," interrupted Madison as she regained her composure, "we've got to do something."

Colton looked up and saw the olive drab green fork trucks begin to unload barriers from the flatbeds. He reached over his shoulder and pulled the door lock up.

"Hop in, LaRon, and lead the way."

Colton started the Wagoneer, which couldn't be heard over the roar of the diesel motors at the Loveless Café. He slowly backed up about a hundred yards, where LaRon instructed him to turn into a gravel driveway leading into the trees across the road. They wound their way through the woods until they entered a clearing.

A white craftsman-style home with a black metal roof stood in front of a barn and a couple of small storage buildings. Several raised planter beds full of vegetables were off to the left next to a well with a hand-pump. Colton guessed the home had been built in the twenties or thirties.

As the Wagoneer approached the home, LaRon's mother emerged with two young girls behind her white skirt. She pointed a double-barreled shotgun at the truck. LaRon immediately jumped out of the truck and waved his arms.

"Whatcha doin', boy?" shouted LaRon's mother as she lowered the shotgun, much to Colton's delight. He had his weapon ready to return fire but dreaded the prospect of a gunfight with the widow.

"Ma, I'm just givin' dem directions to the Trace. Dey gonna cut through da woods."

"Then go on now," she shouted. "We don't want dem soldiers up here gittin' in our bidness. Go on!" She swung the barrel of the shotgun to the right side of the house, where Colton could see the entrance to the trail.

"Okay," shouted Colton through his window. "We're leavin' now. Thank you!"

LaRon stood there with his thumbs tucked in his jeans pockets. He managed a smile and waved to Colton.

Colton put the truck in drive and started to pull away. He glanced in the rearview mirror. Alex was in the backseat, frantically digging around in the rear of the Wagoneer. She apparently found what she was looking for.

"Daddy, stop, wait!" she shouted. Before Colton could come to a complete stop, she opened the rear door and bounded out and around the Jeep.

Alex walked toward LaRon, and his mother instinctively raised her shotgun in Alex's direction.

"Alex, what are you doin'?" asked Colton.

Alex approached Laron and asked, "Do you like comic books?"

"Sure do!"

"Do you like *The Walking Dead*?"

"I love zombie ones!"

Alex gave LaRon the comic book given to her by Jimmy Holder. It was the one-hundredth issue of *The Walking Dead* series.

Tears of joy began to roll down LaRon's face. Alex leaned down and gave the young boy a hug. He might now be the man of the house, but inside, he was still just a boy.

CHAPTER 5

DAY FIFTEEN
10:00 a.m., September 23
Natchez Trace Parkway
Leiper's Fork, Tennessee

The Natchez Trace Parkway was a two-lane road running from Nashville to Natchez, Mississippi, an historic town located on the Mississippi River. This four-hundred-forty-mile highway, which locals referred to as the Trace, was traveled for hundreds of years by Indians who followed the early footpaths created by the foraging of bison, deer, and other large game.

When the first European explorers came to the region, led by Hernando de Soto, the path was well worn and later became a wilderness road followed by pioneers and settlers heading west out of Tennessee and Kentucky. Eventually, at the behest of a group of ladies' garden clubs in the South, the Natchez Trace became a part of the National Park Service in the late thirties.

The Trace followed and maintained the spectacular scenery along its route, including the preservation of the swamps and forests, by limiting access to only a handful of access points along the entire parkway.

Over the years, tales of buried treasure, ghost stories, outlaws, and witches became as much a part of the Trace as the road itself. Stories of the demise of the *Kentucks*, entrepreneurs who traveled to and from Natchez to sell their goods, at the hands of outlaws and Indians were commonplace. Then the brutal battles between the *rebs* and the *yanks* during the Civil War were remembered as the Union Army was bent on bringing the South to heel.

The Rymans were feeling better after hitting the open road. This morning, no ghosts of the Trace's violent past invaded their thoughts, and the encounters of the morning were already a distant memory. Mile after mile, the road dipped and turned gracefully through rich fields, grassy meadows, and trees whose leaves were beginning to turn into their autumns shades.

And there was no traffic. Not a single car coming or going. The dreamlike quality of being completely alone in the world was only interrupted on one occasion when a lone farmer, sitting atop a Tennessee Walking Horse, was seen herding cattle off in the distance.

"This is more like it, don't you agree, guys?" asked Colton.

The wind blew through Madison's hair and she stuck her head out slightly to catch a deep breath of fresh air. She loved this. In fact, she wondered why they couldn't find a place here to find a spot, plant roots, and make a new life.

Alex must've been thinking the same thing. "Daddy, maybe we could find a farmer around here to take us in. You know, sleep in the barn or something until things settle down and we can go home?"

Colton, who was maintaining a steady fifty miles an hour, wheeled the Wagoneer through a set of curves. As they entered a wooded area, he replied, "It does look inviting, honey, but we don't know any of these folks. What if we take a chance and drive up someone's driveway and find out they're dangerous? We could lose everything, including each other."

The open fields were suddenly gone and Colton continued to wind his way through the woods. The two-lane highway seemed tight as the shoulder of the road gave way to a steep embankment on both sides with no guardrail.

"I know that, Daddy, but we have to trust someone," replied Alex.

Colton had unconsciously picked up speed during his conversation and was now going over sixty when he rounded a bend in the road.

"Whoa!" he exclaimed as he let off the gas and shoved on the brake pedal. He immediately checked his mirrors and looked for an option to pull off the road. There wasn't one.

The three cyclists toting heavy backpacks and bedrolls apparently were caught off guard as well. One rider overreacted and pulled over to the shoulder, losing his balance, which caused him and his now destroyed bicycle to tumble down the hill toward the overgrown brush. The other cyclists stopped to assist their friend, but hurled curse words and shook their fists at Colton.

"Sorry," yelled Madison as Colton continued to drive past them.

"Should we stop to help them?" asked Alex.

"I didn't run him off the road," replied Colton. "Again, it's like I was saying. We can't take the risk. They'll figure it out."

The family drove in silence for several minutes as the road opened up into farmland again. As they approached an intersection that included an exit to Leiper's Fork, Madison saw something that was straight out of the eighteen hundreds.

"Look, to the right," she exclaimed. "Slow down for a minute, Colt."

Colton slowed the truck at the overpass and the Rymans watched as four sets of horses and carriages came down Highway 46 toward Leiper's Fork.

"Hey, their wagons are loaded with baskets of vegetables," said Madison.

"Another one is holding piglets!"

Colton came to a full stop at the overpass and the Rymans exited the Wagoneer to take in the spectacle. Colton whispered into Madison's ear, "Help me keep an eye out for those bicyclers, okay."

Madison nodded and turned her attention back to the wagon train.

"Hey," shouted Alex to a teenage boy in overalls who led the first wagon with another, younger boy. "Where y'all goin'?"

As the wagon made its way through the underpass, the younger boy hollered, "Ya sure are purdy!"

Alex blushed and smiled at the boy, whose brother immediately gave him a playful shove. He then responded to Alex's question. "There's a market in Leiper's Fork. We're takin' this stuff to sell or trade."

Alex leaned over the guardrail as the first wagon passed beneath them. The next buckboard contained the boys' parents.

"Y'all could get a pretty penny for that truck," said the father. "In fact, I'll trade you my whole last wagon full of pigs fer it. You can have the wagon too and the horses. I tell you what else, you can have them young'uns drivin' it also. But you gotta feed 'em!"

The man started roaring in laughter, but the woman on the seat next to him didn't seem to think it was as funny. She grabbed his green John Deere cap off his head and began to swat him with it.

"You lay off them young'uns," she hollered. "Or I'll whoop ya!" That last part echoed from underneath the bridge as the horses continued to clomp their way to Leiper's Fork.

"There you go, Alex," started Colton. "I could make a deal with Farmer Bob there, trade for the pigs and the wagon and the young'uns. Who knows? I could marry you off to the boy and get a dowry or somethin'."

"Daddy!"

"Colton Ryman! You stop that, or I'll whoop ya," shouted Madison as she chased Colton around the truck.

CHAPTER 6

DAY FIFTEEN
10:55 a.m., September 23
Natchez Trace Parkway at I-840
Near Boston, Tennessee

Alex's parents were still teasing her about getting married off to Farmer Bob's oldest son. He was cute, but it looked like he was missing a front tooth. Alex was sure she'd seen him spit out his tobacco juice—a definite deal breaker.

For several minutes, she had to endure a series of bad jokes.

"What do you get if you cross an angry sheep and a moody cow? An animal that's in a baaaaaaaad mooooooooood!" If the opening salvo wasn't bad enough, then the jokes devolved into pure silliness.

"You may be a farmer if—your dog rides in the truck more than your wife!"

"You may be a farmer if—you know cow patties aren't made of beef!"

"You may be a farmer if—your No Trespassing sign reads *beware of wife!*"

Guffaw, guffaw.

Alex had had enough, so she sought out her iPhone, which she'd charged the day before. *Time for some music.* She opted for some of Jake Allen's classics. She had to get used to it 'cause she was sure he and her daddy would find plenty of opportunities to sing together.

As the music filled her headphones, her mind wandered to that two-week vacation at Shiloh Ranch, as the Allens called it. She really did have a good time fishing and eating down-home Southern-style cooking. Although her interaction with then thirteen-year-old Chase was awkward at times, she remembered that they were inseparable. They'd spent their days walking through the woods or along the banks of the Tennessee River. Sometimes they'd fish or ride their four-wheelers through the many trails that traversed the perimeter of the Shiloh National Military Park where the Allens' property was located.

The evenings were fun too. Every night involved a campfire, singing, and trading stories. The Allens' caretaker, Stubby Crump, was from McNairy County, as was his wife, Bessie. They'd lived their entire life in southwest Tennessee. Stubby's military career and short-lived minor league baseball stint made for some interesting conversation. Alex remembered Stubby as being quick with the one-liner jokes, but she was especially fond of Bessie's cooking. When they made it to Shiloh Ranch, Alex was sure the Crumps would keep them well fed, despite the circumstances.

It was several years ago when Alex was a preteen and didn't fully understand the workings of the male species. She'd changed a lot since Chase tried to impress her with teenage boy machismo and the ability to dip tobacco. He was always clowning around, doing his best to garner her undivided attention. But it wasn't until he took his shirt off to show Alex how to use the rope swing over the lake that she realized he was kinda cute. Alex closed her eyes and wondered if he'd grown up much now that he was seventeen.

Between the music and the steady rumble of the old truck on the highway, Alex began to drift off to sleep. She'd stayed up all night, watching over the house, before they'd pulled out early that morning. In just five hours, they'd been through more drama than the average family saw in a year. It was time for a break from the excitement, and a nap.

*****

"Colton!" yelled Madison.

"I saw them," he replied as he pressed the gas pedal down to pick up speed, at the same time glancing back and forth between his rearview mirrors. "They came out of that gravel road like a bat out of—"

"They're gaining on us!" interrupted Madison. "They're gonna catch up!"

Colton mashed the gas now, pushing the upper limits of the Wagoneer to seventy miles an hour and the point where the wheels started to shake. This change of speed and the rattling of the truck's chassis caused Alex to wake up.

"What's goin' on?" asked a sleepy Alex. She stretched her arms and worked the kinks out of her neck.

"We're being followed," said Colton.

"More like being chased," added Madison.

Colton wound his way through the narrow stretch of woods and a series of S-curves, which caused them to sway back and forth. There were no exits and no places to hide. He pressed forward as he gripped the wheel, intent on outrunning the chase vehicle, which appeared to be an old white pickup truck.

Their pursuers were not giving up, but they weren't gaining either.

"Madison, how far is it to the next side road, exit—anything?"

Madison fumbled with the map and found their location. "Colton, you know, there aren't many ways to get on here. There's a gravel driveway here and there, like the one those guys shot out of. But nothing else for miles. The eight-forty loop is up ahead, but there doesn't appear to be an entrance or exit ramp."

Colton sped past two teen boys walking down the road, who waved their arms and ran after them for several yards before giving up. He continued to check his mirrors, quietly hoping the chasers would relent. No such luck.

"Did you see how many passengers?" asked Colton.

"Two men in the front seat," replied Madison. "I think there might be a dog in the bed of the truck."

Colton raced around the curve, throwing Alex against the left-side passenger door.

"Whoa!"

"Sorry, honey," replied Colton. "Alex, dig out the AR-15. Can you shoot at them if you hang out the window?"

"I-I think so," she replied, suddenly waking up in a hurry. She pulled the rifle out from under some pillows behind her seat. "I can't promise that I'll hit anything."

"Colton, let me do that," protested Madison. "Why would you want Alex to shoot at those men?"

Colton began to slow the truck and tapped on the front window, pointing ahead towards the Interstate 840 overpass.

"Because you're gonna have to shoot at them. We're trapped!"

CHAPTER 7

DAY FIFTEEN
11:05 a.m., September 23
Natchez Trace Parkway at I-840
Near Boston, Tennessee

"Daddy," shrieked Alex, "they're coming!"

Colton brought the truck to a stop and leaned across Madison to get a better look. The white pickup slowed to a crawl and then stopped a quarter mile away, apparently surprised by their prey's sudden change in behavior. Colton grabbed the AR-15 and exited the truck. He pulled the charging handle and steadied his nerves.

"Listen to me," started Colton, leaning in through the door. "I think this is an ambush. There are people crouched below the guardrail at the overpass up ahead. The car below it is parked at an angle. There may be more people waiting for us behind it, or they may all be up on the bridge."

"What're you gonna do?" asked Madison.

"There are less people behind us than in front of us," replied Colton. "I'm gonna try to scare these guys off, and we'll backtrack. There has to be a way around this overpass."

"What if they don't *scare off*, Daddy?"

"Then we'll shoot our way through," replied Colton. "Now, have your guns ready and stay down. Madison, the overpass will be out of your gun's range. Don't waste ammo if they begin shooting. Just stay down, okay?"

"Got it," she replied. "I love you."

"I love you too," he replied.

The angle at which Colton had parked the truck obstructed the view of the driver's side of the Wagoneer from both the pursuing pickup truck and the people manning the overpass. He had an element of surprise that the attackers wouldn't expect. There was no time for negotiation. With TEOTWAWKI came a life without rule of law. Colton had learned that the only way to establish rules in a threatening situation was with deadly force.

Colton was comfortable using the AR-15. It had served him well when battling the COBRA marauders last week. He'd never been a gun owner, much less a gun guru. In that short battle that day, he'd learned the AR-15 was accurate, easy to use, and provided sufficient firepower to get the job done.

Colton peered around the back of the Wagoneer. The pickup was clearly in range. His plan was to throw some rounds in their direction with the hope they'd turn and run. He gave the overpass one more glance. Growing impatient with their prey, the occupants of the bridge popped their heads up to observe the Wagoneer. Despite the distance, Colton could make out five silhouettes, including possibly two children. There was no activity in the car below. Either way, he didn't like the numbers.

Colton began to second-guess whether the people on the bridge were lying in wait after all. They might be onlookers, just like his family was at the overpass near Leiper's Fork. *Did he have it all wrong? Was this an ambush or a simple misunderstanding?*

The blast of birdshot that rained down on top of the Wagoneer's roof provided him his answer. One of the men had exited the pickup and was shooting at them with his shotgun. However, at this distance, the birdshot had little effect other than to provide Colton a reminder that these jerks meant business.

He answered their first shot with a volley of six quick rounds out of the AR-15's muzzle, which flashed in the shade of the trees. His rounds skipped along the asphalt like a stone across a pond's surface. He didn't hit anything, but he did chase both men behind their truck to seek cover.

A pit bull roared viciously from the pickup bed. Another round of bullets sailed in his direction, this time from a handgun. They careened along the asphalt and past him into the trees. Colton returned fire, raising his aim considerably and hailing another eight rounds upon the men.

This time he found his mark, peppering the hood of the truck with bullets and blowing out their windshield. Fluids began to spill out of the pickup's engine, possibly from the radiator.

"Colton," shouted Madison, "are you all right?"

"Yeah," came the reply as another shower of birdshot fell harmlessly around them.

Colton stuck his head up over the rack containing the generator and sent another half dozen rounds in their direction. One hit the spot, blowing the right front tire of the pickup, disabling it for good.

"Daddy, you blew out their tire," said Alex as she stuck her head out the driver's side rear window.

"Get back in there, Alex," said Colton as more bullets from the handgun sailed past, getting closer to them with each effort.

Disabling the pickup was a blessing and a curse. On the one hand, Colton's option to backtrack was taken away from him. The pickup blocked the road and there were two armed men behind it. But it also meant they couldn't give chase. He could press forward through the overpass with only the group of three to five adults ahead.

"Get ready to go forward!" he announced as he fired off another few rounds in the direction of the pickup to hold them at bay in case they decided to chase on foot.

Colton jumped behind the wheel and tried to start the truck. It wouldn't turn over. He sat there in dumbfounded silence—almost in shock. *Has our engine been hit?* He tried it again. Nothing.

Bird shot pelted them again. Colton turned his attention to the rear of the truck. They were coming. Frantic now, he turned the key over and over again. Nothing.

"What's wrong?" he shouted.

"Daddy, they're coming!"

"Colton," said Madison, "the gear shift."

"What?"

"The gear shift is still in drive. Hurry, put it in park and try again!"

In his haste earlier, Colton had turned off the ignition, but in the unfamiliar truck, he'd forgotten to put it in park.

The approaching men were close enough now for Colton to hear one of them rack another round in the shotgun and fire. This time, the pellets found their target with more force, causing the rear window of the Wagoneer to shatter.

Alex shrieked as tiny shards of glass entered the backseat. Colton gathered himself, threw the Wagoneer in park, and fired the engine. He immediately put it back in drive and lurched the nearly fifty-year-old truck forward.

As their Wagoneer took off toward the I-840 overpass, Colton began to lose sight of the two men, who continued to trail their truck. Feeling a little more comfortable with the space between them, Colton quickly analyzed his approach to the bridge.

He was still unsure as to whether the occupants of the overpass were a threat. They hadn't shot at them, although from that distance, unless they were skilled snipers, it would've been a waste of effort. In addition, he was almost certain two of the five people up there were children. *Would adults be that stupid to place their young children in the line of fire?*

"Madison, use the AR-15. Get ready to shoot, but don't unless we're fired upon first."

"Why?"

"I don't know if the group ahead is with these other people," replied Colton. "I thought I saw five heads look over the guardrail, including two children. They could just be stranded."

"Okay," said Madison hesitantly. "But expect the unexpected."

CHAPTER 8

DAY FIFTEEN
11:15 a.m., September 23
Natchez Trace Parkway at I-840
Near Boston, Tennessee

As the Rymans put sufficient distance between them and the two men behind them and the pit bull, which briefly gave chase, they focused their attention on the overpass. Colton approached slowly because he was unsure what might be hiding behind the stalled vehicle under the bridge. The Trace was also heavily wooded on both sides and could contain more members of the ambush team.

Madison hung out the window with the AR-15 pointed at the overpass. Colton positioned Alex on the right side of the truck to watch for any gunmen in the woods and to have her mother's back. Colton cautioned her against shooting her mom, to which she replied, "Duh!"

At thirty miles per hour, Colton could approach the overpass quickly enough to be a more difficult moving target but also not so fast as to hinder their balance and aim. They were two hundred yards away.

"Gun!" shouted Madison. "Left side of the guardrail. Do you see it?"

"Yeah," said Colton. "They have really good cover. We'll keep shooting at them as we sail past. Hopefully, they won't be bold enough to stand up to get better aim."

Bullets flew past the truck from the two men behind them.

"C'mon, guys," started Alex. "Now these two are catching up and the dog is running toward us too."

"Shoot at them!" instructed Colton as he picked up speed toward the overpass.

One hundred yards away, a bullet skipped off the pavement and embedded itself in Colton's door.

"There's our answer! Fire back!" shouted Colton. He hung his arm out of the driver's window and attempted to take aim at the bridge. He had no expectation of hitting anyone under these circumstances, but they didn't know that. One of the things that Colton had learned from the gun battle with the COBRA bunch was that the other guy was just as afraid of getting shot as you were.

He kept on the pressure, becoming the aggressor now. Colton jammed on the accelerator and sped toward the bridge. He began to methodically shoot toward the concrete guardrail, causing the bullets to ricochet wildly in all directions. They were taking fire now from the middle and both sides of the overpass, but the shots missed them. The shooters were apparently not willing to show themselves to take better aim.

Click—click—click.

"I'm out of bullets," declared Madison.

"Alex, give Mom another magazine."

"I don't have any more loaded ones."

Colton looked up in the rearview mirror. "Really?" *Note to self,* he thought as he shook his head.

"No, I didn't think about—" started Alex as a bullet shattered one of their headlights, causing Madison to duck behind the dash.

"Switch to your sidearm, Maddie," said Colton as he mashed the gas. "I'm gonna speed up now, but they think they have the advantage. Look!"

The two men on the ends now stood and pointed their rifles at the Wagoneer. They had clear shots and were getting closer to finding their target. Colton fired upon the man on the left, causing him to drop to the highway.

Madison hesitated for a moment and then began firing wildly toward the concrete railing. This was sufficient to cause her target to seek cover. Colton raced under the bridge, thankful that there wasn't anything in his way behind the stalled sedan.

As they emerged on the other side, shots rang out once again, but skipped harmlessly behind the truck, only dinging their trailer hitch rack. Within minutes, they'd confronted the threat and narrowly avoided a disaster. Colton continued to hold his breath as he mashed the accelerator, giving the Wagoneer all the speed it could muster. He was doing seventy-five as he roared away and navigated the next bend in the road.

CHAPTER 9

DAY FIFTEEN
1:00 p.m., September 23
Johnson Chapel Baptist Church
Natchez Trace Parkway
Near White Oak, Tennessee

"Look, Mom, there's a church," said Alex as she pointed to the right side of the road. Appearing through a clearing in the woods was a small white church with its steeple barely rising above the tree line.

"Colton, do you think we could take a break?" asked Madison. "The shoulder seems flat here. We might be able to make our way into the woods a little bit and rest. Whadya think?" She rubbed his shoulders and ran her fingers through his hair. He appeared to be very stressed out by the events of the day. It was time to catch their breath and get something to drink.

Colton steered the Wagoneer off the road and slowly made his way through a clearing created by utility poles providing power to the tiny church. He turned to Madison and Alex, gesturing for them to look around for signs of life. After he drove several feet through the field, Colton stopped, surveyed the surroundings, and shut off the motor.

Colton turned to Alex. "Have you reloaded the magazines?"

"Yes, Daddy," replied Alex, hanging her head. "I didn't know."

Colton reached out and patted his daughter on the leg. "Look at me, honey. None of us know. This whole ridiculous world we're in wasn't even a blip on our radar three weeks ago. Now look at us. We're the stars of a post-apocalyptic action movie!"

Alex managed a smile for her father, so Madison decided to

lighten the mood and continue the subject. "Which actress would you like to play your character, Alex?"

"Well, maybe Jennifer Lawrence?" replied Alex. "She'd be pretty good. What about you, Mom?"

"Um, the girl that played on *Heroes*, Ali Larter," replied Madison.

"Oh, good choice," crowed Colton. "She's, um—"

"Careful, husband," roared his missus.

"Daddy, who would be a good actor to play you?"

"Clint Eastwood," he replied. Colton did his best Harry Callahan impression. "Go ahead, make my day!"

"Great, you get Ali the hottie Larter, and I get ninety-year-old Clint Eastwood." Madison laughed. "No way. Alex, would you pass the water and the magazines?"

"Sure," replied Alex, who picked up on the new vernacular inserted into the daily lives of the Ryman family. "Would you prefer *Soap Opera Digest* or *US Weekly*?"

Alex provided everyone a bottle of water and their reloads and started to open the door before Colton stopped her.

"Listen, guys, it appears quiet, but take nothing for granted. Let's clear the area first before we relax."

"Okay, Daddy."

"Aye-aye, sir!"

The three of them exited the vehicle and made their way around the church, which appeared to be deserted. Colton tried the front door and it was unlocked. He cautioned them against making any noise as he eased the door open with a slight creak.

A rush of stale air greeted them as they eased one by one into the open, one-room sanctuary. It was empty except for the hand-carved pews lined up neatly in rows. The Rymans were greeted by the sight of the chapel's portal in full bloom with colors emanating from the beautiful stained-glass windows.

It had been a few weeks since they'd attended church services together. Although each of them prayed from time to time, the thought of attending worship service was the farthest thing from their minds.

"Do you think they'll have Sunday service again?" asked Alex as she holstered her handgun and walked up to the pulpit. The simple oak piece stood alone on a raised stage, which enabled the preacher to look down upon his congregation. A solitary cross hung high on the wall behind the pulpit. A piano and folding chairs for six choir members finished out the furnishings—simple and unassuming, as many felt God intended.

"I found a Bible," said Madison, who turned the first few pages to see if it bore a family's name. Traditionally, the family Bible was handed down from generation to generation, recording information such as births, baptisms, marriages, and deaths.

"It belongs to the Johnsons," she announced. "I wonder if they built this old church for their families and their neighbors?"

Madison handed the Bible to Colton, who began to thumb his way through until he found 2 Corinthians. He took Madison's hand and they sat in the front row together, where Alex joined them.

"In Corinthians, the apostle Paul wrote about the many trials and persecutions he had endured," started Colton. "He wrote *we're troubled on every side, yet not distressed; we are perplexed, but not in despair; persecuted, but not forsaken; cast down, but not destroyed.*"

Colton carefully closed the Johnson family Bible, then took the hands of his wife and daughter and held them on top of it.

"Let's pray. Dear Lord, thank you for my life and family. We thank you for the divine protection you've given us, your children, who walk this Earth in faith. We choose to focus on your great love for us and your protection of our family rather than give a place in our souls to fear of those who would do us harm.

"We declare, according to the scriptures, that the wicked who walk among us cannot touch us. We pray that you continue to guard us, guide us, and wrap your blanket of protection around us as we persist on our journey. In Jesus' name we pray, Amen."

"Amen."

CHAPTER 10

DAY FIFTEEN
3:40 p.m., September 23
Natchez Trace Parkway
Near White Oak, Tennessee

Alex studied the map and scanned both sides of the road for landmarks. She found that navigating their way was easier using the old-fashioned methods rather than relying on her GPS. This allowed Alex to keep up with small cross streets, and simple observations enabled her to spot gravel roads that approached the Trace.

When they left the church, she'd set the Goal Zero folding solar panel on the dashboard of the Wagoneer, with her iPhone attached. The afternoon sun was providing it a solid recharge, which seemed to take just over an hour. She hoped to listen to some more music later 'cause it took her mind off things.

"Slow down up ahead, Mom," said Alex as she laid the map in her lap and picked up the binoculars. Alex looked toward the overpass ahead, using just her left eye. She rotated the center focus ring slightly until the bridge abutment became less blurry. Then she did the same with her right eye, using the adjustment ring on that lens. The bridge was crystal clear now. "This afternoon sun is getting brutal. It almost hurts my eyes to look through the lenses."

"How's it look?" asked Madison, glancing into the backseat to check on a sleeping Colton.

Alex didn't answer for a moment as she scanned the cross street identified on the map as Leatherhood Road. She didn't see any indication of activity.

"I think we're good," she replied after a minute. "Mom, this is gonna take forever. We've still got eighty miles to go."

"Well, think of it as being halfway home," said Madison as she started to roll the truck forward. Colton had warned her to take it easy on the gas as well.

"Or halfway away from home is more like it," said Alex, who folded her arms and stared out into the desolate woods.

Madison continued to drive and Alex finally picked up the map to look for the next potential road crossing. She felt guilty for what she'd said. After a minute or two of silence, she spoke up.

"Mom, have you thought about turning around and going back? I mean, at least at home we kinda knew what to expect."

"Of course, honey," replied Madison, who checked her mirrors again. "I've run the options through my mind repeatedly."

"You mean, in between getting chased and shot at," interrupted Alex.

"Yeah, then too." Madison laughed. "I admit that this morning was much more than I expected. I envisioned a roadblock here and there, maybe people walking in the road, like those two. A gunfight was possible, but not expected."

Madison hugged the left shoulder of the road to give the travelers a wide berth. A man and woman in their forties shuffled down the road, carrying backpacks and Whole Foods grocery bags in each hand. Their clothes hung on them like a sheet draped over an old chair.

"You're right," said Alex as she stared at the couple in her mirror until they were out of sight. "I guess it could be worse."

Madison continued driving while Alex reassumed her role as navigator. She checked the charge on her iPhone and, satisfied it was ready, disconnected it from the solar panel. The Goal Zero was designed to fold up and store in a backpack, or under the bench seat of a 1969 Jeep Wagoneer after TEOTWAWKI.

"What are you thinking, Alex?"

"I don't know. Honestly, it's the first time I've had a chance to think since we left home."

"Contemplate."

"Huh?"

"You're contemplating, you know, like contemplating life," replied Madison.

"Yeah, I guess I am. I mean, whadya think life is gonna be like now?"

Madison took a deep breath before answering. "Well, I kinda look at it from the perspective of short term versus long term. Short-short term is from here to Shiloh—the next seventy miles or so."

"I believe it will be better than the first half of our trip, don't you? I mean, we're farther away from the city."

"I agree," replied Madison. "It couldn't get any worse, right?"

Alex held the map up and glanced over it toward the road ahead. She then traced her finger along the route on the map. She grabbed the binoculars and gave her mom instructions.

"Up here, Mom, around this sharp curve that turns left. Ease up until you see the long straightaway."

Madison did as instructed, and once the nose of the Wagoneer created a clear line of sight for Alex, she stopped.

"There's a man on a horse about half a mile down the road. It looks like he has several dogs with him. Hang on."

Madison studied the map while Alex observed the horseback rider. His dogs were barking and excited, and then they took off into a field with the man in hot pursuit. They were hunting something.

"Okay, Mom. He's gone."

Madison continued driving and picked up the conversation. "It's hard to talk about the long-term predictions of what our lives will be like because we don't know how long it'll take the government to get the power back on. For one thing, we don't know how widespread this problem is. Do you think the solar storm affected the entire planet?"

"I hope not," replied Alex. "If it did, who would be able to fix things? Think about it. What if Europe, Russia, China and Japan have all lost power? There isn't anybody left."

"That's part of what I mean. You can't really think long term until you know all the facts. It may be some time before communications and power are restored."

"What if it takes years?" asked Alex.

"That's where the short-term scenario comes in—survival."

Alex leaned back in her seat and chuckled. "I have no problem surviving. The solar storm doesn't scare me. The prospect of growing or hunting food almost sounds like fun. What scares me is people. The only people you can trust is your family."

"I guess I have to agree," said Madison. "I think people, when given a choice, tend to stick together with like-minded people. Think about it, who wants to hang out with someone that constantly disagrees with you or who doesn't share the same values or interests?"

"Exactly," replied Alex. "Our neighbors had their own selfish interests. Then there was that gang who wanted to take advantage of the situation. Today, we were chased by a mob who wanted to take our things. Even the National Guard was setting up roadblocks to confiscate everything for the government."

Alex opened up the glove box and retrieved a brown-sugar cinnamon Pop-Tart out of an open foil pack. She broke it in half and offered it to her mom. The girls took a moment to enjoy the sweet snack.

"Listen, there are ordinary people out here that make up what I consider to be *civilization*," said Madison as they passed another man on a horse, sitting quietly in the middle of a field. "Like that guy. People come in all shapes and sizes, but we've learned they'll do unpredictable, unspeakable things during a crisis. Our country has never experienced a prolonged catastrophic event like this. There have been regional disasters like earthquakes, storms and wildfires, but nothing has challenged America like the collapse of the grid."

Alex pondered this for a moment as she tried to recount the events of the last two weeks. She could count on one hand the number of *civilized* people she'd encountered.

Madison continued. "Think about before the collapse. When we were running errands or you were playing golf, we'd see young people walking to and from school, elderly people shuffling down the sidewalk to the mailbox, construction workers tearing up the streets, et cetera. All of these people have dealt with the collapse differently, but I believe they have several reactions in common."

"Like what?"

"Well, for starters," replied Madison. "Just like us, they were confused and afraid. Some were in denial and many became angry. One thing they all share is a sense of desperation."

Alex continued to follow their route on the map. She applied her mom's advice to what she'd seen and experienced so far.

"Okay, I can agree with that," said Alex. "Here's what I think. Never underestimate desperate people. You never know how far they'll go to take what you have. With that said, who can we trust?"

"Trust no one."

CHAPTER 11

DAY FIFTEEN
4:30 p.m., September 23
Natchez Trace Parkway
Near Fly Hollow, Tennessee

"Mom," said Alex, pointing down the highway to a stalled car with the hood raised. Madison slowed the truck as they exited the woods and entered the long stretch of farmland. She glanced around but didn't see anyone else.

"I see it," said Madison. "It looks like two cars. Is it a wreck?"

Alex examined the accident scene through the binoculars. One of the vehicles had its hood raised and was parked with its front bumper against the grill of the other car. She couldn't make out how bad the damage was, but they appeared to be right up against each other.

"Hey, there's a body up there," exclaimed Alex. She leaned forward in her seat unconsciously, attempting to get a closer look. A young woman was sprawled out on the pavement, wearing shorts and a white T-shirt, covered in blood. On the asphalt next to her was a towel near her outstretched arm. "It is! Mom, it's a woman and she has blood all over her shirt. She's lying on the road next to the car with the driver's door open."

"Do you see anybody else?" asked Madison as she continued to allow the truck to slowly roll forward.

Alex looked again. "Yes, there's another woman slumped over the steering wheel of the car with the hood raised. I can barely make her out, but her long hair is blowing in the wind."

"Wake your dad," said Madison.

"Mom, the woman on the ground is waving for help. She's

bleeding. We've got to do something!"

"Okay, wake up, Colton." Madison continued to inch forward and was now a hundred yards away, allowing her to see the scene clearly. There were some fluids spilled around both of the engines. The woman on the ground was trying to lift herself off the ground to get their attention.

"What's going on?" asked a groggy Colton as he rose up in the backseat.

Suddenly, smoke began to pour out of the car with the hood raised. It billowed out of the rear windows on both sides, making it difficult to see as the winds carried it across the road.

"There's a wreck up ahead blocking the highway," said Alex. "There are two women hurt. One is bleeding and the other one must be unconscious or dead."

"Let me see," said Colton as he propped his arms on the back of the bench seat. He reached for the binoculars. "I don't know about this, guys."

Madison was still slowly creeping forward, yard by yard. Smoke was pouring out of the car on the left and she thought the driver moved.

"Did you see that? The woman driving the other car. I think her head moved. Colton, her car might be catching on fire!"

They were now fifty yards away. "Maddie, stop!" yelled Colton, prompting Madison to ease to a halt. "Stop now! There's something wrong. These cars—these cars are too new. They wouldn't be running to—"

The rear passenger door flung open and a man reached into the truck and grabbed Colton's arm. Another man appeared at Madison's window and reached for the steering wheel.

"Get off me," yelled Colton.

"We're surrounded!" yelled Alex as another man began reaching for her door lock.

"Leave us alone!" yelled Madison. Madison mashed the gas pedal, but the engine just revved. She tried it again as the man groped for the door handle and the steering wheel.

"Get out of here!" yelled Colton, who was on his back, kicking at the man who'd climbed part of the way into the backseat. The man stank and his long stringy hair dripped sweat on Colton.

"Goooo!" hollered Colton. Madison, while forcing the gas pedal to the floorboard, realized the man had pulled the gear shift into neutral. She forced it into drive and the truck surged forward, leaving her assailant tumbling to the asphalt.

The man, whose crazed eyes darted all around the back of the truck, continued to grab at Colton until he caught sight of the AR-15. Shifting his focus, the man now sought the Rymans' best weapon.

Madison jammed on the brakes, throwing him off balance. This enabled Colton to kick his attacker in the throat.

"ARRRGGGGHHHH."

The throaty groan indicated the man couldn't breathe. Colton kicked him again, this time in the chest, which sent him back through the window and tumbling onto the gravel shoulder of the road. He rolled down the embankment into a field, clutching his throat.

The other two men caught up to the truck again. They were attempting to grab the generator and gas cans. This time, Madison threw the truck in reverse, running over one of the men's legs with a thump and noticeable crunch, causing him to scream in agony.

"Mom, watch out!" screamed Alex as one of the women jumped on the hood of the truck and swung a tire iron onto the roof of the Wagoneer with a thud.

Just as the woman was about to take another swing toward the windshield, Madison sent the truck forward, throwing the woman off balance. She dropped the tire iron and held onto the windshield wipers to avoid falling off.

Madison gained speed to nearly forty miles an hour and then jammed on the brakes, throwing Colton and Alex forward and the crazed woman off the hood. The woman flew off the truck, still clutching the wiper blades, which she'd ripped from the Wagoneer, and cracked her skull as she rolled over and over on the pavement, leaving a trail of blood from her head.

Their pursuers were relentless. The other woman began grabbing at Alex through the window. Alex pushed off the door and tried to kick at the woman.

"Get off my daughter!" screamed Madison, who started forward again, hoping the momentum of the truck would cause the woman to fall. With her focus on Alex's attacker, Madison didn't notice the body of the dying woman on the road and unexpectedly ran over her.

The pronounced bump threw all of the Rymans up in their seats, causing them to hit the roof of the Wagoneer. It also caused Alex's assailant to lose her grip and fall to the ground with her legs pinned under the right rear tire. This bump was not as severe, but caused sufficient damage in the form of two broken legs to Alex's attacker, bringing an end to the threat.

Madison gripped the wheel and didn't stop as she drove the Wagoneer on the shoulder around the staged wreck. It was several miles before any of them breathed.

Madison gritted her teeth. She was mad. She'd just killed someone. For no reason! *Stupid. Stupid. Stupid!*

She finally relaxed and let out the air that filled her lungs. She had to remind herself that the bumps in the road were meant to slow them down, but not stop them completely. She continued to drive until she was alone again with her family.

CHAPTER 12

DAY FIFTEEN
5:45 p.m., September 23
Natchez Trace Parkway at I-840
Near Fly Hollow, Tennessee

Colton finally convinced Madison to pull over. He thought she might be in shock after what had happened. He opened the door for her and helped her out. Then he simply held her tight in the warm setting sun and allowed her to cry for as long as she wanted.

Assault, in the pre-collapse world, could include pushing, slapping, punching, and other forms of bullying. People used all sorts of weapons, both physical like knives, sticks, or rocks, and nonphysical, like words. The old adage that *sticks and stones may break my bones, but words will never hurt me* held true in some respects, although the use of words to assault another had gained traction in the world of social media and the Internet.

Post-collapse, assaults were taken to the highest levels of human depravity. The taking of another man's life became normal and, in some cases, accepted behavior. Physically attacking another was now considered a part of survival rather than an illegal act.

Without rule of law, in a post-TEOTWAWKI society, physical assaults were punished with like-kind means—*an eye for an eye*. Most people didn't know that the origin of the concept of *lex talionis*—the law of retaliation—dated back to the earliest civilizations and meant a retaliation authorized by law in which the punishment corresponds in kind.

Victims of assaults didn't care about the punishment in store for their attacker. They just didn't want to be a victim again. They were shocked, angry, and afraid of a possible repeat of the attack. Oftentimes they questioned themselves in pursuit of answers as to why this happened to them.

In a post-collapse world, it was hard to convince someone that survival included constantly being under attack by those who wanted what they had. Socially moral people would choose to take the high road in this new norm and focus on defending the ones they love and their belongings.

Or they became the aggressor and focused on taking what they didn't have with no morals or standards as to what methods they employed. These *aggressors* were the threats to the rebuilding of society. While the socially moral individuals tried to recover from the catastrophe and search for solutions, the morally depraved sought to use the weakness of the world around them as an opportunity to better their position.

Ordinarily, the law of the jungle, every man for himself, kill or be killed, was kept in check by the laws of society. Post-collapse, those laws were discarded, and those survivors of a catastrophic event who didn't recognize that the law of the jungle was no longer kept in check succumbed to the attacks of their aggressors.

Madison finally stopped sobbing and Colton wiped away the tears from both of their faces. He held her and tried to take the pain away. She'd killed someone, defending her family. There was no shame in that.

Alex had been walking the road, watching for travelers through the binoculars. She returned to Colton and Madison with the AR-15 slung over her shoulder by the strap.

"Mom, Daddy," started Alex, pointing over her shoulder with her thumb. "There's a man walking this way alone. He appears to be weak, but we should probably leave."

Madison sniffled and shook her head. "Yeah, let's go. I'm ready."

Colton helped his wife get settled in the backseat as Alex took her position in the front—riding shotgun. After everyone was in place, Colton fired up the Wagoneer and continued west.

"Colton, I'm so sorry," said Madison from the backseat as the truck sped past the lone walker on the highway. He didn't even look in their direction. Madison continued. "I should've known that was trouble. I should've driven right past them."

"You didn't know, darlin'," said Colton. "It looked innocent enough and those people genuinely appeared to be in trouble. It was an elaborate setup that could've fooled anyone."

"Daddy," interrupted Alex, "I need to check this next overpass. I'll tell you when to stop, okay."

Colton nodded and continued another half mile, at which point Alex had him pull over. She jumped out of the truck with the rifle under one arm and the binoculars held in the other. He was impressed with her adaptation to this new way of living.

"I wish I could be strong like Alex," said Madison as she began to tear up again. Colton turned around and leaned over the seat to hold Madison's hand.

"Listen to me, Maddie," he started. "You saved us from getting hurt back there. It was your quick reactions behind the wheel that threw those marauders all over the pavement."

"But I killed that girl." She was sobbing again.

"She got what she deserved," said Colton reassuringly. "You can't just go around attacking people without cause. When you do, punishment will be meted out. You absolutely did the right thing."

Madison shook her head with a halfhearted acknowledgment. She looked exhausted. Alex jogged back to the truck and announced through the window that it was all clear.

"Daddy, we'll have to stop again in a few miles. Also, I just wanna point out that the sun is beginning to set. It'll be dark in about an hour."

"Alex, how many more crossroads do we have before we hit the Duck River?" asked Colton.

Alex referred to the map and did some calculating. She replied, "Two more after this next one. Then it's a long stretch until we hit the Duck River Bridge, which, at this pace, is about an hour away."

Colton turned to Madison again. "I've got an idea, Maddie," started Colton. "I don't want to cross that bridge at night, so we'll hit it early in the morning. It's a straight shot to Savannah and on to Shiloh from there. Whadya think about finding a spot to get settled in for the night. I'll cook you dinner."

"Oh boy, I can hardly wait." Madison laughed as she regained her composure. "Methinks I've had enough for one day."

CHAPTER 13

DAY FIFTEEN
6:15 p.m., September 23
Fattybread Pond
Near Williamsport, Tennessee

"Here we go," said Colton as he gingerly turned the Wagoneer off the road and up the embankment. "We'll find a spot up on this hill behind those trees. And if Alex's calculations are correct, there should be a pond and lake up here."

"I confirmed it on the GPS, Daddy," started Alex. "If the truck can make it up there, we should be only another hundred yards away from the clearing."

Colton spun the tires on some pine needles as he wound his way through the overgrown four-wheeler trail. He knew he was close when he saw a deer stand up ahead. Deer hides usually sat on the perimeter of a clearing. One last incline and they'd be there.

"Hold on, y'all!" Colton gunned the engine, and after a hop or two over some rocks, the Wagoneer emerged on top of the hill. The boys at T-Ricks would've been proud.

"Very nice, dear." Madison laughed. "It ain't the Ritz-Carlton, but I like it." It warmed Colton's heart to see that Madison had recovered somewhat from the attack just hours ago. Maybe they could look at this as a little camping expedition and put the post-apocalyptic world out of their minds. But before they did that, they'd better check the perimeter before it got too dark.

"Okay, listen up," started Colton. "It looks pretty secluded up here, but we need to walk the perimeter and make sure there aren't any surprises. I'll walk clockwise and you all go the other way. We'll meet on the other side of the lake."

"What are we looking for, Daddy?"

"I don't know. Look for fresh footprints, a well-worn trail into the woods, and signs of a campfire. Stuff like that." The girls pulled their weapons and began the trek around the roughly one-acre pond, which appeared to have been formed by a sinkhole. Cattails surrounded the bank and occasionally a bird would fly and rest on top of a sausage-shaped spike before flying off for a more stable resting place.

The woods could be a dangerous place for those unprepared or who hadn't spent much time in the wild. Nature could be unforgiving and a lack of respect for the dangers could be deadly. Bears, feral hogs, and venomous snakes could all cause the unwary camper serious problems.

In addition, aside from Mother Nature, the post-apocalyptic camper might have to contend with the most dangerous animal of all—their fellow man. Colton was fully aware that they might not be the only humans in the area. He planned on setting up some type of perimeter security to warn them against the four-legged critters, but sleeping with one eye open was the only defense against the two-legged vermin.

As he walked around the edge of the woods, Colton was becoming more comfortable with the campsite. It was concealed well off the highway without an obvious access route. They also maintained the high ground over anyone who might wander up the trail.

He would resist the temptation to build a fire, despite their hidden location. A fire in the middle of the night would be a signal to anyone walking in the area. They had battery-operated lanterns for lighting, and the temperatures this time of September were near a very comfortable seventy degrees at night.

He had slept a couple of hours in the back of the truck earlier today, as had Alex. He'd let the girls sleep first and he would roam around the perimeter to keep an eye on things. It was a clear evening, allowing plenty of light from the moon to give him decent visibility.

It only took a few minutes before he met up with Madison and Alex on the other side.

"Did you see anything, Colt?" asked Madison.

"Nothing at all," he replied. "I suspect whoever hunts this area cut the four-wheeler trail up the hill and built the deer stand at the top of it. It doesn't appear that anyone else comes up here."

"So whadya think, Daddy?"

"Let's go for it, my fellow happy campers."

They made their way back to the truck and discussed whether they should pitch a tent, find a spot to roll out their sleeping bags, or sleep in the truck. Nobody voted for sleeping in the truck. The nearly fifty-year-old seats were not comfortable.

Colton cautioned against just laying the sleeping bags out in the open because of snakes, ticks, and mosquitos. After a hurricane had blown through Florida in July, mosquitos were transported into Middle Tennessee and they brought the Zika virus with them. The Zika virus was more aggravating than it was deadly for most people, but in a post-apocalyptic world devoid of doctors or pharmacies, there was no sense in pushing their luck.

As a result of the process of elimination, they chose the safest route, which was the tent Madison had purchased the day the lights went out. Colton laid down the rear seat, which gave him access to the back of the Wagoneer. He pulled out some more bottled water for them, his planned dinner, and the tent, which the girls quickly set up.

Colton took the same approach to security as he had that first night. He strung a fishing line between the trees that were closest to the truck. After dinner, he would use the empty cans filled with pebbles from around the edge of the lake to create a rattling warning system. After the girls got settled in the tent, he'd walk the perimeter, but he'd mostly stay up in the deer stand. This would give him a clear field of vision for the entire surroundings, as well as the ability to watch the wooded trail between them and the Trace. Overall, he was very pleased with the setup.

"We're ready for inspection, Scoutmaster Ryman," announced

Madison as she gave her husband a hug around the waist. She whispered in his ear, "Thank you for taking care of us."

He turned to her and kissed her. "We all take care of each other," he whispered. "Now, let's check out this tent." Colton walked around and pretended to test the ropes and stakes, but he could already see that it was sturdy. He was playing along for fun. They needed to laugh after this *eventful* day.

"Excellent work, scouts. As your reward, in lieu of merit badges, I promised you a gourmet meal. Find a place to sit and I'll be right back."

"We can hardly wait, right, Mom?"

"Oh yeah." She laughed.

Colton made his way to the truck and shuffled around in the back. As it grew darker, Alex turned on a couple of the battery-powered Coleman lanterns to give them some light. She placed them on the ground to keep them hidden from the road.

"Here we go," said Colton. He gave them each a can of Vienna sausages, Crown Prince sardines, and some Ritz Crackers. "In addition, we have a choice of condiments, which include French's mustard and Tabasco. Bon appetit!"

"Well, aren't we lucky, Alex?" Madison laughed.

"Sure are, Mom. Would you like to trade your Vienna sausages for my sardines?"

"Deal."

The three of them enjoyed their camping cuisine and helped Colton create the security system. After they'd cleaned up, Colton dug out some Tootsie Pops he'd found at Mrs. Abercrombie's home the evening they discovered her body. Madison wasn't aware he'd found them there, so she shouldn't get upset by the memory.

"I used to be a Boy Scout, you know," said Colton.

"No way, Daddy. Really?"

"Yup, and when we went on camping trips, we used to sing this song just for grins and giggles. It's called a repeating song. I know it's goofy, but humor me, would ya?"

"Sure," replied Madison. "Get us started."

"Okay, here's what you do. I'll sing the lyrics and you guys have to repeat them right back to me."

"No prob."

"Okay, here goes," started Colton. "I say boom—chucka—boom."

"What? Mom, really?"

Madison was in stitches, doubled over in laughter. She nodded her head and said, "C'mon, Allie-Cat. Just this once."

"I'll start over," said Colton in all seriousness.

"I say a boom—chucka—boom."

"I say a boom—chucka—boom," said the girls, who repeated each phrase.

"I say a boom—chucka-lucka—boom."

"I say a boom—chucka-lucka—boom."

"I say a boom—chucka-lucka—chucka-lucka—chucka boom."

"I say a boom—chucka-lucka—chucka-lucka—chucka boom."

"All right?"

"All right!"

"Now slow," said Colton, slowing the pace. "I say a boom—chucka-lucka—chucka-lucka—chucka boom."

The girls repeated slowly. "I say a boom—chucka-lucka—chucka-lucka—chucka boom."

"Now fast. I say a boom—chucka-lucka—chucka-lucka—chucka boom."

"I say a boom—chucka-lucka—chucka-lucka—chucka boom."

"Okay?"

"Okay!"

"We're done!"

"Thank God!" Madison and Alex laughed as they rolled on the ground, delirious in laughter.

CHAPTER 14

April 20, 1978
Spring Break
Galveston, Texas

There was a time in the life of Betty Jean Pusser when she woke every morning with fear and anxiety and didn't know why. Fear was a given that she factored into the events of the day like a stone that never left the sole of your shoe. An adult might've called the ability to live with that kind of fear a form of courage. If so, for Betty Jean Pusser, it might have been courageous, but it wasn't very much fun.

She lost her fear on a Saturday during spring break of her senior year in 1978, when her grandmother let Betty Jean join some of her high school friends on a trip to Galveston Beach, fifty miles south of Houston. This was her first trip away from home and her grandmother was none too pleased about it, but there was no stopping her from going. Despite her delicate appearance, nobody stopped Betty Jean Pusser.

She and her friends had a fine day playing Frisbee on the white sandy beach, which eventually grabbed the attention of some young men from Little Rock. The guys invited the girls to play a friendly game of Nerf football, which lasted until evening.

They built a bonfire as the sun set and the guys brought sacks full of food from Whataburger. Before long, a bottle of Jim Beam was making the rounds and then out came another. Betty Jean declined at first. She was sensitive to the criticism leveled at her father for allegedly being drunk the night of his fatal accident. Betty Jean was always on a mission to defend her father's reputation, and not drinking alcohol was her way of proving that she didn't have the *drunk* gene.

One of the boys, Preston Atkins, was particularly sweet on Betty Jean. When he invited her to take a swim out to the sandbar near the Galveston Pier, she agreed to join him. The Gulf of Mexico was not only murky and cold, it was also a favorite hangout of tiger sharks. She was flattered at the older boy's attention, and she would've never done this by herself, but he seemed nice and harmless—not as drunk as the others.

They waded through the breakers and Preston reached over and held Betty Jean's hand. This sent a chill through her body, causing her back to tingle through her sunburn. The only sounds were the gulls and the water slapping against their bodies.

"C'mon." He laughed as he let go of her hand and dove headlong into the dark water. Betty Jean inhaled deeply, dove into the first wave, and kept stroking through the next one and then the one after that until she caught up with Preston at the sandbar.

The water became suddenly frigid, causing her to shudder. The waves sliding over her became heavy as concrete, causing her to lose her balance and fall into the arms of Preston. He was pretty, in an Elvis sort of way—lots of jet black hair with beautiful, yet haunting eyes.

Her world became surreal as the hotels and palm trees on the beach became miniaturized. Preston held her and whispered in Betty Jean's ear that he would keep her warm. Then he kissed her. It was dreamy, not like the clumsy attempts of the boys back home. Her body warmed and responded, and she kissed him back. It felt good.

Then Betty Jean felt her heart seize. The fear was back. Not because of Preston, but because they were surrounded by jellyfish— big ones with bluish-pink air sacs and tentacles that could wrap around your neck or thighs like swarms of underwater yellow jackets.

Preston reacted quickly by swooping Betty Jean up in his arms and running with her across the sandbar as fast as he could until he sank in to the deeper water. She swam toward the shore like an Olympian, with Preston eventually catching up as the incoming waves gave them a boost.

By the time they hit the beach, however, they were laughing, exhilarated by the thrill of escaping the menacing creatures. Holding hands, they ran up the beach to join the others by the bonfire.

Preston told the story to the riveted crowd, and Betty Jean became mesmerized by the fire's sparks twisting into the night sky. She was on top of the world. This time, when the bottle of Jim Beam made its way around the fire, she partook.

And she had another, and another, and another.

As the fire began to die down, she and Preston laughed with the others as jokes were told and funny stories were exchanged. From time to time, they shared a kiss, and as the night got colder, they huddled under a blanket together.

"Hey, you wanna go back to my room where it's warmer," Preston whispered into her ear. His warm breath stirred feelings in her that she'd never experienced.

Betty Jean nodded and the two left with the blanket and half a bottle of Beam. They giggled as they ran toward the Central Hotel, leaving the bonfire and Betty Jean's friends behind.

Once inside the room, they shared a drink and a kiss. Preston pressed himself against her. She liked it. This was different. He was nice. She had held out when the boys made advances toward her in the past, like her grandmother said. But this was the *right time*.

"Turn out the lights, Preston," said Betty Jean as she removed her bathing suit and stood naked, waiting for him to return. She took another swig of the whiskey and allowed it to soak into her body. She was drunk, but she didn't care. This was the *right time*.

Preston turned off the lights and was making his way back to her when the door swung open. It was Preston's friends, all five of them. They flipped the light back on and Betty Jean scrambled to pull the bedspread over her naked body.

"Well, well, well. What do we have here?" said one burly teen.

"Yeah, *Presto*, ya been holdin' out on us?" Another one laughed as the six boys all circled the bed, staring down at Betty Jean. She pushed herself against the headboard and drew the covers up under her chin. Her eyes pleaded with Preston to do something. He didn't.

After passing the bottle around until it was empty, one of them pulled the covers away from Betty Jean. She was naked and unprotected. The assault lasted for two hours, during which time she stared at the door, waiting for her daddy to walk through with his stick. He never saved her. She was demeaned, beaten, humiliated, and raped—repeatedly. By two in the morning, they'd passed out and left Betty Jean lying on the floor in a pool of urine and blood.

At least it was over.

*****

DATELINE GALVESTON, TEXAS
From United Press International Wire Services

TEXAS HOTEL FIRE KILLS 12; 20 STILL MISSING

Firemen dug eight charred bodies out of the still-smoldering debris of the Central Hotel on Galveston Beach Sunday morning after it was destroyed by a fire that police are calling arson.

The bodies of six men, four women, and two children were among the first to be pulled from the remains of the charred building hours after the five-story hotel collapsed into a pile of burning rubble.

It was shortly after 3 a.m. when the fire started in three locations, police said. It spread rapidly, sealed off the Central Hotel's narrow entrance, and quickly burned the building to the ground.

Fire department officials immediately declared the tragedy to be the work of an arsonist. One guest who escaped through a window said he smelled gasoline and turpentine. Also, he said each of the guest room doors was held shut by a rope, which was tied to the door handle and then wrapped around the porch supports outside of the walkway. Fire officials also said that the hotel's entrance and fire exits were jammed shut with scrap wood, preventing them from being opened.

Witnesses said people were jumping from the upper stories to avoid the flames, only to be crushed when the building suddenly collapsed.

Policeman Rick Singleton said, "There was a lot of them lying on the sidewalk here with broken backs, legs and arms. Others simply were buried in the flaming rubble. It was horrific."

Nobody stopped Betty Jean Pusser.

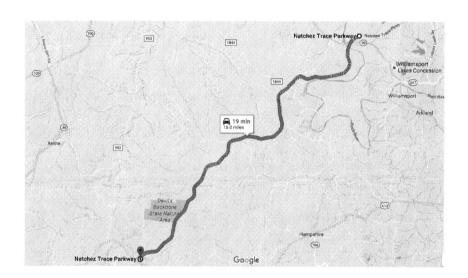

CHAPTER 15

DAY SIXTEEN
7:00 a.m., September 24
Fattybread Pond
Near Williamsport, Tennessee

"Good morning, sunshine," said Madison as she crawled into the tent and presented Colton with his beloved Starbucks insulated coffee tumbler with the commemorative Nashville logo honoring the city as the Music Capital of the World. She planted a kiss on his cheek and waved her hand over the coffee, fanning the aroma into his nostrils. "Wake up and smell the coffee, big boy."

"I'm awake," groaned Colton. He wasn't really sleepy, but he was sore from the combination of the uncomfortable Wagoneer, the cramped deer hide where he'd spent much of the night, and the unforgiving ground full of lumps and stones.

Colton sat up and took a long sip of the dark roast coffee brewed by Madison using the gear she'd picked up before the solar storm. Nothing awakened Colton's senses like his first sip of coffee in the morning. On this particular occasion, it really hit the spot.

He gave his wife a kiss and whispered, "I love you, Maddie."

She hugged him and replied, "You should."

Colton chuckled as he took another sip, dribbling a little down his shirt.

"Nicely done, Mr. Sweet Talker."

Alex poked her head inside the tent. "Hey, guys, take a look at this."

Madison scrambled out first and Colton reached for his pistol and crawled out on all fours, holding the coffee in a death grip.

"What is it?" he asked.

"Shhhh," admonished Alex. She pointed, directing their attention across the clearing. "Look. The other side of the lake. Do you see them?"

"Beautiful," said Madison. "They're nibblin' on the cattails."

Two does and two fawns had entered the clearing and were nibbling on the cattails' spikes before washing down their breakfast with water. The lake and the surrounding plant life provided the animals of the woods their own swamp supermarket.

Cattails were full of nutrients and provided a means of cover for deer. No plant produced more edible starch than common cattails—not potatoes, rice, or yams. One acre of cattails could produce over three tons of flour and supply an abundance of essential vitamins like A, B, C, potassium and phosphorus.

"Think about this for a second, y'all," started Colton. "If you were lost in the woods and found cattails, you've actually found the four things you need to survive—water, food, shelter, and a source of heat by using the old stalks. We used to have an old saying in Boy Scouts—*you name it, and we'll make it from cattails.*"

The does must've detected the Rymans' presence because they both immediately shot their heads up and looked across the lake. The babies, still unaware of the threats to their existence from man, continued to bow their heads to enjoy their yummies.

Without warning, they hopped onto the bank of the lake and bounded into the woods, white tails bouncing up and down effortlessly. In a flash, mommas and little ones were gone.

"Cool," said Alex. "How could anyone shoot something so beautiful?"

"I don't know, Allie-Cat," said Colton. "They're so innocent and vulnerable. Before the collapse, I didn't get the point. Afterwards, obviously, you'd kill a deer as a source of food. For me, I'll eat everything else first."

"Me too," said Madison.

Alex started to walk back toward the truck and then she added one more thought. "I'd shoot another person before I'd shoot one of those deer."

When she was out of earshot, Colton leaned in and whispered to Madison, "Do you think she was kidding, or should we be worried about what's going on in her head?"

Madison shrugged. "The violence doesn't seem to faze her. Maybe she's accepted it as part of life now?"

"I guess," said Colton. "She made the statement so matter-of-fact like that, I think she meant it. I'm gonna have to talk with her about boundaries, I guess."

They started walking back to the truck as Alex began to take down the tent. Colton retrieved the binoculars from the truck and took out the map. He spread it across the hood of the Wagoneer and reviewed their route to Savannah, where the bridge crossed the Tennessee River.

On paper, their route was pretty straightforward. They left Nashville on the Natchez Trace Parkway and would take it directly to the intersection of U.S. Highway 64, which turned west towards Memphis. The plan was to cross the Tennessee River and travel the last fifteen miles or so south to Shiloh.

Common sense told Colton to avoid population centers like small towns and even refugee routes. He tried to anticipate the mob mentality, which would've followed normal traffic patterns like Interstates 40 or even Highway 100, which led directly to Memphis. He also thought those were likely routes to encounter the National Guard.

He'd thought about what other refugees would be looking for, such as sources of water, food, and safe camping areas. South of Nashville toward Franklin was a logical destination for those people fleeing the city. He ran it through his mind repeatedly and his conclusions always supported this direct route.

He'd learned a lot yesterday, however. In theory, the Trace's lack of ingress and egress to side roads was a plus. The map provided him this analysis. However, the steep embankments and nonexistence of a shoulder became a real problem, as they'd learned with the two dangerous encounters yesterday.

During the first day, they'd been caught up in logical choke points—strategic, narrow routes where they became trapped by their attackers. He studied the map and traced the route to Savannah. Colton then took Alex's iPhone and looked at the GPS rendering of their route.

He tried to identify bridges, overpasses, or long stretches of wooded areas that might put them in a similar position as yesterday. It was critical that they establish at least two alternative routes to take to avoid getting trapped again. Yesterday, they'd been lucky. Today, they'd be smart.

"Hey, Alex, would you mind giving me a hand?" he asked as Alex finished folding up the tent with Madison.

"Sure, Daddy."

Colton began to untie the tarp and remove the bungee cords to access the gas cans. While standing watch, it didn't take him long to realize that the one-hundred-fifty-mile drive to Shiloh could easily double in length if they had to wind their way through the backroads to avoid potential hostile encounters. They had already used half a tank of fuel as a result of their evasive maneuvers yesterday.

"What can I do?" asked Alex.

Colton continued to unwrap the trailer hitch receiver to reveal the four five-gallon gas cans. That was when he saw the holes in two of the cans.

"Crap!" said Colton.

"Oh no, Daddy. Are they empty?"

Madison joined them. "What? Oh no," she said.

The two cans on the right side of the Wagoneer had been emptied during the shoot-out at the I-840 overpass. The gas had spilled along the ground while they were driving and nobody noticed.

Colton picked them out of the grate and jiggled them. Each contained a gallon or less. All he could do was shake his head.

"It is what it is. Alex, take what you can out of these and fill the tanks. Go ahead and top off the tank with the other two. I think you'll have some left over."

"What should I do with the empty gas cans?" asked Alex.

"You know, keep them. Stow them back on the rack and cover the whole rig with the tarp. We might have a use for them at some point."

Madison walked up and rubbed Colton's shoulders. "We should be all right, Colt. We only have about seventy miles to go."

"Yeah, we should get there. The Wagoneer is a gas hog. If we can avoid any more shoot-outs and significant detours, we'll have more than enough."

"Yeah, see?" added Madison.

Colton smiled and hugged his wife, who always made him feel better when he was down. He loved her more every day.

"Thank you, darling," he replied. "Listen, I wanna walk down and check out the two bridges that cross the Duck River. One is the long span that's part of the Trace. The other is a side road below to the north. It may take us longer, but we have to have several route options as we move forward to avoid more of yesterday's excitement."

"Amen to that!" She smiled and looked upward to Heaven. "You go ahead. Alex and I will get the truck ready to hit the road."

CHAPTER 16

Colton slipped and landed on his backside, finishing the walk down the trail to the Trace in a bruised and bumpy fashion. He looked back up the hill to determine what was responsible for the rude loss of footing. He slapped the dirt and pine needles off his jeans and checked the road to make sure it was clear.

It was about a mile to the Duck River Bridge, which would take him fifteen to twenty minutes. Based upon the map and his assessment of the terrain, driving up to the bend that led to the bridge would lock them into a position they couldn't back out of.

The Duck River wound its way for over two hundred fifty miles through Middle Tennessee. It was a scenic river and a favorite of Nashvillians who enjoyed canoeing, fishing, swimming, and camping. Colton recalled a conversation he'd had with Jake Allen about the river. It contained more species of fish than all the rivers of Europe combined. It was full of freshwater mussels too.

As a rural river, it was fairly clean except for pesticides, which ran off the farmland during heavy rains. But the local farmers had taken steps to prevent this practice, and before the collapse, the Duck River provided fresh water to a quarter million surrounding residents.

"This would have been a perfect place for a weekend cabin or a bug-out place," Colton muttered aloud as he walked closer to the bridge. He'd barely had time for the girls at home, much less for long

71

weekends at a cabin. It hadn't made sense to make a purchase like this on any level.

How could he have known they'd need a bug-out location? He'd never really paid attention to stuff like this before. Of course world events concerned him, but the saber rattling of foreign countries had been in the news his entire life and nobody had fired off the nukes yet.

In Nashville, he never thought they were susceptible to things like hurricanes, earthquakes, or wildfire. It was true that this area of Tennessee was in the heart of Dixie Alley, one of the deadliest tornadic regions in the world. But they had places to hunker down for that at home and insurance to pay for the damage.

The solar storm was completely off his radar. Now, in hindsight, of course, he could see how a small cabin on the river would have been a fun place to hang out with Madison and Alex during normal times, as well as provide them a place to survive after a catastrophe.

As Colton got closer, the entrance to the bridge came into view, but it was immediately engulfed in a thick white fog along the Duck River. The fog formed when cooler air moved over and mixed with the warm and moist air at the river's surface. The moist air cooled and became saturated, causing the fog to form and rise up along the valley walls.

"NOOOOOO!" came a man's voice through the dense condensation.

"Please, sir, just take what we have," a woman's voice pleaded. Her words carried through the fog.

There were two bridges that crossed the Duck River here. One, a long very elevated span, was part of the Natchez Trace. Even at its high elevation above the river, the bridge was awash in thick fog. Another bridge, just a hundred yards to the north of Colton's position, was part of a country road that led from Williamsport to his south, towards Centerville.

A gunshot rang out and Colton immediately ran into the woods for cover. The man was moaning in pain. Colton was unable to discern whether the activity was on the upper or lower bridge. The fog was thick and the sounds echoed off the valley walls.

"Pleeeeeeease!" the woman begged, and then there was another gunshot, followed by her haunting cries. "No, Billy, please God, no!" The next sound Colton heard was a splash below.

Colton tried to get a better view of the two options through his binoculars but still couldn't see. He had no way to calculate when the fog would lift. He did know that his family was only a mile away from this carnage and he wanted no part of it.

The woman could be heard running, her bare feet slapping on the concrete.

"Git 'er!" shouted one of the men.

Many feet were now in pursuit of the woman who'd just witnessed her Billy get shot and unceremoniously thrown into the Duck River. She was running for her life.

Colton felt for his weapon and contemplated helping her. The road dropped in elevation considerably as it entered the river basin. Even if he could get to her, he'd have to shoot his way out and escort a distraught girl uphill out of the fog. On the other hand, a few warning shots might scare them away and he could rescue the girl.

"Run, you idiots!" the leader shouted at his men, and the girl's pursuers picked up the pace.

The sounds of the footsteps were getting closer. They must be on the upper bridge! He started walking in that direction to get a better look. He was dangerously close to where the fog began. If the girl emerged, with the men chasing close behind, he might be discovered.

Colton weighed his options. He could fire warning shots and encourage the girl to keep running. But if the marauders had a vehicle, they could chase Colton down before he could run a hundred yards back toward his own family.

Colton paced the road, slapping the side of his head with the palms of his hands. *You've got to decide! Please, God. What do I do?*

"Gotcha!" shouted one of the men. Colton could hear the girl hit the road and scream in pain.

It was too late to help. There was nothing he could do. He'd debated with himself too long. Colton let out a gasp of air, leaned over, and then looked to God for guidance and forgiveness.

After a moment, he turned and quietly walked back to his own girls.

CHAPTER 17

DAY SIXTEEN
8:00 a.m., September 24
County Road 50
Williamsport, Tennessee

Colton didn't want to discuss the details of what he'd observed at the Duck River Bridge, and Madison didn't press him. Whatever had happened, it had a profound effect on him. When Colton returned to their camp, he looked around to make sure everything was secure and simply announced they'd have to make a detour to the south toward Williamsport. Neither Madison nor Alex questioned why. They knew him well enough to know he'd talk about it when he was ready.

Colton and Alex studied the map together before he worked his way down the trail and back onto the Trace. Instead of continuing, he pulled off into a cornfield on the south side of the highway and drove down a rut-filled dirt road. Eventually they found a gravel drive and made their way over to Highway 50, which led into the small town of Williamsport.

They drove down the narrow, two-lane highway through a tunnel of trees. The leaves on the sweet gum trees were in full fall pigments, while most of the others were starting to turn. As the days grew shorter, the leaves would begin to paint the Tennessee landscape with an autumn palette of color. If the weather of the last few weeks was an indicator, the succession of warm, sunny days would bring about spectacular displays of autumn hues throughout the state.

The truck cleared the tree canopy and arrived in a valley of rich farmland. Off in the distance, they could see a farmer plowing a field, using a quarter horse harnessed to an old-fashioned plow. He was either preserving the fields for spring or, more likely, planting winter rye, wheat, or barley.

Madison thought of one of her favorite songs by Hank Jr., "A Country Boy Can Survive." In a world thrust back into the nineteenth century, those closest to the earth, the farmers, were best suited to change their way of living to adapt to the drastic adjustments needed to survive.

"Daddy, the highway crosses the Duck River up ahead into the town of Williamsport," said Alex. "It should be right around this curve."

Colton touched the brakes and then pushed them down in earnest as the Wagoneer came upon a roadblock manned by two police cruisers, one county and one from the city of Williamsport. The vehicles were wedged between a guardrail and a tall bank covered with kudzu.

He eased past a road to their right, which led them away from the roadblock, but instead chose to approach the uniformed deputy and a younger man wearing a cowboy hat.

"Colton, do you think this is a good idea?" asked Madison. "The road we just passed takes us toward Savannah."

"I know, but I want to talk to this officer," said Colton. He continued to ease toward the roadblock, where both the deputy and the younger boy pointed rifles at them. Colton was only a hundred feet away when they shouted at him to stop.

"That's close enough, mister," the deputy shouted. "Road's closed to Williamsport. In fact, these cars don't run, so they can't be moved. You need to turn yourself around and go on now, ya hear?"

Colton put the truck in park and began to open the door to exit. Madison heard the distinctive sound of a shotgun being racked.

"Colton!" she yelled after him as he exited the vehicle anyway.

Colton raised his hands away from his body and shouted to the deputy, "I just need some directions and I need to tell you something. Here, I'll hold my arms out where you can see me."

Colton kept walking toward the roadblock and Madison began to survey all parts of the intersection to make sure they were alone. She expected an ambush of some sort, but thus far, nobody else appeared.

"What's he doin', Mom?" asked Alex. "I mean, this may not be safe. Wait, look. They're shaking hands."

"Are you kidding me?" asked Madison. "He's over there making friends. Look, he's waving us over."

"No way," said Alex.

"Seriously, he's telling us to come out and join them."

"I know that, Mom. I'm just not gonna do it."

Madison studied the body language of the two men manning the roadblock. They'd both lowered their weapons and were freely talking with Colton. Colton glanced toward her again and waved his arm.

"You know what, let's go join him. He wouldn't tell us to come out if it wasn't safe."

"No," said Alex defiantly.

"Come on, Allie. Don't you wanna talk to some nice people? I mean, all the others have tried to kill us, right?"

"Okay, good point. You first though."

"Very funny." Madison laughed.

When Madison and Alex arrived, they were greeted with smiles and friendly faces. While the adults talked, Alex and the young man copped a squat on the hood of the sheriff's department cruiser.

As they walked away, Colton spoke in a hushed voice to the deputy. "Listen, while they're out of earshot, I need to tell you about something that I haven't even discussed with my wife yet."

Madison immediately gave Colton a puzzled look.

He smiled and nodded to her, then continued. "This morning I walked up to the bridge crossing the river up on the Trace. I think a man may have been murdered. I mean, it was really foggy and I couldn't see, but I heard the shot and then something that sounded like his body being dumped in the river. Can you check it out?"

"I wish we could," answered the deputy. "We've heard reports of a group of bikers who've taken up residency at both bridges up there, kinda like trolls. Folks who try to cross get attacked and their stuff is confiscated. Sometimes they're let through; other times, um, well, it depends."

Madison's interest was piqued. Now she understood why Colton was solemn when he returned from his surveillance. "Depends on what?"

The deputy looked down, shook his head, and kicked some loose pebbles. "These guys want what you have—anything and everything. If you resist, they shoot you and throw you in the river. We've received reports of bodies flowing downriver for days. Even if you don't resist, if you, well, excuse my bluntness, ma'am, look like you and your daughter, then it doesn't end well."

Madison could read between the lines. "Why don't you do something?"

"We can't," the deputy replied. "We don't have the manpower to take them on. There are almost twenty men up there, heavily armed. We can't risk losing our own fathers and sons while leaving the town unprotected in the process."

"But—" Madison attempted to argue before Colton cut her off.

"Honey, I understand where the deputy is coming from," started Colton. "Sadly, I wrestled with the same issue when I was standing at the bridge, listening to the screams and gunshots. I felt helpless and conflicted. In the end, I decided to do what's best for my family—come back alive to them."

The three adults stood quietly, considering what Colton had said. He was right, of course. They all knew it. Sadly, this was the world they lived in now. Alex and her new friend were laughing, trading barbs about city girls versus country boys.

The boy laughed. "You know, I could use a cute little city girl like you to ride in the middle of my pickup to make me look good."

Alex, always quick on her feet, especially with young men, shot back, "Ride where, cowboy? We've got the only runnin' truck in these parts."

"Minor detail," he said, having been one-upped. He then hopped down onto the pavement and fell to one knee. He removed his hat and held it close to his chest. Using his best country drawl, he pleaded his case.

"Dawlin', sometimes your knight in shining armor turns out to be a country boy in mud-covered boots. You're from the city, and I'm from the country. You got the whole world at your feet, right here. Whadya say, Miss Alex?"

Alex doubled over in laughter, which immediately reminded Madison that a good life could be had after the crap hit the fan, if you could just find the right people to live it with.

Chapter 18

DAY SIXTEEN
11:00 a.m., September 24
Natchez Trace Parkway
Near Keg Springs, Tennessee

"Just ahead, Daddy," said a rejuvenated Alex after having a little social interaction with the young man at the Williamsport checkpoint. The guy was sweet and different from the boys she used to hang around with at Davidson Academy. Country guys were unassuming and seemingly uncaring about their appearance. Their clothes were not all about brand names and expensive embroidered logos. Functionality and durability guided their wardrobe. She could get used to their country-boy charm too.

Colton slowed, looking for the power lines that the deputy said would be in this vicinity. Apparently, all of the locals who used the Trace would drive along the makeshift road created by TVA for maintenance of the high-voltage towers that traversed the state. He slowed the truck as they came into view, and then slid down the shoulder of the road.

"I have to say, it's times like this when I realize how lucky we are to have the Wagoneer and its incredible durability," said Colton as the girls bounced out of their seat with each bump in the dirt road. "I doubt the Corvette I traded could've made that maneuver."

Madison and Alex both shot Colton a look. "Well, Mr. Off-Roader, congrats on your acquisition, but could you slow it down a bit until we hit the pavement," said Madison. "Neither my top, nor my bottom, can take too much more of this wagon-trail ride."

Colton slowed as they approached the Trace. To the east, a group of five men and women walked slowly toward the Duck River Bridge.

"Should I warn them about what's ahead?" asked Colton.

"Nobody warned us," replied Alex dryly. "Besides, how do we know they won't start shooting at us as their way of saying *thanks for the info?*"

"That's pretty cynical, dear," replied Madison.

Not receiving any support for the warning idea, Colton resumed their journey westbound on the Natchez Trace. Alex sat quietly and saw that her dad was looking at her through the rearview mirror.

"What?" she asked.

"Nothing," replied Colton.

He drove on quietly for another minute and then she spoke up. Alex wasn't that much different from other teens in that she could seem moody and reserved. When they were young, they needed to be nurtured and guided through life. But as most teens got older, they sought independence and respect. Even though their attitudes, behavior or body language said otherwise, teens like Alex still needed their family support system.

"Daddy, when you negotiated deals for your clients, how could you tell if the other side was being fair? You know, trustworthy."

Colton chuckled a little as he responded. "Over the years, I learned the hard way. Some people are far better liars than others."

"When you meet someone for the first time, it's hard to tell if you can trust them," added Madison. "Your first impressions can often be wrong. It takes time to really get to know somebody."

Colton slowed the truck as an overpass came into view. Madison observed the surroundings through the binoculars, scanning for anything out of place.

"I would always study the person's eyes," said Colton. "Maintaining eye contact doesn't necessarily mean the person is telling the truth; it's possible that they're accomplished liars."

"Is that why poker players wear sunglasses at the table?" asked Alex.

"Yes, in part," replied Colton. "When sitting across the table from someone for hours, the other poker players may be able to establish a pattern between card playing and eye movement or positioning."

Madison interrupted. "I think we're good to go."

As Colton started them rolling, he continued. "They used to say that you can tell a liar by their shifting eyes or looking down when they speak untruthfully. I've found that's not always the case. They could be an insecure person or simply distracted."

"So how could you tell?" pressed Alex.

"As for eye contact, I'd study their pupils," replied Colton. "If their pupils increased in size, they were more likely to be tense and nervous. That was an indication to me that I had the upper hand."

"What about body language?" asked Alex. "I could tell if a kid was up to something just by the way he acted sometimes."

"Great question and that really deals with the situation we're in now," replied Colton. "Before the collapse, things like eye contact and body language were used for my negotiations all the time. For someone like you, it helped you determine if a new classmate might be someone you'd want to become friends with. Today, it takes on a whole new importance."

Alex perked up and slid to the edge of the backseat so she could lean between her parents. "Yeah, this is what I'm getting at. For three weeks, we've been running into people that I'd normally trust, and they end up shootin' at us. It's gettin' old, Daddy."

Colton and Madison began laughing at Alex's matter-of-fact assessment. They rounded a curve and two men working on an old tractor in a field waved to them as they drove by. Out of habit, Colton gave the horn two quick taps as the Rymans waved back.

"Okay, let me tell you what I've learned over the years, and we'll apply it to the new way of life," started Colton. "Just like before the solar storm, paying attention to what's going on around you is the key. Most people float through life, oblivious to imminent threats to their safety. Madison, how many times have you swerved in your car to avoid another driver who was texting or distracted?"

"Daily," replied Madison.

"Now, imagine if you were distracted too, oblivious to the other bad driver," said Colton.

Madison made two fists and bumped them together, then allowed her fingers to wiggle to her lap. "Boom." She laughed. "Followed by a lecture from my husband, an even worse fate."

"No lectures, just lessons," said Colton. "Situational awareness is about the observations of your surroundings, including the people in close proximity to you."

"Like studying their eyes and body movements?" asked Alex.

"Yes, eyes. But also body language, which is something we all give off, mostly unconsciously. The way we carry ourselves speaks volumes as to what our postures, facial expressions, and hand positions mean. The longer you have to study a person, the more accurate you can be in your assessment."

Colton slowed to avoid several buzzards picking at the carcass of a dead critter in the road. He continued.

"Here's the thing. Body language can give you advanced warning about the actions that a person or group of people are about to undertake. It kinda gives you a window into their mind and emotions, as well as their intentions. In a world like the one we face now, where determining friend from foe isn't easy, body language is an early warning device built into every single human being."

Madison placed the map on the dash and looked ahead. "You can keep going, but there's another bridge overpass up ahead. I'll keep watching it."

"Daddy, what should I watch for?"

Colton took a sip of water and wiped the sweat off his face. It was a hot day for September. "On the one hand, our faces are the most expressive body part we possess. On the other hand, it's the most easily manipulated. Most people will crack nervous grins and will exhibit numerous facial twitches. Just ignore the signs that can be controlled and manipulated, and focus on those that cannot, like their pupil dilation that we just talked about. Watch for their pulse to increase, usually indicated by a visible pounding pulse in their neck or temples. If they suddenly break out in a sweat or their breathing becomes more rapid as their mouth remains open, there is increased anxiety in their system."

"A warning sign," added Alex.

"Exactly," said Colton. "Here's something I learned from growing up in Texas, where boys fought each other for the heck of it. A person's shoulders and chest reveal a lot. If their shoulders are tight and raised rather than hanging relaxed and natural, then they might be about to swing on you. Also, most men tend to breathe through their belly while women breathe through their chest. If a man starts to breathe through his chest, then chances are he's ready to fight."

Madison slapped the dashboard and Colton immediately slowed down. She adjusted the binoculars to get a better look. As Colton moved forward, Alex could see what her mom was watching.

"Hey, look, it's a boy on a bike," exclaimed Alex.

The boy was standing on the side of the road, next to his bicycle, but at the sight of their truck, he jumped on it and sped away.

"Wow, look at him pedal," said Madison. "He's givin' it all it's worth!"

Colton picked up speed and followed the kid as he pedaled as fast as his short legs would allow.

"Hey, kid, slow down," said Alex. "We're the good guys."

As Colton got closer, he laughed. "Should I put it in neutral and rev the engine a little bit? You know, kinda growl at him like that car in Stephen King's book?"

Madison slugged him. "No, Colton Ryman, you will not. Leave that boy alone. In fact, give him some space."

"Okay," said Colton. He continued with his thought. "You see, Alex, that boy doesn't know we're the good guys. Ordinarily, he'd have probably sat there on the side of the road and waved to us as we drove by. In this violent world, where you don't give folks the benefit of the doubt anymore, you almost have to assume they're up to no good."

"Which is why he's running from us," said Alex. "Are there any other signs we should watch for?"

"I think the last thing, which I learned from television and movies, is to keep an eye on their hands and feet," replied Colton. "Well, maybe feet not as much. I've never seen feet kill anyone in the movies. But always watch their hands, especially if they suddenly reach into a pocket or hover around the waist of their pants. A balled-up fist is obvious. Slipping their hands under their coat to draw a pistol can be more subtle."

"Really, it's all about assessing the other person until you can get a comfort level, right?" asked Madison as she studied the map.

"To an extent," replied Colton. "Never let your guard down around strangers. Your ability to identify these early warning signs will give you valuable seconds in which to act."

Colton continued them on their way as they passed two stalled cars with their windows broken out. He moved to the side to avoid the broken glass. As the Wagoneer turned around the bend, a brown road sign indicated they'd just entered the Devil's Backbone Natural Area.

Alex, who had craned her neck to analyze the stalled cars, looked forward and asked, "Daddy, where did the boy go?"

CHAPTER 19

DAY SIXTEEN
Noon, September 24
Natchez Trace Parkway
The Devil's Backbone, Tennessee

The first arrow struck the hood of the Wagoneer and careened harmlessly over the roof. The second arrow hit the windshield dead center, creating a hole before it imbedded in the seat between Colton and Madison and barely stopping before it would have traveled into Alex's chest.

Colton instinctively jerked the steering wheel to the left to avoid being hit again, but the barrage caught them all by surprise. From the woods lining the highway, arrows were hurled in their direction. They whizzed by, but close enough for Colton to hear the swoosh of displaced air.

"Roll up your windows!" shouted Colton as another ricocheted off the door post of the truck's frame.

"Go faster, Daddy!" said Alex, and Colton happily obliged. He pressed the gas just as an arrow embedded in their tire. The arrow's shaft banged against the wheel well, creating a fast clicking sound like baseball cards beating against a bike's spokes.

Colton disregarded the sound and punched the gas. If the tire was going to go flat, he wanted to get as far away from these wild Indians as he could.

"Daddy!" screamed Alex. "There's one grabbing at the trailer rack."

Colton sped up as a boy no older than ten held on. Colton swerved the truck back and forth, trying to shake the kid. Finally, he slammed on the brakes, causing the boy to ram his head against the rack and lose his grip. Colton floored the gas pedal and surged ahead, leaving the boy in a heap on the asphalt road.

"Get down, both of you!" shouted Colton as more arrows pelted the truck.

"Up ahead," yelled Madison, pointing a hundred yards deeper into the Devil's Backbone. "They're blocking the road with bicycles, chairs, and even tree limbs. Colton, they're just kids."

Colton had to make a decision. They didn't have enough fuel left for another detour. He couldn't drive through the debris. If he did, he might blow out all four tires. He either had to stop them or turn around. He glanced in his mirrors. They were being chased by a dozen or more of the hellions.

Suddenly, an arrow flew in the tailgate window, which had been broken out in the shoot-out. It stuck in a case of bottled water, causing the spray to soak Alex.

"Daddy!"

"I know, honey. Maddie, take the AR and shoot at them."

"What? They're just kids."

"Mom, they're trying to kill us! They almost did kill me. See?" Alex yanked the arrow out of the Jeep's bench seat and showed her mom.

Madison didn't hesitate as she pulled the charging handle on the weapon and hung it out the window. As she fired, the sound of brass clinking on the pavement could be heard, and the screams of the kids diving for cover echoed off the tree-lined road.

Alex quickly rolled down her window and held her arm out. She fired off a few rounds at the chasing kids to their rear.

"Daddy, did it slow them down?"

"Yeah, do it again on this side."

She repeated the action and this backed down their pursuers.

Colton approached the debris pile and gave it a quick assessment. He decided to remove the pile on the right side of the road, which should give him enough room to pass.

"Here's what I'm gonna do," started Colton. "I want you to stay in the car but keep shooting at these brats to keep them from firing off arrows at me. I'm gonna clear a path."

"Are you sure?" asked Madison. "We can just turn around."

"We don't have the gas to spare," replied Colton. "This won't take long. Just cover me, okay?"

"Okay, Daddy, be careful."

"Love you!" shouted Madison as Colton bolted out of the truck.

A quick glance at the left front tire revealed that the arrow was stuck in the thick part of the tread and was not a threat to causing the tire to go flat. Colton ran in a low crouch as he reached the pile of debris. Arrows were flying high over his head due to their trajectory. The kids were hidden under the road in an underpass that did not appear on the map. Tents and makeshift lean-tos lined the gravel road beneath him.

Madison and Alex periodically fired at the young marauders as Colton frantically tore through the pile, casting bikes and furniture to one side or the other.

Suddenly, an arrow, much smaller than the others, flew past him and stuck in a wooden chair. A man was standing behind a tree about sixty yards to the north. He was reloading his crossbow for another attempt to kill Colton.

Colton fell to the pavement as another arrow embedded itself into a fallen tree branch next to him. Colton didn't hesitate. He jumped up and drew his weapon at the same time. He sent three rounds in the direction of the man, who dodged behind the tree. Colton waited while the man reloaded. He planned on steadying his aim and shooting the man as he emerged for another attempt with the crossbow.

Colton never got the chance.

CRACK—CRACK—CRACK. CRACKCRACKCRACK!

The man, who was dressed as a Boy Scout scoutmaster, turned into a bullet-riddled heap of blood and rolled down the embankment into one of the tents below. Colton knew he was dead.

"Oh no!"

"Mr. Jennings!"

The shouts from below, coupled with the cessation of the arrows, gave Colton the head start he needed to get back to the truck. Two more kids drew aim on him from the woods to his right as he ran back to the truck, but they were quickly sent scampering into the woods by Alex's warning shots.

Colton slid into the driver's seat and gunned the truck toward the debris. The arrow barrage had stopped, and now more than a dozen young boys were huddled around their dead scoutmaster.

As Colton sped away, ignoring the repetitive clicking of the arrow stuck in the tire, he thought he saw an aberration in the shadows of the tall pines to his left. Had Colton known the folklore surrounding the Devil's Backbone, he might have seen the ghosts of the five dozen unsuspecting Creek Indians who were slaughtered in a predawn attack in 1813.

The Creeks had underestimated the depravity of man too.

CHAPTER 20

DAY SIXTEEN
3:40 p.m., September 24
Natchez Trace Parkway
Gordonsburg, Tennessee

Colton knelt in the grass next to his wife and held her hair back as she finished throwing up. Her vomiting and crying had now been replaced by the dry heaves. Alex could tell her dad ached because of the despair her mom was undergoing. Mom had protected him and might have saved his life, but she'd left a bullet-ridden corpse in her wake. Nobody should have to go through what just happened. Alex knew. She'd been there.

"Colton," she sobbed, "they were just kids. Boy Scouts!" Madison began to cry again as Alex brought Colton a wet towel and a bottle of water. Alex pulled the bill of her cap down over her eyes to shield them from the sun and returned to her guard duty but stayed close in case they needed her.

"Maddie, I know. They were misguided by a man who thought they needed to attack others to survive. You saved my life back there. You did what *you* had to do for your survival and mine."

"Colt, this isn't me," she said, breathing heavily but able to gulp down some water. She sat back on her heels and took the wet towel to wipe her face and chin. "I don't think I'm made for this life. Really, I can't do it."

"C'mon," said Colton as he encouraged her to stand and get away from where she'd retched. "Let's go lean against the truck and get you some crackers. I even have a Sprite that will help settle your stomach. How's that sound?"

Madison nodded and walked with Colton to the Wagoneer, but not without looking up and down the highway first. She was visibly shaken and nervous about her surroundings. Recovering from this might take some time for Madison.

"Daddy, there are some people walking this way, 'bout a mile in front of us," announced Alex. "We'll need to get movin'."

"How many?" asked Colton.

"Looks like three, a man, woman, and child. They've got backpacks but no rifles that I can see."

Colton straightened Madison's disheveled hair. She'd stopped crying and finished off her water. She nibbled on some crackers as her emotional reaction started to subside. Without Colton having to ask her to get in the truck, she smiled and nodded before she took up a spot in the back of the Wagoneer.

He gently closed the door behind her and then took a moment to remove the arrows that were stuck in the gear strapped to the roof. Colton also snapped the shaft of the arrow stuck in the tire. He didn't want to remove it completely in case it had penetrated the inner wall of the tire. For now, at least, the arrow's head sealed any puncture hole it might have created.

"Let's roll," said Colton as he slapped the roof of the truck. This startled Madison, and Alex could see her dad instantly regretted it. "I'm sorry, darlin'."

"It's okay," mumbled Madison.

Alex jumped in the front seat and set the binoculars on the dash. She readied her weapon just in case.

"Alex, how does the overpass look at Columbia Highway?"

"It's clear," she replied. "I think you can drive by them quickly so we don't take any risks. At the overpass, just keep going. I'll continue to watch through the binoculars."

Colton fired up the truck and took off toward the approaching family. As they passed, the parents grabbed their son and slowly stood to the side of the road. The young boy waved as the truck sped around them.

"Daddy, how have they survived on the road like this?" asked Alex.

"I don't know," Colton replied. "It could be they're like us. They held out at home as long as possible and now they're headed for a better spot."

"They hope, right?"

As the truck roared past the bridge overpass without incident, Alex thought about the number of people who were probably wandering out of Nashville and other big cities. She was surprised they'd not encountered more travelers on foot or bicycle.

Also, she expected to see more stalled cars. It could be that folks heeded the warning to shelter in place once the news broke about the solar storm coming. That made sense. But where were the refugees? Where were the masses of tens of thousands of people who, like them, wanted to flee the violence and carnage of the city? Were they holding out, hoping for a quick recovery?

Are they dead? Alex contemplated the possibility that the vast majority of people fleeing the city simply didn't make it. The ones who did make it out to the countryside appeared to be resorting to violence for survival. She immediately wondered if that would ever end.

Alex studied the map for the next point where a road crossed the Trace. She couldn't get this trip over with fast enough. By her calculations, they only had forty miles or so to the Tennessee River, but the shadows were growing long on the highway once again.

"Yeah, they hope, Allie-Cat," her dad finally responded. He must have been thinking the same things as his daughter.

Colton continued down the road as they began to make pretty good progress. But then it always seemed that way before something happened.

"Daddy, let me jump out here and take a look," said Alex. "The overpass is right around this curve. After that, we'll enter the Laurel Hill Wildlife Area." Colton pulled to a stop and nodded. He'd been deep in thought and Alex didn't engage him in idle conversation. Her daddy seemed worried about her mom. Alex knew Madison would snap out of it because she was tougher than her daddy realized. Alex, however, was not gonna try to talk him out of his concern for her mom.

Alex jogged along the shoulder and noticed a motorcycle turned over in the weeds off to the side of the road. She immediately drew her gun and scanned the area after dropping to one knee. Alex tossed a stone in the vicinity of the motorcycle just to see if she could stir up any movement. The woods remained still and quiet.

She holstered her weapon and ran up to the outside edge of the curve to get a better look. Once again, luckily, there was no activity. They had made it through the last several overpasses without incident. That one underpass had been another story.

She waved the truck forward and continued to monitor the woods around the fallen motorcycle. As her dad pulled up, Alex turned her back to the woods and leaned in the window.

"Daddy, there's an abandoned motorcycle over the embankment. Do you think it runs?"

"Honey, I don't know anything about motorcycles, but from what I understood listening to the folks on the radio coming back from Dallas, their electronics would be fried just like other newer vehicles."

"Okay," said Alex. As she opened the door to the truck, she was startled by the rustling of the weeds behind her. She immediately drew her pistol and turned toward the noise. The tall grasses swayed as a feral hog entered the clearing, followed by three pint-size piglets.

Alex let out a huge sigh of relief and put her gun away. "Daddy, it's a momma pig and her three little pigs. They're so adorable!"

Alex started toward the sow and her piglets, but Colton called her back. "Alex, don't get too close. These wild hogs can be dangerous, especially if you threaten the momma's babies."

Alex stopped and accidentally kicked some gravel in the road. The female hog heard this and let out a series of grunts and growls as she turned toward Alex. Alex backed up a few paces and felt for her weapon. After a moment, the sow squealed, turned and ran into the woods, followed immediately by her babies.

Make no mistake, regardless of species, there is nothing more dangerous than a mother protecting her young.

CHAPTER 21

DAY SIXTEEN
5:40 p.m., September 24
Natchez Trace Parkway
Laurel Hill Wildlife Area, Tennessee

They approached the entrance to the Laurel Hill Wildlife Area with caution. Their last trek through a Tennessee State Park didn't end so well. Alex calculated that they were only ten miles from the east-west route of U.S. Highway 64, which would take them directly into Savannah. It would've been hard to vocalize the frustration held inside by Colton for the slow pace they were forced to take. Between gas conservation and the constant surveillance of crossroads and overpasses, they were moving like a herd of turtles.

Despite his anxiousness to get to the safety of Shiloh, he wasn't going to place his family at any additional risk. Taking the backroads involved more population and potential for roadblocks, although he was beginning to wonder how it could be any worse than what they'd experienced thus far. If they had to go around the massive wildlife area, they'd add a couple of hours to the trip and burn an extra few gallons of gas.

It was getting dark and Colton didn't want to lose sight of the potential threats up ahead, so they followed their normal routine as they carefully entered the park. Colton parked the car and gave Alex instructions.

"I want you to stand guard outside the truck," started Colton. "Before I forget, be sure to refill the magazines, okay?" Colton glanced into the backseat one last time to check on Madison, who was still sleeping.

"Okay, got it, Daddy," replied Alex. "Daddy, we're getting closer to the final stretch."

"Yeah, let's see what we've got up ahead and then we'll go," said Colton as he started a slow jog toward the turn into the park. Around this stretch of road was a mile-long cleared area surrounded by trees. With binoculars, he'd be able to get a good idea of what was ahead.

It didn't take Colton long to get a view of what they faced, and the decision was an easy one—turn around. He hustled behind a guardrail on the outside of the curve and took up a position that was relatively concealed. Just a hundred yards away was a series of encampments with roaring fires built around each.

He could see several deer hanging upside down from trees, their skins removed, and blood dripping from the lowest part of their bodies allowing gravity to bleed out the dead animals. There were several men field dressing their kill, and some of the women were cooking the meat over the fire.

The scene was surreal in comparison to what they'd observed the last couple of days. These families were working together to feed themselves and had created perimeter security for the camp. There were a couple of men standing on the road, holding their rifles at a low-ready position and smoking cigarettes. There was a similar set of sentries at the other end of the encampment.

Colton wanted to believe that these people were not cut from the same cloth as the marauders on the Duck River Bridge, or even the crazed kids at the Devil's Backbone. He didn't know and realized he couldn't take the risk of being outgunned by a group of seasoned hunters, much less a dozen or more of them.

Curiosity kept Colton from running back to the truck and turning around. He didn't see any cars, but there were a variety of all-terrain vehicles parked throughout the camp. Colton wondered if the ATVs worked despite the solar flare. As he studied the interaction between the people, there didn't appear to be any indication of hostility. It could be the folks knew each other and were possibly there for a hunting trip or family get-together. In any event, they appeared close-knit and probably wouldn't appreciate the intrusion of the Wagoneer rolling through their camp.

Colton jogged back to the truck and joined Madison, who was awake and stretching her legs. She ran to Colton and gave him a hug like she hadn't seen him for weeks. A kiss sealed their embrace.

"Well, hello to you too." Colton laughed.

"I feel so much better," said Madison. "The nap worked wonders. What did you see?"

"We have to turn around, so I'll tell you about it on the way around Laurel Hill. Let me just say it was encouraging."

"In what way?" asked Madison.

"Well, they looked like a decent enough group of people, which gives me hope that survivors who want to rely on themselves rather than taking from others actually exist."

Madison laughed. "You'd think a group of Boy Scouts would have adopted that self-reliant mind-set too."

"I believe their leadership was lacking," said Colton. "The scoutmaster's bad judgment resulted in him paying the ultimate price. As much as I admired the interaction I just observed, I think we'll drive around, just in case."

Madison squeezed her husband around the waist and gave him a peck on the cheek.

"I agree," added Madison, releasing their hug and looking around at their desolate surroundings. "After the collapse, out here, it's better safe than sorry because too much of the time, sorry means you'll be dead."

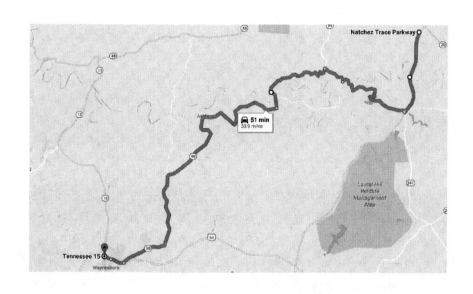

CHAPTER 22

DAY SIXTEEN
6:20 p.m., September 24
Highway 99
Perry Hollow, Tennessee

Alex found them a suitable highway that circled around the Laurel Hill Wildlife Area and dropped them just west of the Natchez Trace Parkway–U.S. Highway 64 intersection. Once they picked up Highway 64, they were only a couple of hours from Shiloh.

Colton drove along the Buffalo River, one of many small tributaries that crossed the mid-state and fed both the Tennessee River and the Duck River. Farmland was abundant along these river bottoms, evidenced by several farmhouses and barns, which began to appear on both sides of the road. Fires could be seen near the homes, as people on these backroads didn't seem to worry about passersby coming onto their property. Once again, Colton questioned his decision to take even a secondary highway like the Trace out of Nashville, but that leg of the journey was behind them.

The road opened up into the middle of a huge cattle farm with hundreds of head on both sides of the highway. For over a mile, they drove past the enormous source of food, not once thinking about killing a steer for themselves. It never crossed Colton's mind, perhaps because they weren't hungry enough to take such drastic measures.

Before they entered the woods again, Colton spied a barn well off the road and outside the fenced grazing pasture containing the cattle. As it was getting darker, he thought they could pull off the road, park behind the barn, and get a good night's sleep without being threatened.

"Hey, let's go camping again." Alex laughed. "This time, we can sleep with the cows and mules in the barn instead of the bugs and the snakes by the lake."

"We wanted you to have a well-rounded experience while on the road, young lady," said Colton.

"Yeah, *well-rounded*," chimed in Madison. "Listen, this is less of a camping trip than it is a homeless family pulling over for the night."

Colton parked the truck and then walked around the barn to make sure they weren't seen. The Wagoneer was well-hidden, so he was comfortable with his choice. He helped the girls unpack the tent and get set up. Although they could've found a place to sleep in the barn, they chose not to run the risk of trespassing in the event the property owner showed up. There was no need to antagonize people who were already on edge.

"Daddy, do we need to set up the perimeter security?"

"You know, Alex, I think we're okay here. Let's keep one person awake to stand watch. We'll eat first and then get some rest. I wanna start just before dawn in the morning."

"We're really close now, aren't we, Colt?"

"Thirty miles to Savannah," he replied. Madison ran and gave him another hug. She was ready to get settled in somewhere, anywhere.

They built a small fire and enjoyed their favorite camp food, Vienna sausages and sardines. This time, they had peanut butter and crackers for dessert. The Rymans actually enjoyed rehashing the day's events, although they didn't bring up the killing of the scoutmaster.

Alex told her parents a little more about the young man they'd encountered back in Williamsport. She wondered aloud what it would be like to date a country boy. That quickly shifted into what it would be like to date a country star, which got Colton's hackles up. No way, no how, he'd insisted. The teasing of Colton accelerated as Alex created an imaginary list of country music personalities she'd bring home to her daddy, just to gain a reaction. She'd just suggested Kid Rock as a possible beau when the whinny of a horse sent them scrambling for their weapons.

"There'll be no need for those, folks," said a gravelly voice out of the darkness as a man sitting high on a quarter horse overlooked their camp. Colton continued to reach for his pistol when the sound of the hammer cocking on a rifle caught him by surprise.

"Let's not do that, young man," said an elderly woman, who walked her horse around the Wagoneer into their view.

The man eased closer and Colton could see he had a double-barreled shotgun pointed at his chest. He slowly stood with his arms spread away from his body.

"We don't want any trouble," said Colton sheepishly. "My family and I are just passin' through. We thought this was a safe place to sleep for the night."

"Yes, sir," added Madison, who also stood to shield the man's view of Alex. "We'll clean up our mess and be on our way."

"There'll be no need for that," he responded gruffly. "All of y'all stand up where I can see ya. Keep your arms spread away from your body. You too, young lady. On your feet."

Alex obeyed the man and the Rymans stood in a huddle with their arms held wide. For a minute, nobody spoke as the fire continued to send dancing flames into the sky, casting a shadow of the family on the broad side of the barn.

"What's your name, son?" asked the man.

"My name is Colton Ryman, and this is my wife, Madison, and our daughter, Alex. We're really sorry."

"You kin to Cap'n Tom?"

"Yessir," replied Colton. "My family was part of the Rymans who went out west with Davy Crockett in the late eighteen hundreds. They settled in Texas."

"You'uns from Texas," asked the lady behind them.

"I was born there, but Madison is from Nashville," replied Colton. He intentionally referred to Madison and Alex by name, hoping to personalize them in case these people had plans on killing them. He hoped it would make it harder for them to do so.

"What brings you way out here from Nashville?" asked the man.

"The city became too dangerous," replied Colton. "We're making our way toward Shiloh to join up with some friends. It's been, um, rough going so far." Colton dropped his arm and took Madison's hand in his. She became emotional and spoke up.

"Please don't shoot us," said Madison, sniffling as she held back the tears.

"Whadya think, Ma?"

"Well, your granddaddy did work on Cap'n Tom's riverboats back in the day. That makes this young man practically family."

"Yes'm, I agree," said the man as he stuffed his rifle into a scabbard attached to his saddle. His wife did the same and the man quickly dismounted. He approached Colton and extended his hand.

"My name is Richard Linn, but you can call me Dick."

"Pleasure to meet you, sir," said Colton, shaking the man's hand heartily after wiping the sweat off his palms onto his shirt.

"My name is Shirley," said the lady as she dismounted and tied her horse to the bumper of the Wagoneer.

"Oh, thank goodness." Madison laughed, wiping the tears off her face as she gave Mrs. Linn an unexpected hug.

"Well, okay, dearie, we're pleased to meet y'all as well." Mrs. Linn laughed.

Colton turned to comfort his wife and said, "She, I mean, we've had a rough day."

"Yeah, my mom had to—"

"Alex," Colton quickly interrupted, "why don't you get these nice folks a bottle of water. Or we have some Cokes, but they're warm."

"No, young lady, don't you bother with that," said Mr. Linn. "We're only gonna stay for a moment. Colton, you seem like good folks, but I trust you'll be hospitable and not make a mistake and reach for those weapons. I'm pretty fast on the draw." Mr. Linn patted the pearl-handled revolver sitting in a leather holster on his hip.

"No, sir. We appreciate you being kind to us. If we could just stay the night, we'll be out of your way first thing in the morning."

"Okay then," said Mr. Linn. "You're headed to Shiloh, you say?"

"Yessir," replied Colton. "A friend has some property on the river and it's kinda secluded. We thought it would be safer than what we experienced in Nashville."

The Linns and the Rymans spent the next couple of hours trading stories. Shirley gave them a big sack of beef jerky that she kept in her saddlebags. Dick shared the news that the Pickwick Dam to their south was closed and heavily guarded by the military. Apparently, the power outage was creating concerns about the Tennessee River spilling into the valley below.

He also told them it was a wise move avoiding Interstate 40. Refugees fleeing Memphis and Nashville were being rounded up and placed into FEMA camps in Jackson. Vehicles and guns were being confiscated, and people were dying within the confines of the camp due to the deplorable conditions.

Finally, they learned a little bit about Savannah. The Linns hadn't run across anyone coming out of the town, so they presumed it must be pretty safe. There was a former civil defense radio station broadcasting that you could pick up as you got closer to the town.

They were also told that the mayor of Savannah was one tough old bird who ran the town on the straight and narrow.

"What's the mayor's name?" asked Madison.

"Betty Jean Durham, the daughter of former Sheriff Buford Pusser. Folks round these parts call her Ma Durham."

CHAPTER 23

September 20, 1984
Home of Leroy & Betty Jean Durham
Adamsville, Tennessee

Over the last twenty-five years or so, tiny Adamsville, Tennessee, had seen more than its share of violence. In the sixties, many argued that Sheriff Buford Pusser should've left the criminals alone to make their money. After all, liquor, prostitution, and gambling were victimless crimes. In a free country, they'd said, these things would be legal everywhere. All a man had to do was drive to Las Vegas and they could get their fill of all of the above without breakin' the law.

Sheriff Pusser had walked tall, carried his big stick, and made it his life's mission to clean up McNairy County. After the spectacular crash that took his life in '74, violent crimes died down. This respite in the murder rate did not result from superior law enforcement, but rather agreements reached with the criminal element via handshakes and envelope exchanges.

Then there was the murder of the Tindles in '76. No one suspected Betty Jean of being the shooter, although her grandmother had been the target of the investigation for a while. The crime remained unsolved, officially, but everybody in the county *knew* it was one of the Pusser women.

After the brutal rape of '78, Betty Jean became pregnant. A failed attempt to end her pregnancy by ingesting a bleach and gunpowder mixture landed Betty Jean in the hospital for three weeks, after which her grandmother insisted that she carry the child to term. For the remainder of her pregnancy, she watched over Betty Jean like a hawk.

A healthy baby boy, Buford Pusser II, was born on Martin Luther

King Jr.'s birthday in '79 and life went on for Betty Jean. She raised her child with the help of her grandmother until she met Leroy Durham, the newest addition to the McNairy County Public Works Department. The two wed and soon thereafter Betty Jean gave birth to another boy, Leroy Durham Junior. Newly minted Papa Leroy immediately took to fatherhood but insisted that Betty Jean's first born become a Durham. So, Buford Pusser II became Roland Durham, nicknamed Rollie, as in Rollie Durham—the birthplace of that illiterate fool Leroy Durham's favorite cigarettes.

Leroy was a heavy drinker and frequently abused the small-framed and somewhat frail Betty Jean. Betty Jean took her licks, but she made up for her inability to fight back with a mouth that absolutely wore Leroy out. Their arguments were legendary around town as the neighbors frequently called 9-1-1 in fear for someone's life in the Durham home.

Thursday, September 20, 1984, started out like most days except the big news was the bombing of the U.S. Embassy in Beirut, Lebanon, by the terrorist group Hezbollah. While most of the town was talking about the third such attack in two years, Betty Jean was looking forward to the debut of *The Bill Cosby Show* that evening. She was none too happy when Leroy came home, cracked open a bottle of whisky, and announced they were going to Selmer for a patriot rally to show support for three young men who'd enlisted in the service that day.

Initially, she refused, but Leroy, of course, showed her the error of her ways right quick like. Betty Jean, who'd been forbidden to allow her grandmother to be alone with the boys by Leroy, hastily arranged for a sitter to watch over the youngsters.

The night in Selmer was full of bravado and alcohol-fueled speeches as McNairy County celebrated sending three pimple-faced teens off to join the Army. Leroy got drunk, Betty Jean got mouthy, and the return trip to Adamsville was a WWE event on four wheels.

Betty Jean immediately went to bed, barely speaking to the fifteen-year-old girl she'd labeled a hussy when she'd arrived to babysit earlier in the evening. Betty Jean always resented the girls who could fill out a pair of Daisy Duke shorts and a crop top like some pin-up chick in a magazine.

The news of what happened didn't reach Betty Jean until she showed up for work the next day at the Pickwick Electric Cooperative office. Leroy, who took the sitter home, had been caught having sexual relations with that hussy in the backseat of the Durhams' car parked in the girl's driveway. As the story went, the hussy's father discovered the two and his daughter immediately cried rape, despite Leroy's arguments to the contrary.

Because Leroy was drunk and the girl was only fifteen, rape charges were levied and a trial date was set. The family lived in shame, as Betty Jean was ostracized and her boys were ridiculed at school.

It was a miserable period for Betty Jean, but things brightened up when the hussy got pregnant by a black fella in Selmer and ran off to New Awlins or Birmin'ham or some such. It didn't much matter, as Leroy was off the hook without a witness to prosecute him.

But he wasn't let off the hook in the court of public opinion. A few days after the charges were dropped, a mob of locals showed up in the front yard of their modest, split-level home. They began to shout at the Durhams and then hurled Molotov cocktails at their house. Three of the fire-bombs found their way into the living room, where a drunk, passed-out Leroy Durham occupied the sofa.

Amidst the flames, Betty Jean scrambled around and gathered up her two sleepy-eyed boys in their matching Scooby-Doo pajamas and ran out the front door. She was about to turn and wake Leroy when the boys were pelted with eggs. Dozens of rancid eggs, allowed to spoil for this special occasion, rained on top of their heads.

Betty Jean gave the house another look; it was fully engulfed in flames.

He weren't no good anyway. He weren't no 'count.

"Git!" shouted one of the mob.

"Yeah, go on now, Betty Jean. We've had 'nuf of ya!"

"Git outta McNairy County!"

The mob was closing in on them and Junior started to cry as he clutched his momma's leg. It was her five-year-old, Rollie, who made the decision.

"C'mon, Ma. Let's go."

That night Betty Jean Durham and her boys drove across the Tennessee River on the Harrison-McGarity Bridge into Savannah, leaving McNairy County behind forever.

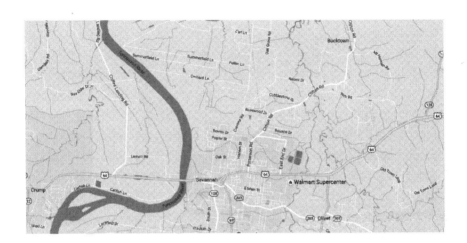

CHAPTER 24

DAY SEVENTEEN
9:00 a.m., September 25
Highway 64, Savannah Highway
Waynesboro, Tennessee

Anxiety isn't ordinarily a condition associated with positive feelings and emotions. Most often, anxiety causes you to focus your attention on negative thinking and creates a mental environment that's prone to noticing only negative events in your life while overlooking the positive aspects that surround you.

It can be hard to believe that many times anxiety is diagnosed when a person is exhibiting periods of euphoria, excitement and happiness. Happiness is always considered a positive emotion and runs contrary to everything we know about anxiety.

In the post-collapse world, highs and lows are amplified. Small setbacks seem insurmountable. Minor advances appear to be leaps and bounds. In the world of psychobabble, euphoria can take over one's psyche as the natural result of a temporary absence of negative emotions. During this brief period of euphoria, it's natural for humans to trigger such complete feelings of relief and happiness as though you're ready to take on the world. Unfortunately, this euphoria can cloud your judgment, resulting in obvious danger signals being ignored.

"On the road again," sang Colton, turning the Wagoneer westbound onto Highway 64. The drive through the intersection at Waynesboro was uneventful, as the small town, which was located primarily south of the turn on to Highway 64, appeared to be either abandoned or folks were staying inside their homes.

"C'mon, Daddy, it's too early for singing."

"How 'bout another song, one of your mom's old favorites," said Colton. "Highway to the danger zone—"

"Colton, I'm gonna have to agree with the kid," interrupted Madison. "Zip it!"

Colton ignored them and kept up the fun. "Hey, Allie-Cat, did you know that your mom used to have a *thang* for Tom Cruise from when he was in the *Top Gun* movie? She even had a poster of him in her room."

"A thang?" Madison chirped. "You had a *Sports Illustrated* poster of Christie Brinkley in yours. What were you thinking when she smiled at you every day, young man?"

"Ewwwww!" groaned Alex.

"You can thank your grandmothers for sharing these two tidbits about our teenage years with your parents," said Colton. Colton slowed as they passed Kelly Mobile Homes. Several of the trailers in their inventory had become temporary lodging for travelers. Clotheslines were stretched between the mobile homes, and fires were smoldering in fifty-five-gallon drums from last night's activities.

"I'm amazed at the difference in this wide, four-lane highway and what we've been used to on the Trace," said Madison. "I think we'll be able to travel without stopping constantly to observe bridges and crossroads."

"Notice all of the stalled cars," added Colton. "These folks obviously got caught out here at the time of the solar storm. I'll betcha they moved into those mobile homes back there."

The road started to narrow and the Rymans were once again traveling on a two-lane highway.

"So much for our superspeedway," said Madison. "I'll take binocular duty if Alex handles the map." She passed the maps to the backseat and immediately took up her watch. She had to be careful staring through the binoculars for too long while they drove. It had a tendency to make her stomach queasy.

"Okay, Daddy," started Alex. "You should be good to go for a while until the road turns four lane again near Clifton Junction. As we approach the town, there are two side streets that can take us around if need be."

"Good deal, Allie-Cat," said Colton. "Now, which song do we wanna sing next?"

"No song!" the girls replied in unison.

"Fine," said a dejected Colton. "Hey, wait, I know. What was that AM station they told us about last night? WORM or something like that?"

"Yeah, 1010 AM," said Alex. Madison set down the binoculars and tuned the radio to 1010. The broadcast was full of static, probably due to the tall rocky inclines on both sides of the highway during this stretch. She fiddled with the dial some more until it provided a better signal.

BEEEP—BEEEP—BEEEP.

"This is a test. For the next thirty seconds, this station will conduct a test of the Emergency Broadcast System. This is only a test."

BEEEP—BEEEP—BEEEP.

"Good evening, this is Gerald Hart, owner of WORM, 1010 AM, Savannah's Pure Gold Station and a designated participant in our nation's Civil Defense Program."

"Wait, he said evening," said Alex.

"Probably a recorded message," added Colton.

"We are honored to be one of several dozen small AM band radio stations around the country that has participated in our nation's Civil Defense Program since the 1960s. In conjunction with the United States military and upon directives of the President of the United States, this station will broadcast news alerts from time to time in times of a natural disaster. Stay tuned to WORM, 1010 AM, Savannah's Pure Gold Station, for further updates. Now, we return you to our regular programming."

Predictably, an Elvis Presley song streamed through the radio. Colton turned down the volume, although he was prepared to join in the chorus of "Blue Suede Shoes."

"Whadya'll think of that?" he asked.

"It sounds like civilization to me," replied Alex.

Madison took up the binoculars and continued to scan the road ahead. "You know what seemed odd to me?"

"What's that?" asked Colton.

Madison scooched up in her seat and turned to face both Colton and Alex. "I wanna hear the recording again, but it was almost if it had been made prior to the solar storm. The radio station's owner read something, um, I don't know, *generic*."

Colton thought about this for a moment and was about to weigh in when the beeping sound came across the speakers again. He quickly turned up the volume and a raspy woman's voice could be heard.

"Good afternoon to all of those who can hear my voice. I am Mayor Betty Jean Durham of Savannah, Tennessee. We are located on the banks of the beautiful Tennessee River about one hundred miles east of Memphis and ninety miles south of Jackson, Tennessee.

"We have all been delivered a jolt by this catastrophe. Loved ones have been lost here, as well as around our nation.

"Our tiny community plans to do its part to rebuild West Tennessee and help others survive. I am reaching out to those of you who might be able to assist us. For now, I must tell you that we are only capable of taking in specific types of families. Please do not come to Savannah at this time unless you meet one of the following criteria.

"First, if you have an operating vehicle, you and your immediate family only are welcome. Second, if you are active-duty military or law enforcement, you and your immediate family only are welcome. Third, if you are a physician or medical support personnel, you and your immediate family only are welcome.

"I apologize for those who've been displaced and are looking for a new home. The time will come when we'll be able to help you. For now, we have to get on our feet, using the people I've just invited; then we'll be able to help others.

"Here in Savannah, we are a group of Americans who take great pride in preserving our heritage and dispensing our Southern charm.

The time will come when we'll be able to extend our hospitality to all of you."

BEEEP—BEEEP—BEEEP.

"This is a test. For the next thirty seconds—" Colton turned down the radio.

"Okay, now that was obviously current," he said. "Sounds like she's trying to single-handedly create a recovery effort in this small town."

"It does kinda make sense," added Madison. "Although Savannah is small, it is the largest town on the Tennessee River in West Tennessee. And it's the largest town for nearly a hundred miles."

Alex leaned over the bench seat with the map in her hand. "Daddy, Clifton Junction is up ahead. I don't know if there's a town located where the roads intersect, but you might wanna slow down so I can take a look."

Colton slowed and worked his way through Haggard Hollow until the road intersection came into view. He motioned for Madison to slide him the binoculars down the dashboard. He studied the intersection for a moment and continued forward.

"Here's what I think," said Colton. "These small towns can't handle an influx of refugees with nothing but the clothes on their backs. They'll need shelter, water and food, but offer little or nothing in return. A town's resources are limited. The deputy said as much during our conversation back in Williamsport."

"It sounds like she's being pretty selective about who she wants to invite in," said Madison.

"Yeah," said Colton slowly. "That's true, but it also makes sense. Her first concerns would be the town's safety, hence the additional people with military and law enforcement background. Then, she's rightfully concerned about the health of her citizens and the strong potential for the spread of illness or disease. Without operating ambulances and Life Flight helicopters, Savannah could become a center of medical facilities for the residents in the surrounding counties."

Alex leaned forward again. "What's with the cars?"

"Now, that's a good question," replied Colton. "I can only guess that those individuals would be put into some type of service working for the county using their car in exchange for some form of compensation."

"Like an ambulance or for police duties," added Madison.

The Rymans drove on in silence for a moment, each analyzing what they'd learned and attempting to visualize the promise that Savannah held.

CHAPTER 25

DAY SEVENTEEN
10:00 a.m., September 25
Highway 64, Savannah Highway
Savannah, Tennessee

"I'm excited, but kinda nervous too," said Alex as the divided highway came into view and homes started to become more prevalent. "Daddy, do we need to check out these side roads? I mean, we don't wanna let our guard down, right?"

"No, honey, of course not," replied Colton. "We have a nice, wide road to work with and we're just a few miles from town. It sounds to me like this mayor's got it together. If there's any sign of trouble, I've got plenty of room to maneuver."

Alex scooted along the rear seat and pressed her nose against the window. "Look, guys, they're picking corn over here. Can you see the people walking down the rows, filling their bags slung over their shoulders?"

"Sure enough," said Colton as he accidentally started to drift toward the grassy median while he rubbernecked the activity. Madison gently reached over and grabbed the wheel to put him back on track.

"Look on this side," said Madison as the Vulcan Quarry came into view. "I see people working on the side of that mountain, and it looks like some kind of machine is operating."

Alex slid to the other side of the truck to get a better look. There was activity. People were working. It appeared normal.

"Well, I'll be dogged," said Colton as he pointed in front of them. An old school bus with different colored paints covering it slowed to

114

turn into the Vulcan Quarry. Colton started laughing hysterically. "They're using their turn signal. I bet they never thought they'd have to do that again."

"Unbelievable," said Madison as Colton slowed the Wagoneer to get a better look at the rare sight of another operating vehicle. "It looks like *The Partridge Family* bus."

"Who?" asked Alex.

"Never mind, honey," started Colton. "It's before *our* time. Your mom, on the other hand—"

"Zip it, Mr. Ryman," said Madison. "You're old enough to remember *The Partridge Family* too."

"Reruns, maybe." Colton laughed as he picked up speed.

Alex caught a glimpse of two armed guards walking out of the shack near the entry of the quarry, contacting others on their radios.

After a moment, Madison spoke up. "You know, I think I can understand why people would locate here rather than finding some place out in the woods."

"Yeah, me too," said Colton. "People like us don't know anything about living off the grid. We haven't learned how to be self-sufficient, you know, like living off the land."

Madison agreed and added, "At least in a town like this one, there may be limited resources, but they at least have some form of local infrastructure like a government, police, and possibly medical care."

"I think Savannah is about the right size," said Colton. "I'm going from memory here, but it can't be much more than five thousand people living here. If they come together, they can trade goods and services as well as watch each other's backs."

"Also, don't forget the social aspect," said Madison. "All of those folks know each other and the mayor seems to make certain people feel welcome as they start the rebuilding process. I think it would be nice to assimilate into a small community where you can make new friends."

"Daddy, do you think that's what the mayor has done here?" asked Alex.

"It sure looks and sounds like it," he replied. "I know this, we've driven into their community without getting shot at. That's a great start in my book."

They continued toward town, the maps and binoculars set aside, but with noses pressed to the windows, taking in the sights. To their left, workers picked cotton. On the right, another group gathered green beans. It was Alex who noticed something off-kilter.

"Did you guys notice there were armed men standing around the fields where the people were picking crops?" she asked.

"Well, dear, it does make sense," replied Madison. "A group could come out of the woods over there to rob them. I guess the workers feel more comfortable with the guards protecting them, considering the world we live in now."

Alex shrugged. There was something else she noticed, but she decided not to bring it up. Her parents seemed to have a logical explanation for everything. Something bothered Alex about the people on the multicolor bus pulling into the quarry. They looked sad. It was more than the appearance of someone who hated going to work. Those faces seemed miserable.

"Hey, look," said Colton as he pointed to an airport sign. "We can fly out of here for our next vacay!"

The Rymans drove across a small bridge over a creek. They started down the incline when the big box stores of Lowes and Walmart came into view, as did a welcoming committee. Without the ability to stop and turn around, they were in the middle of a roadblock, facing a dozen armed men.

The sign on the shoulder of the road read *The City of Savannah Welcomes You.*

CHAPTER 26

DAY SEVENTEEN
11:30 a.m., September 25
Highway 64, Savannah Highway
Savannah, Tennessee

Savannah, Tennessee, the county seat of Hardin County, was a small town of around six thousand residents and sat on the eastern banks of the Tennessee River. The river divided Hardin County into two distinct geographic regions. The western half of the county was rich bottomland with some hills and ridges—ideal for farming. The land east of the river was higher with a steadily increasing elevation—ideal for quarry operations and industrial production.

Hardin County was also divided politically. In the eighteen hundreds, the mostly rural and agricultural western half of the county was decidedly Democrat and had favored the Southern cause during the Civil War. The eastern side of the Tennessee River had supported the North and contained mainly Republicans. Over time, party affiliations and platforms flipped, and the western half of the county became more conservative.

The Civil War had moved across the county several times, including the historic Battle of Shiloh, which took place between Shiloh Church and Pittsburg Landing in April of 1862. Make no mistake, in parts of the Deep South, nerves were still raw over the divide created over one hundred fifty years ago.

"Don't move," said Colton as he abruptly brought the truck to a stop next to the concrete barricades blocking the road. The roadblock was set up across the five lanes of Highway 64 in front of Lowe's on the right and Walmart on the left.

117

Colton slowly took his hands off the wheel and placed them on the dashboard next to Alex's solar panel and charging iPhone. Madison followed his lead and Alex quickly placed her hands on the top of the bench seat in front of her. "We don't have any choice but to hope for the best here. I'm sorry, guys."

"Colton, it'll be fine," said Madison. "They're just protecting their town. Once they hear we're passin' through, they'll allow us to continue on our way."

The men guarding the highway slowly walked around the Wagoneer with their rifles pointed at the Rymans. They looked in all of their windows and raised the tarp to reveal the hitch rack's contents.

"I've got one male, two females," announced one of the men. A man dressed in jeans and a black tucked-in polo shirt approached from the rear of the guarded area. He was unarmed except for his smile. He walked up to the driver's side and made a circular motion indicating he wanted Colton to roll down the window.

"Hello," said Colton sheepishly.

"Well, greetings, weary travelers, and welcome to Savannah," said the man. "My name is William Cherry with the Hardin County Chamber of Commerce." Colton thought he heard snickers in the background from a couple of the men, but he couldn't be sure. He focused his attention on the man's face.

"My name's Joshua Dalton," lied Colton. "This here is my wife, Carol, and my daughter Rennie. We're just passin' through."

"Well, Mr. Dalton, we'd be happy to oblige you folks, but I hope you understand, these are unusual times and we have to be mighty careful who we allow to cross through our fair city," said Cherry. "My family has lived in these parts since the war and we're a little protective of our family and friends. You can understand that, right?"

Colton glanced at Madison and then surveyed the roadblock. He was trying to get a sense of whether they were in danger or not. The vehicles used by the men appeared to be manufactured in the late sixties or early seventies, similar to the Wagoneer. He also noticed some of the men had two-way radios attached to their belts. If they

118

had communications and operating vehicles elsewhere, running wasn't a good option—especially with a dozen rifles pointed at them. He had to play it out.

"Of course," replied Colton cheerily. "We've heard so many great things about Savannah. And we heard your very welcoming radio broadcast. But we're headed west and would just like to pass through town on 64 if y'all don't mind."

"Where ya headed?" asked Cherry.

Colton hesitated. "Um, Memphis."

"Well now, Mr. Dalton, Memphis ain't exactly a hospitable place right about now. The locals are burning the city to the ground. Ya sure that's where you wanna go?"

Colton tried to make his lie better. "I mean, we're not going all the way to Memphis. Her sister, you know, lives just outside of Germantown. They've got a place—"

"A farm," interrupted Madison, causing Cherry to crouch and look into the passenger's seat at Madison. "My sister and brother-in-law have a farm just outside of Germantown. We're goin' there, you know, to bug out."

Cherry started laughing, which caused some of his men to laugh along with him. "Boys, these folks are *bugging out*," he said sarcastically. "They're *bugging out* to Germantown."

"Right," said Colton, who didn't understand the sarcastic tone of Cherry.

"I have to say, we've had plenty of folks come to Savannah, claiming to be buggin' out, but none were headed to Germantown." Cherry laughed and withdrew from the Wagoneer and summoned two of this men over. After some whispering back and forth, they shouldered their weapons and headed for two of the cars parked in the Lowe's parking lot.

"Daddy, are we gonna be okay?" whispered a concerned Alex from the backseat. Colton's eyes darted around, trying to assess the situation. He didn't want to appear to be overly nervous.

"Honey, I think so," he replied hesitantly.

Cherry returned with his signature grin. "Okay, Mr. and Mrs.

Dalton," he started. "These men are going to be your escorts. Please follow the blue Dodge, and the white Chevy pickup will follow you folks."

"Okay," said Colton as he reached to start the ignition.

"Hold up, Mr. Dalton," said Cherry, which startled Colton. "I'm not done yet. We have certain protocols to follow, you know, for the safety of all concerned. I'm sure you folks have weapons, and we're not going to confiscate them from you. But, out of an abundance of caution, those men in the back of the pickup truck will be watching you carefully. They are deputized and armed with automatic weapons. We can't be too careful. You understand, right?"

"Yes, of course," replied Colton, who was willing to say anything to move out of this tense situation. "We'll follow as instructed. It was a pleasure to meet you." Colton attempted to extend his hand to shake Cherry's, but the man walked away and circled his hand in the air, indicating that the escort vehicles should get moving.

Colton pulled in behind the Dodge and they rolled slowly towards town. As expected, the white pickup with two men dressed in camouflage, dark sunglasses, and backwards-turned caps leaned on the roof of the truck, with guns pointed at them.

By Colton's calculation, it was about three or four miles through town to the bridge crossing the river. He had committed to this course of action and intended to dutifully follow their instructions. There really wasn't a better option at this juncture.

There were things known in life, and then there was the unknown. In between, there were adventures. Colton had no illusions about this new post-apocalyptic world, but there was one thing he knew for certain—don't think you're on the right road just because the road is smooth.

CHAPTER 27

DAY SEVENTEEN
2:30 p.m., September 25
Highway 64, Main Street
Savannah, Tennessee

If nobody knew you—you were a stranger. If Alex had seen someone walking back and forth in front of their home, and she didn't recognize them, they would immediately have fallen under her suspicion. If the person was a neighbor, she wouldn't have given the activity a second thought, other than it might seem odd. But a stranger would stick out and draw additional scrutiny. As they drove into Savannah, Alex understood what it felt like to be a stranger—watched and scrutinized.

"Daddy, all of these businesses are being guarded by men with guns."

"I see them," said Colton. "They must've moved quickly to protect the businesses from looters. That explains why they put a call out to law enforcement and ex-military personnel. They're in need of warm bodies to watch over things."

Colton continued to follow the lead car while Madison and Alex took in the scenery. Except for the occasional burned-down home, the businesses remained intact and under the watchful eye of armed guards.

"Where is everybody?" asked Alex.

"Whadya mean?" replied Madison.

"I see armed guards, but I haven't seen any people yet. Where are the kids playing or the parents walking down the street or anything?"

Another decrepit school bus of workers passed them, headed

toward the quarry. The faces told the same story as the prior busload of workers—despair. Alex took the binoculars from her mother and started to scan the side streets to look for signs of life.

Nothing.

Highway 64 was set to become Savannah's Main Street when another concrete barricaded roadblock appeared and the lead vehicle continued south instead of west toward the river. The Rymans were less than a mile from the bridge that would take them to Shiloh.

"Colton?" asked a worried Madison.

"I don't know, Maddie," replied Colton.

Alex noticed more faces—withdrawn, sullen, and anguished. Eyes peered through curtained windows. The locals poked their heads around the corners of buildings. Children hid behind their mother's skirts as they were hurried out of sight. They were frightened. They were all women and children.

"Look at the old cars," said Colton. "You'd think this was an antique car show at the Tennessee Fairgrounds. Look, Maddie, there's a '69 GTO like mine."

"I saw it, but Colton," started Madison, "most of these cars have out-of-state tags. I've seen Mississippi, Alabama, and Kentucky."

"Okay, but we have Arkansas tags," said Colton. "Maybe folks responded to the radio broadcast. You saw the hospital back there. It appeared there were folks lined up out the front door, waiting to get in."

Alex continued to observe her surroundings. She felt like something was out of sorts.

"Look!" exclaimed Alex. "There, to the left. Do you see those boys running?"

As they slowly drove down Water Street, several teenage boys were shadowing their movement. They would scamper from building to building, using trees and shrubs as cover along the way.

"Curiosity, I guess," replied Colton.

Alex tried to count them—five, six, maybe seven. They were so fast and seemed to disappear so easily. *Why are they following us?*

"Daddy, something's not right here. I can feel it. Mom?"

"Colton, I don't know," started Madison, who suddenly grabbed the dashboard with both hands, bracing for the impact. "Look out!"

The blue Dodge sedan made a sudden swerve to the right and then quickly swung back to the left, effectively blocking both lanes in an attempt to force the Wagoneer into the Hardin County Sheriff's Department. The driver and the passenger jumped out of their vehicle with their guns drawn.

At that moment, the world began to move in slow motion for the Rymans—everything except for Colton's brain, that was. In that moment, the family could sense the mortal danger they were in.

Colton didn't hesitate. He jammed on the brakes, throwing everyone forward. He immediately checked the rearview mirror. Alex glanced backward and saw the grill of the pickup truck filling her view.

"Daddy!" screamed Alex. "What's happening?"

"Colton?"

Colton quickly turned to look at them and said, "I love you."

"What are you doing?" begged Madison.

He opened the door and began to leave, grabbing Alex's iPhone as he went. "Go! You'll find me!"

Colton began sprinting across an open grassy area toward a barn about a quarter mile away. The white pickup threw it in reverse, spun its tires, throwing rancid burnt-tire smell into the air, and sped off across the field after him.

Fear is not real. It's the product of thoughts you create. Danger, however, is very real, but fear is a choice. Colton accepted the danger, but he had no fear.

Chapter 28

DAY SEVENTEEN
2:30 p.m., September 25
Highway 64, Main Street
Savannah, Tennessee

"Mom! Hurry, drive!" shouted Alex, attempting to bring her mother out of her momentary shock. Madison quickly slid under the steering wheel and rammed the truck into drive. The tires spun as Madison launched the Wagoneer toward the men who were approaching with their rifles pointed at the windshield.

Madison whipped the steering wheel to the right to avoid hitting them, but clipped the passenger with the trailer hitch rack, causing him to flip over and roll under the Dodge. He fired wildly toward the Wagoneer in retaliation, but missed his mark.

The driver had better luck, unloading a deluge of bullets into the rear of the truck, which also ricocheted off the Wagoneer's fenders.

"Where's Colton?" hollered Madison as she hopped the curb and sent them both crashing into the ceiling. Several more rounds of bullets flew past the truck and splintered the telephone pole as Madison roared passed. Both of the Ryman women attempted to look for Colton through their side mirrors but had no luck.

"Mom! They're coming after us."

Madison sped up the hill past a dilapidated building and the algae-green swimming pool of the local hotel. She swerved to miss a pothole as the truck gained speed, but then found herself unable to bring the Wagoneer to a stop as she vaulted out of the alley and into the middle of Main Street.

"Which way?" asked Madison. She turned her head back and

forth, temporarily disoriented by the onslaught of activity and bullets.

"Left. Go left!" yelled Alex.

Madison whipped the wheel and floored the gas, barely missing several parked cars in the process. Another round of bullets blew out the windows of the cars next to them as their pursuers entered Main Street, then skidded to a halt and opened fire.

Madison was creating some space between them and the trailing Dodge when Alex shouted, "Look ahead. Two trucks are coming right for us. They're shooting!"

Gunfire erupted from the passengers in both pickup trucks and their bullets ripped up the asphalt pavement in front of the Wagoneer. Madison whipped the truck back and forth, attempting to dodge the bullets, but a few embedded in the Wagoneer's fenders.

"Turn right up here!" shouted Alex, who was fumbling to find their location on the map. "I didn't think of other ways around Savannah. I was just sure this would be okay."

She took the right turn too fast, which threw Alex hard into Madison's shoulder. The rear of the truck slid out from under them and the left rear quarter panel crashed into a metal street sign. Madison overcorrected and the Wagoneer bounced over the sidewalk, sending both girls off their seat and into the ceiling of the truck. She finally brought the truck to a halt as it skidded through a vacant lot up against a tree.

Resting momentarily under the hundred-year-old oak's canopy wasn't an option. The three vehicles pursuing them arrived at the side street simultaneously, resulting in a jumbled mess of cars all attempting to occupy the same space. Shouts and cursing between the men gave Madison an opportunity to get away.

She crossed them up by doubling back, spinning and sliding through the grassy lot toward Main Street. While the pursuing vehicles were wedged together, she hit Main Street with a screech of tires and gassed it towards the bridge crossing the river.

As they rounded the final bend, the concrete barricades came into view and they were greeted with a barrage of gunfire. Alex screamed as a round skipped off the hood of the truck and dinged the passenger side of the windshield. Other rounds careened off the road and past them as Madison deftly whipped the truck past the Huddle House into a gravel parking lot behind three parked eighteen-wheelers.

THUMP—THUMP—THUMP.

The shooters were emptying rounds into the trailers and attempting to skip bullets under the chassis. Madison moved forward, using the big trucks as cover.

"Mom, the three cars are coming!" shouted Alex, pointing to her right. "Two are on Main Street and the other is on the side road right in front of us. You've gotta go!"

Madison gunned it through a yard and drove onto a road that ran northbound, parallel to the river. She sped up the residential street, which was completely empty except for a few parked cars. In that moment, Madison thought it was odd that all of this activity and gunfire didn't bring people out of their homes.

She continued to the north as Alex fumbled with the maps to find their location. "Mom, these maps won't help us because Savannah is too small. There isn't a city map available."

"We have to get out of town," said Madison calmly.

"What? We can't leave Daddy!" protested Alex.

The Dodge sedan rounded the curve behind them and came into view. Their pursuers were gaining speed. Madison looked in the mirrors and reminded herself—*one thing at a time.*

The road took a sudden right turn and Madison braked to slow the heavy Wagoneer. As she did, she saw a circular driveway that led behind a house on the right. She pulled into the driveway and raced around the back. They were now alone and well hidden from the street.

"Help me watch," instructed Madison as she took a deep breath, exhaled, and pushed the hair out of her face. Alex turned and looked between the older homes, which were closely spaced together. They had a narrow, thirty-foot-wide space to observe the street from, but it was enough to notice their speeding pursuers.

First, the Dodge sedan raced past their position, followed less than a minute later by the two pickup trucks. Madison and Alex held their breath for a moment before they started looking for a way out.

"We can't stay here," said Madison. "They have too many men and operating vehicles."

"Radios too," added Alex as she gathered up the AR-15 out of the backseat. She grabbed an extra magazine. She'd made sure all of them were full.

"Let's work our way through these backyards and put some space between us," started Madison. "We need to get out of town and regroup. Then we'll come back for your dad."

Madison drove through to the next street and turned north.

"Mom!" shouted Alex as a car sped through the four-way intersection in front of them. "He saw us. We've gotta hide or something."

The car spun its tires in reverse, throwing black smoke into the air. It was one of those old muscle cars—a Dodge Charger. Lightning fast, the car spun around and was headed for them before Madison reacted.

She turned right into a driveway and looked for an exit through the backyard. She faced a six-foot-tall privacy fence instead. Panicked, she looked for a way out. She started to back out of the driveway when the Charger squealed to a stop behind her before backing up to follow them. Madison was out of options.

"Hold on!" she shouted and floored the gas pedal. She roared toward the wooden fence and crashed through it, sending shrubs and fencing over the top of the Wagoneer.

The truck bounced over a landscape berm then clipped the side of a swing set as it swerved and slid through the backyard. The Charger was right behind them!

Madison didn't have time to think. She slammed the accelerator and crashed through several low-hanging tree limbs before crashing through the fence again at the back of the yard.

"Pool! Pool!" shouted Alex as the back door neighbor's inground swimming pool suddenly came into view. Madison veered to the right, throwing up grass turf and dirt, barely missing the pool decking but plowing through some lawn furniture.

The Charger behind her wasn't as lucky. The debris obstructed their view and the driver was slower to react. The car, and its occupants, dove nose-first into the deep end and flipped upside down before it sank.

Madison didn't wait around to see it submerge completely. She wheeled the Wagoneer through the backyard and out onto the driveway. She hit the street at full speed, whipping the steering wheel back and forth to adjust the top-heavy Wagoneer.

They dashed up the street until a car suddenly appeared from their left. *How many are there?* Madison quickly zigzagged to the right, narrowly missing the new participant's front end. The sedan pulled out behind them and the passenger began firing at them.

"Mom, what do I do?"

"Shoot back!"

Alex pulled the charging handle and leaned out of her window. She fired a few short bursts from the AR-15, which slowed the chasing sedan down.

"They slowed down!" exclaimed Alex.

Madison was approaching sixty miles an hour now and thought she was getting away. Then she glanced to her left and saw two cars speeding alongside on the road next to them. Between the houses, she could see the occupants looking toward her.

"Alex."

"I see them, Mom. They're gonna cut us off."

"Seatbelt, dear," said Madison calmly. "We're not gonna stop." She floored the gas and the truck began to shake when the out-of-balance tires hit seventy miles an hour.

They approached the four-way intersection as the two cars to the left took the curve in their direction. The first car hit the intersection first and was going too fast to stop. It skidded sideways and slid into an oak tree on the other side after spinning three hundred and sixty degrees.

Madison didn't slow the Wagoneer as the second vehicle, which resembled Sheriff Andy's car from Mayberry, slowed into the intersection. A smallish man who resembled Deputy Barney calmly stepped out of the driver's side. He was wearing a sheriff's uniform with a broad-brimmed, brown cowboy hat.

The man began to pull his pistol when Alex opened fire. She didn't hesitate to empty ten rounds into the old-school sheriff's car, sending the man crawling for cover behind it. Madison slowed to drive between the two vehicles as Alex continued firing upon anyone who showed their head. As they got closer, Alex shot out their tires.

Madison gave it gas and roared past, but not before she locked eyes briefly with the sheriff of Hardin County. There was something very wrong about Savannah other than the fact that her husband was on the run and they were being hunted like escaped fugitives. She'd find their way out of town to safety and return to find her husband.

CHAPTER 29

November 2008
Main Street
Savannah, Tennessee

The days following the election of the first black President of the United States overshadowed the local political story in tiny Hardin County, Tennessee, just as Mayor-elect Betty Jean Durham knew it would. If the truth were known, Betty Jean never thought she had a chance to win a county-wide race that was known for its low democratic turnout and heavy money influence in favor of incumbent Republicans. But when it became apparent in June of that year that the democrats were going to nominate their first black candidate for the highest office in the land, Betty Jean shrewdly saw the playing field even out for a mayoral run in democrat-friendly Savannah.

The incumbent Republican mayor and the Hardin County sheriff had both become embroiled in scandals in the fifteen months prior to that November 2008 election. Mayor Wally Walters was finally caught with his paws in the city's cookie jar, helping himself to United Way donations raised by local businesses for a park along the river. He resigned in disgrace and his temporary replacement didn't have a nose for politicking. Not like Betty Jean, anyway.

Hardin County, like most of the South, was full of yellow dog democrats—a term originating in the 1800s for voters who would *vote for a yellow dog before they would vote for any Republican.* The eastern half of the county was full of 'em and Betty Jean knew that all it would take was to get 'em to the polls.

For her to win the mayoral race, she had to make sure the black voter turnout was strong, which seemed to be a given considering the democratic presidential candidate. But she also needed to get other typical democratic constituencies to the ballot box on Election Day.

As it turned out, democratic voter turnout hit an all-time high for the entire county, and Republican voters stayed home, unenthusiastic for Senator John McCain or their local mayoral candidate.

The day after the votes were tallied, Betty Jean was mayor-elect. The town was shocked, but she'd won fair and square. However, that was only half the story of Betty Jean's rise to power and prominence in Hardin County. There was another candidate running for office— Leroy Durham Jr., her youngest boy.

Junior, as all of his deputy buddies called him, wasn't much to look at. He was scrawny like his ma. He used to get bullied as a kid and teased about his appearance. He grew up fightin', like his ma, and defendin' the memories of his famous granddaddy, Sheriff Buford Pusser.

Most folks would've agreed that Junior's older brother, Rollie, would've been better suited to be sheriff. Like their granddaddy, Rollie was a hulk of a man that didn't need his granddaddy's big stick to whoop the tar out of anyone. Rollie, however, found himself in trouble with the law as he turned eighteen and his ma hustled him off to the Marine recruiting office in Memphis before he could get charged with runnin' 'shine. Rollie was destined to become a jarhead.

When Betty Jean saw the possibility of victory in November for her mayoral race, she approached Junior with the wild-eyed scheme to run him for sheriff at the age of twenty-seven. He'd told his ma that she was plumb out of her ever-lovin' mind until she smacked him upside the head and reminded him that his granddaddy became sheriff of McNairy County when he was just twenty-seven.

After a night of explainin' to Junior the *perks* of his being sheriff and how the two of them could run Hardin County together, he jumped on board against all odds. He started a campaign despite the ribbing and condemnation of his few friends in the Sheriff's Department.

Well, as luck would have it, the scandal surrounding his opponent hit the fan as the proverbial October surprise broke just prior to Election Day. Several female employees of the Sheriff's Department came forward and accused the incumbent sheriff of demanding sex in exchange for promotions. The sixty-five-year-old married sheriff was given a carefully orchestrated perp walk just ten days prior to Election Day, which spread to all corners of Hardin County.

Junior became the instant favorite to win, but the Republicans inserted a perfectly acceptable substitute for the disgraced incumbent—the female head of the Savannah Police Department. Betty Jean, however, was undeterred. She always had a backup plan.

Two days before Election Day, Betty Jean was engaged in some pillow talk with her lover and former boss—Mr. Billy Joe Abernathy, the operations manager of the Pickwick Electric Cooperative substations that serviced the western half of Hardin County from Shiloh in the south to Saltillo in the north. Of course, Betty Jean was careful to keep hidden her affair with Billy Joe's counterpart, the operations manager for Tennessee Valley Electric Cooperative, the electricity provider for the eastern half of the county. Betty Jean never put all her eggs in one basket, don't you know.

Now, for those folks who've been payin' attention, the western half of Hardin County was full of Republicans. Betty Jean needed to suppress the vote, and after their night of sweet luvin' and promises of future trysts, old married Billy Joe promised to do her a favor. He agreed to cut the power to his district during the last four hours of Election Day when Republican voter turnout was the heaviest.

In the event of a power outage, the protocol was to switch to a paper ballot process for the remainder of the voting day. The ballots would then be delivered to Savannah, the County Seat, where they would be tallied and added to the electronic totals. Once the paper ballots arrived in Savannah, manipulating the vote count was easy for Betty Jean thanks to her friends in the county canvassing office.

The vote for sheriff was close, and it was surprisin' to everyone in the county, except for Betty Jean, but the local county judge certified it. Junior was *The Man*!

It'd been many years now. Re-elections had come and gone. Ma

Durham and Junior had kept a firm grip on Savannah and Hardin County without challenge. Both Ma and Junior continued to worship, publicly now, the memories of Sheriff Buford Pusser.

By the way, folks have always wondered about those two. 'Cause, you know, their bond to each other was strong—sorta like Norman Bates and his momma.

CHAPTER 30

DAY SEVENTEEN
2:30 p.m., September 25
Hardin County Sheriff's Department
Water Street
Savannah, Tennessee

Colton knew he might die, but his gut told him it was the only way to save his family. Those men never had any intention of letting them cross through town and over the river to Shiloh. When they were diverted by their escorts down the backstreet and Colton saw the dozens of parked vehicles with out-of-state tags, his gut instinct told him it was a trap.

Once the alarm bells rang in his subconscious, the abrupt maneuver of the Dodge to block the road told him they were being herded toward the Sheriff's Department for a reason. He made a judgment call and he hoped Madison and Alex were able to use the distraction to get away.

He was now running for his life. The pickup was a hundred yards behind him but gaining quickly. Colton was not in the best of shape, but his adrenaline surge made up for his lack of athleticism. He ran off the gravel and onto the grass, where his footing was less sure.

POP—POP—POP.

The sound of gunfire echoed off the sheriff's office walls and caused Colton to instinctively duck. He stumbled and almost lost his footing.

CRACKLE—CRACKLE—CRACKLE.

Fireworks? He was nearing the woods when he stepped into a hole, lost his balance, and sprawled face-first onto the rough ground. His face bloodied, Colton rolled over and reached for his gun. He was going to make a stand.

Gunfire erupted, but it was not aimed at him. The pickup truck slid to a stop, spraying gravel and chunks of grass for thirty feet toward Colton. The men turned their attention to a block retaining wall near the buildings across the vacant lot. They immediately opened fire in that direction, tearing off chunks of plaster from the masonry. Although the sound of gunshots filled the air, Colton couldn't see anyone shooting back.

He didn't take the time to analyze what had happened or lick his wounds. He scrambled to his feet and ran into the woods. After scratching and clawing through some dead honeysuckle vines, he found a well-worn path and ran down it.

Later, Colton couldn't recall how long or how far he'd run. He put as much distance between the sheriff's office and the men chasing him as he could. After thirty minutes or so, he ran past an electric substation, where he stumbled upon a creek and finally stopped.

Colton's heart was pounding out of his chest and he got the cold sweats. At first he thought he was having a heart attack, but then he realized it was an anxiety attack. He took a deep breath and exhaled.

Colton was afraid, but that was okay. They'd been through a lot since they'd left Nashville, but this was different. He was separated from the girls and now he was second-guessing his decision. He replayed those moments over and over again. He could've driven across the curb and tried to drive away.

He took another deep breath and put the what-ifs out of his mind. He'd made a decision; now he planned to ensure it was the right one. Colton leaned over the creek and washed his face. He didn't realize how badly scraped his hands and arms were. The cold water stung a little, but it was also refreshing.

He leaned back on the bank and collapsed, staring up at the dormant power lines that crossed through the woods toward the south. Colton wondered if they'd ever carry electricity again. The thoughts of electricity and the girls reminded him of his lifeline. He felt around in his pockets and found Alex's phone. He powered it up and quietly said a prayer thanking God that it worked. Now, he had to hope the girls figured out why he'd taken it with him.

Colton relaxed for another moment and then considered his next move. He expected the bridge to be blocked with a similar armed guard contingent as they'd encountered on the east side of town. Most likely, all of the major highways in and out of Savannah would be covered.

The night before, they'd talked at length about the military occupation of the Pickwick Dam. Colton doubted Madison would've headed south. Besides, her initial getaway took her in the opposite direction from where he ran.

Colton pulled up the map on Alex's phone. There was only one major road that ran toward the north and that was County Road 128. It was probably heavily guarded and Madison would avoid it. He also knew they wouldn't attempt to find him during the daytime. It was too risky.

Colton shook his head and slammed his hands against the ground in anger, sending pain through his arms. They should have discussed alternative routes and rally points in case they got separated. Both of those things were common sense that hadn't crossed his mind as they'd gotten closer to Savannah. He'd thought it would be a straight shot across the river and they'd be easily at Jake's place before dark. Now he wondered if he'd ever see his family again—alive.

The barking dogs brought him out of his dejection. From his days in Texas, he knew the difference between dogs barking for the sake of making noise and those that were on a mission. These were huntin' dogs and they were getting louder. The manhunt was on and he was fairly certain they were after him.

He hopped up and weighed his options. Evading a good tracker wasn't like what folks saw on television, where the pursued ran through a creek to the other side. Colton knew that good trackin' dogs picked up a fugitive's scent again where he exited the creek because his scent would mix with the water that dripped off him to the ground.

The water would delay the dogs and their handler, which was the best way to escape their tracking him. Colton ran into the creek and waded toward the east for about a hundred feet until the water got near waist high. Then he emerged on the north side of the creek and started running along an area cleared for some power lines.

After a while, he darted back into the woods toward the creek and made his way along a path created by hogs or deer. Colton found another shallow part of the creek and walked into it and then up the hill on the other side. He traced his steps backward into the water and then waded farther to the east about fifty feet. He hoped this would confuse the dogs as well.

Colton continued this process and began to run through the woods again until he came to a clearing and a gravel road that took him south. The rumble of a truck with a loud muffler could be heard ahead. Colton knew he was getting near the main road.

The sound of the dogs barking grew faint. They either pulled off the hunt, or they had to go around the creek at a road crossing somewhere. Either way, Colton was relieved at the breathing room the distraction provided.

It was still too early to hide, and the longer he stayed in these woods, the more likely it was that he'd get cordoned off. He had to make a run for it and get out of the immediate area. He pushed through the brush until he came upon a street running north and south. Colton crouched in some dense underbrush and studied the Google Maps app on Alex's phone. This was CR128.

Crap! He was only five blocks from the sheriff's office. He was still right under their noses!

Colton felt like this was the best route out of town to rendezvous with the girls, but with all of the businesses that lined this road, he'd surely be seen in broad daylight. And, like Alex, he'd noticed there wasn't anyone on the street. It was too risky for him to be out in the open.

He inched closer to the road and watched for traffic. It was deserted. He studied the four houses across the way. There didn't appear to be any activity. Colton thought if he could cross the road, the tracking dogs wouldn't be able to follow his scent across the asphalt. Out of precaution, he'd lead them in a triangular path before running to the houses across the way.

Colton took a deep breath, assessed the surroundings one more time, and ran onto the road. He performed his triangulation avoidance maneuver and ran between the older, craftsman-style homes. At the third home, he discovered a set of double doors leading to a basement root cellar. Finding it unlocked, he slipped down the concrete stairs into the dark space.

He pulled out Alex's phone and lit up the display. Colton took in his surroundings. What he found in the basement would've scared him on a normal day.

CHAPTER 31

DAY SEVENTEEN
6:00 p.m., September 25
Off Clifton Road
Bucktown, Tennessee

Madison drove through the backyards of the neighborhood and worked her way over to the adjoining streets as they found their way north out of town. She knew this was risky, but driving across the bridge was out of the question, and she wasn't going to leave Colton alone on this side of the river.

Madison and Alex were barely a mile out of town when the countryside opened up into the type of rural landscape they'd driven through since they'd left Nashville. Soon the houses became fewer and far between, eventually making way for large stretches of farmland and woods.

They'd picked a random side road, which led them up into the hills overlooking the Tennessee River valley and the town of Savannah. Madison checked the odometer and began measuring their distance as soon as they cleared the city limits. By their estimation, it was approximately five miles back to the center of town.

At a clearing, they drove off the one-lane road and bounced along a well-worn trail created by years of off-roading by locals. The ruts created were barely wide enough for the Wagoneer to follow, but the path led them behind a tree stand that shielded them from the view of any passersby, not that they expected any. A little further up the mountain, the elevation allowed them a clear view of Savannah to the south and the Tennessee River to the west. If the search for them continued into the night, they'd be able to see the vehicles' headlights.

After they found a secluded place to park, Madison grabbed a comforter out of the back of the Wagoneer and spread it out on the ground. They both agreed they'd stop, drink some water, and digest what had just happened to them. Despite their concerns for Colton, now was not the time to make any rash, hasty decisions.

They let go of their emotions as they both realized how close to death they had been. Then their concerns turned to the whereabouts and safety of Colton. They both calmed down after several minutes of discussion and then quiet reflection.

Alex finished off her water and replaced the cap for future use. "Mom, the arrows the other day destroyed several of the bottles of water. We only have six or eight left."

"Okay," said Madison. "We'll need to unpack the back of the truck anyway to find a few things."

"Like what?"

"For starters, we need my cell phone and the Eton crank weather radio," replied Madison. Do you remember where they're packed?"

"Why do we need your cell phone? Let me get mine." Alex started to get up to retrieve her phone when Madison reached out and held her arm.

"Don't bother," said Madison. "Your dad took the iPhone."

"He did? When?"

"He grabbed it as he ran off," replied Madison.

"Why would Daddy take my iPhone?"

Madison looked down to the ground and gathered the courage to explain. "Honey, we've always trusted you. You know that, right?"

Alex hesitated and gave Madison a puzzled look. "Yeah, I know. What's this about, Mom?"

"Well, when your dad and I purchased the iPhone for you, we added an app."

Alex sat up and crossed her legs. She clasped her fingers together and studied Madison's face. "So? What kind of app?"

"It's called Footprints," replied Madison. "It's sort of a *find my kids* app. Footprints uses geo-tracking technology to keep up with the location of your iPhone while you were out. We could follow where you went and how long you stayed at a particular location. You know, stuff like that."

Alex stuck her jaw out and nodded her head. "Really?" she stated sarcastically.

"Yes, honey. Again, it wasn't because we didn't trust you. It was, well, you know. We're your parents and we worry."

Alex started laughing as she stood. "Mom, all of the kids laugh about Footprints. There are a couple of app killers to disable them temporarily or hold the location in place until you go back and allow geo-tracking to pick you up again."

"Are you kidding me?" asked Madison, looking up to her daughter.

"Nope. It's kinda like that Newton's Law of Physics—for every action there is an equal and opposite reaction. Well, for every so-called parental control, there's a whiz-kid hacker out there who figures out a work-around."

"Why haven't I heard of this work-around?" asked Madison.

"Kid code," replied Alex.

Now it was Madison's turn to stand. She jumped to her feet and shook her head.

"What is kid code?" asked Madison.

"You know, it's kinda like girl code," replied Alex. "Girl code has those certain rules that cannot be broken. You can't date another girl's boyfriend. You can't lie directly to a girlfriend's face, which includes lies of omission. You never disclose secrets that were told to you in confidence."

"Yeah, I remember girl code," said Madison.

"Kid code is the same thing, except kids actually stick to it, whereas girls always break girl code," started Alex. "The first rule of kid code is you never tell your parents something that could go against the best interest of your fellow kid. Parents *always* think they know what's best for kids and they'll ruin anything that *we think* is best for us."

"Like the Footprints app-killer thing," said Madison.

"Exactly."

Madison pondered this for a moment as she watched the sun begin to set across the Tennessee River. Madison wished she could remember her high school days better. She couldn't specifically recall a kid code from those days, but she was sure there was one.

"Okay, *kid*, let's get organized and find your father," said Madison, changing the subject. It was getting dark. *Time to mount a rescue.*

"What's the plan?" asked Alex as she helped Madison unpack the trailer rack in order to gain access to the Wagoneer's tailgate. Alex and Madison hoisted the generator out of the way and emptied the last of the gasoline into the truck's gas tank.

"Let's dig out a few things," said Madison as they lifted the rear hatch. "Be careful with this glass." They picked out the shattered rear window, which had been shot out in the I-840 gun battle.

"You know what, Mom," started Alex as she removed the contents of the back of the truck onto the grass. "None of this scares me anymore."

"You're joking, right?" said Madison.

"No, seriously. Ever since I shot that Holder man, I've come to accept this way of living. I'll admit, and I didn't really let you know this, but I was messed up that afternoon after I shot him."

Madison stopped unpacking and turned to her daughter. "Come here, honey. Your dad and I knew that was traumatic. Taking another person's life is something nobody should have to deal with, especially a teenage girl."

Alex chuckled and said, "No, you don't understand. I wasn't upset. That's what I'm trying to tell you. I had to get my head together that afternoon because I couldn't figure out why it didn't bother me."

"Oh."

"Yeah, I guess I'm just one of those natural-born killers." Alex laughed.

"Alexis, that's not funny," said Madison sternly.

"C'mon, Mom. Of course I'm kidding. I'm just sayin' that since that day I've come to accept that we're going to be shot at, often. And we're going to have to shoot back to survive. I no longer look at the people trying to kill us as human beings. They're animals on the attack and we have to do what it takes to defend ourselves."

Madison looked at her daughter and wished she had Alex's fortitude. She simply nodded her head, indicating she understood, and then finished cleaning out the truck. As she did, Madison realized being a mother included learning about the strengths you didn't know you had and facing threats you didn't know existed. Somewhere over the last sixteen years, Alex had become ahead of the learning curve.

CHAPTER 32

DAY SEVENTEEN
8:00 p.m., September 25
Pickwick Street
Savannah, Tennessee

Colton had fallen asleep amidst the six full-size stuffed Bengal tigers that inhabited the disagreeably dark, damp basement underneath the home on Pickwick Street. At first glance, the taxidermy tigers appeared to be staged for the purposes of causing any intruder to run screaming into the night. Their menacing fangs and piercing eyes were frighteningly realistic. But after careful inspection, with his weapon drawn, Colton realized that the basement was full of paraphernalia and trophies from the local high school, whose mascot was obviously the tigers.

Colton found a place in the corner of the basement where an old recliner had been discarded. He made sure Alex's iPhone was on and that it still had a decent charge. He wrapped himself in a maroon and white Hardin County High stadium blanket and quickly fell asleep with gun in hand.

It had been several hours when the shuffling feet on the wood floors above him caused decades-old dust to fall onto his face, waking him up. He could barely make out the muffled voices from the occupants of the home, but it appeared to be several people. Colton checked Alex's phone and saw that it was eight o'clock. He was pleased to see that the battery had also retained its charge.

He considered his options. Colton was well-hidden here. If he were a hiker lost in the woods, he would stay put. The worst thing that he could do was wander in the wrong direction, expending energy and putting the girls at risk chasing after him. Second, he had adequate shelter and safety.

Colton doubted that the locals were going to give up looking for him. As if to reinforce that belief, Colton heard a car pass in front of the house, which caused the shuffling upstairs to stop momentarily. *Are they hiding too?*

Under these circumstances, he felt helpless. There really wasn't a clear choice on which direction to travel. He knew nothing of his surroundings and had no idea where the girls had escaped to. In the end, he forced himself to wait—with his new pals, the tigers.

He wandered around the basement, using the illuminated iPhone as his source of light. Workbenches lined the perimeter of the room, which also included a wood-burning furnace and two water heaters.

He found a plastic cup amidst the Hardin County High gear and emptied some of the water out of the water heater into it. It smelled okay, so he gave it a quick taste. Winner! Colton quickly gulped down the pint-size cup and filled another. He took his time with this one as he started to survey his surroundings. Other than some tools and boxes filled with high school stuff, most of the contents of the basement were unexciting.

Then Colton spied a padlocked box on top of one of the cabinets. It looked somewhat like a guitar case, except it was rectangular in shape and longer. Curious, he figured out a way to pull the case down and examine it. Colton found a five-gallon bucket and turned it upside down so he could use it as a step.

Colton reached over his head and slid the case towards him, which brought a cloud of dust into his face. He resisted the urge to sneeze, but he couldn't.

ACHOOOO!

The force of the sneeze caused Colton to lose his balance on the bucket, and he crashed to the dusty floor with a loud groan—the much sought after case on top of him. As this happened, the illumination on the iPhone timed out. He was in the dark, sprawled out on the floor. And it was deathly silent above him.

Did they hear my fall? There wasn't any movement, and Colton held his breath, straining to hear. All of a sudden, the people above him ran through the house. He could hear voices and the sound of someone descending the stairs of the home, taking two at a time.

Colton scrambled to his feet and fumbled in the dark for the phone. He knocked over the water and it drenched the iPhone. In that moment of panic, he was glad he'd purchased Alex the iPhone 7 model, which was waterproof for those days she hung out by the pool. It was amazing how the mind raced in a moment of stress to matters unrelated to the threat at hand.

He found his way to the stairs leading to the outside. He hastily climbed up them—three—four—five. Colton hit the top and started to burst through the doors just as they were opened up for him. Colton stumbled and fell onto the dewy grass outside.

Colton rolled over onto his back, where he faced four shotguns and half the starting linebackers of the Hardin County Tigers football team.

CHAPTER 33

DAY SEVENTEEN
9:00 p.m., September 25
Clifton Road
Savannah, Tennessee

Moving at night was much easier than during the daytime. Madison and Alex cast their fashion sense aside as they put on the darkest clothes they had, dressing in all of the *ninja attire* they could find among their belongings. Alex even succumbed to her mother's wishes and wrapped a passé Mickey Mouse fanny pack around her waist to carry extra magazines for the AR-15. It was a trade she was willing to make for the right to carry the best weapon the Rymans possessed.

The fanny pack also carried another essential tool Alex had grabbed at the Holders' home that day—a FLIR Scout mini-thermal monocular. Jimmy Holder had shown her how effective it was to see in the dark one day when he turned out the lights in the Holder basement. At first, Alex thought this was a ploy by the younger teenage boy to make a move on her. But he was showing her how the night-vision device worked.

The one-handed button design and compact size made it ideal for the type of activity the Ryman women were undertaking tonight. Under most circumstances, in an urban environment, there would be too much ambient light for the thermal monocular to work. But tonight, other than the headlights of the sheriff's posse traversing the streets of Savannah, it was pitch black.

Madison carried her phone and the ETON crank radio in a Louis Vuitton backpack. Colton had provided a halfhearted objection to the inclusion of the LV bag, but when Madison explained it was the only small backpack accessory they had, he reluctantly gave in. She was glad she had it now because it could easily hold the LifeStraw, two bottles of water, the radio, and extra ammo for their two nine-millimeter handguns.

Madison also brought the Midland two-way radios she'd purchased at Walgreens in the hours before the solar storm hit. The black handheld radios could monitor and transmit over fifty common channels with up to a thirty-six-mile range. It took about an hour to charge each of the two-ways using the truck's cigarette lighter. She and Alex each had one in case they got separated. More importantly, they could scroll through the channels, listening for chatter from the locals who were hunting for them and Colton.

After they got the necessary gear together, they began to work their way into Savannah.

The girls had been ecstatic and rejuvenated up on the mountain when they'd powered up Madison's iPhone and activated the Footprints app. They'd immediately located Colton via the app. His position had not changed the entire time—a residence on Pickwick Street, the same county road that they were on. This location was about three-quarters of a mile east of the point they were separated, so it was natural to assume Colton was hiding out and waiting to be found.

They walked for about two hours as they carefully made their way into the neighborhoods on the north side of Savannah. The number of vehicles crisscrossing the streets in search of the Rymans had lessened.

They ducked in behind a utility fence as a vehicle approached. After it passed, they slipped in behind a house, turned up Alex's squelch, and scanned through the channels, listening for activity. Although the Midland boasted a thirty-six-mile range, that must've meant mountaintop to mountaintop across the Grand Canyon. It wasn't until they were within a mile of other radios did they actually pick up any discernible conversations.

"I've got something, Mom," said Alex as she pulled the radio away from her ear and turned up the volume.

"*Whadya want us to do? Keep lookin'? Over.*"

"*Nah, Junior said pull back into town. He's got two cars headed to the Clifton Road bridge over the creek now.*"

Alex laughed and elbowed her mom. "Junior?" She snickered.

Madison laughed with her. "I reckon," she replied mockingly. The conversation between the men continued.

"*Them women ain't that stupid, are they? They ain't comin' back after we run 'em off.*"

"Hey!" protested Alex. "They didn't run us off."

"And we ain't stooopid," complained Madison.

"*Don't matter. Come on back into the station. Junior is organizing a search of the town. We's goin' door to door to find that feller that run off.*"

Alex and Madison began to elbow each other and then spontaneously laughed out loud. This was followed by high fives and a jumping chest bump. You'd think these two had just won the Super Bowl.

In their minds, they did. Colton was alive and safe.

CHAPTER 34

DAY SEVENTEEN
9:00 p.m., September 25
Pickwick Street
Savannah, Tennessee

"Spread those arms and legs," said one of the men standing over him. They kicked his legs apart and Colton willingly spread his arms. One of them reached down and grabbed his gun out of his paddle holster. "Now, don't move."

Colton tried to get a better look at his captors, but it was a dark, cloudy night. He counted four sets of legs, all men, dressed in jeans. Two of them appeared to be older teenage boys, heavyset, wearing high school letterman jackets. A third boy wore jeans and a camo sweatshirt, while the fourth man, maybe fortyish, wore shorts and a pullover long-sleeve shirt.

They whispered between themselves before addressing Colton. "On your feet, buddy, real slow like. No sudden moves, ya hear?"

"Okay," groaned Colton. He was really sore from the escape earlier in the day and the tumble out of the basement just now. "I don't want any trouble."

"Well, sir," said one of the younger men, "from what we've seen of ya so far today, you ain't nuthin' but trouble. C'mon now." The young man helped Colton to his feet and began to dust off his back.

"We need to git inside, boys, before they drive by again," said the older man.

"Yeah, I wanna get back on that Bearcat," said another.

"Come along, bud," said the older man to Colton as he led them around to the front of the house. As the group arrived near the porch, he raised his fist and looked both ways down the road. He then waved them forward and the boys picked up the pace and headed to the front porch, leading Colton into the house.

"Check his pockets," said the older man. One of the boys quickly began to pat Colton down from behind. He pulled the iPhone out of his pocket and handed it to the man. "Is that it?"

"Yeah, Coach."

Coach? Colton was beginning to get the picture.

"C'mon," said the man identified as Coach. He led Colton into the kitchen and pointed to a breakfast table and chair. "Let's pull up a couple of seats and get to know one another. Okay by you?"

"Sure," replied Colton. Colton slowly eased into a chair and left his hands on the table where they could be seen. He didn't want his movements to be misinterpreted, resulting in a mistake by a nervous teen with a gun. He also couldn't lie this time. They had Alex's phone, which would provide them his true identity. "My name is Colton Ryman and I'm from Nashville. My family and I were simply passing through when these men—well—I don't know what their intentions were for sure."

"We do," said one of the boys, who had more to say until Coach raised his hand, indicating for him to keep quiet.

"Where ya headed?" asked Coach.

"West, toward Memphis," replied Colton. He didn't feel the need to disclose his true destination.

"Mr. Ryman, my name is Joe Carey, but they call me Coach. This here is my son, Beau. These other two boys are the Bennett brothers, Jimbo and Clay."

Colton let out a huge sigh of relief. He was safe. "It's a pleasure to meet you folks," started Colton. "I didn't mean to break into your cellar, but I needed a place to hide and regroup. Those men were chasing me with dogs and guns."

"Yessir, we know," said Beau. "Me and the boys saw you pull down Water Street and we followed you until they tried to steer you into the jail. You did the right thing in runnin'."

Colton rubbed his hands together and got emotional. "I hope so.

I'm worried about my wife and daughter. I left them alone to fend for themselves. I don't know if they're okay. I don't—"

"Now, hold on, Mr. Ryman," said Coach Carey. "We believe your family is safe. They got away."

The boys started laughing. Beau spoke up to explain. "Yessir, they got away all right, and tore up the north part of town in the process. They drove that Wagoneer like a couple of crazed lunatics. Your wife led them boys on a chase that would make *Fast & Furious* proud. She took out a fence, led Boone together with his pride and joy Dodge Charger into a swimming pool, and shot out Junior's tires."

"Classic!" said either Jimbo or Clay Bennett, giving each other high fives. Colton couldn't tell which Bennett was which because they were identical twins.

Colton didn't have time to enjoy the news that the girls were safe. Coach and the boys were having too good of a time laughing about the driving prowess of his wife.

"Oh yeah, the best part was Junior losing his mind. We heard over the scanner that your daughter hung out the window and shot out their tires. Junior smacked them boys around for lettin' that happen."

"Who's Junior?" asked Colton.

"Oh, that's a story you gotta hear," said one of the Bennetts.

"All right, boys, I'll tell Mr. Ryman all about it, but we've got some work to do tonight," started Coach. "First off, return the gentleman's gun and cell phone."

The boy set his weapon on the table and Colton immediately holstered it. The man gently placed the iPhone down. Colton pressed the on button to check the power levels. It had nearly sixty percent battery life. He was mad it himself for using it as a flashlight in the basement. It had sucked the life out of the battery.

"You expectin' a phone call, mister?" Beau laughed.

Colton smiled and put the phone in his pocket. "Nah, it's my daughter's phone. We installed a tracking device on it so we could check on her whereabouts when she was out at night."

"Whoa, great idea," said Coach.

"Our momma had the aliens implant a chip in our skull so she

152

could track us." A Bennett laughed.

Beau slapped the side of his friend's head. "That rock's too hard to implant anything in it. That's why we had to put you guys on defense, right, Dad?"

"Hold up!" protested the quiet Bennett. "We've played offense before, right, Coach?"

"Yeah," interrupted Beau, who was now having a good laugh. "Back in the peewee days maybe!"

Coach stood and calmed down the ruckus. "Okay, boys. We've all had a good guffaw. Jimbo, I need you upstairs on the night vision and monitor the scanner. Clay, we're gonna need some help tonight. Round up about five of the fellas. Swing by the shoe store and pick up some M-80s and cherry bombs. We'll need 'em."

"What about me, Dad?" asked Beau.

"Son, take a rifle, a radio, and head across town. Pick up some help and make your way over toward Clifton Road. If they're tracking this gentleman's phone, they'll walk straight down until they hit Cravens."

"What if I see them?"

Coach turned to Colton and asked. "What can Beau say to your ladyfolk that only you and your family would know?"

Colton thought for a moment. "I know what, refer to my daughter as Allie-Cat. It's always been a nickname we've used for her, but she kinda grew out of it. She'll know that I sent you."

"Got it," said Beau. "Dad, if I find them, I'll put the word out so everyone can hear it. It'll be easier for y'all to come across the highway once than me bringing them here and then back across again."

"Makes sense," said Coach. "Let's meet up at Graham Chapel as our rally point. Okay, everybody know their job?"

A chorus of yes sirs was provided as the boys took off in different directions. Colton was impressed with both the comradery and the discipline.

"Let me show you somethin', Mr. Ryman," said Coach as he led Colton deeper into the house toward a back bedroom.

"Sure, but please call me Colton. I'm feelin' kinda old with *mister.*"

Colton followed him into a bedroom and then through a closet door. Inside the closet, Coach opened a false panel entry and they stepped into a well-lit enclosed space that was hidden under the home's staircase. It was eight feet by ten feet and contained guns, ammunition, and maps all over the walls.

For the next thirty minutes, Coach gave Colton the rundown on the history of Savannah's illustrious mayor, Ma Durham, and her boy Junior, the sheriff of Hardin County. Colton also learned how they were profiting from the collapse of the power grid.

It appeared indentured servitude was alive and well in Savannah, Tennessee, and it'd never been uglier.

CHAPTER 35

DAY SEVENTEEN
10:30 p.m., September 25
Clifton Road
Savannah, Tennessee

Madison and Alex had high hopes as they entered the more populated areas of Savannah just after ten that night. By their calculations, only a mile separated them from Colton. They methodically worked their way through the neighborhood streets of Savannah, listening to radio chatter and confirming Colton's location.

They used the backyards mainly, running from one cover and concealment point to another. On rare occasions, privacy fences blocked their route, so they were momentarily exposed to the street as they made their way through front yards.

They'd only seen one other person thus far. An older man sat in a rocking chair, smoking a pipe. Using overgrown boxwoods as cover, Madison and Alex ran past the man's front porch and caught the scent of the aromatic cherry blend as they passed. Alex glanced over at the man and she doubted he saw them. He was off in a faraway, better place at the moment.

"Mom," whispered Alex, "what if Daddy dropped my phone and lost it? We could be walking to the phone, but not him."

"I thought about that, but it doesn't change the plan. We're so close now, Alex. The only major hurdle I foresee is crossing the main drag—Highway 64. We'll be wide open and exposed."

Alex continued to thumb through the channels on the two-way radio. The chatter had died down. "When we get close, we'll find a spot and observe. I've got the night vision. Maybe we'll catch a guard sleeping and run right past him."

"They had a roadblock at Main Street, which forced us toward the sheriff's office," said Madison. "Let's turn down this way and cut across the highway before that roadblock."

They picked up the pace and began jogging through a large backyard when they came face-to-face with a pit bull.

GRRRRRRRRRR.

"Shhh, puppy!" whispered Madison. They stopped dead in their tracks, just out of reach of the growling dog that was chained to a tree. "Please, be quiet. Good doggy!"

GRRRRRRRRRR, BUFF, BUFF, SNORT.

"Walk back slowly, Alex. He can't reach us, but he can surely raise the devil if he wants to."

They slowly stepped back and the pit bull lunged at them. Now he was mad and let the world know about it.

BARK—BARK—BARK—BARK.

GRUFF—GRUFF—GROWL—BARK!

"Jeez Louise," exclaimed Alex. "Run this way, Mom!" The girls took off, running for the cover of other homes. Ordinarily, lights might have come on, glowing through bedroom windows, with faces appearing to determine the cause of the commotion. Alex didn't stop to determine if they'd drawn attention. She wanted to put as much distance between them and the barking dog as she could.

HOOOOOOWL!

BARK—BARK—BARK.

HOOOOOOWL!

"Great!" exclaimed Madison, almost out of breath. "Every hound in West Tennessee is joining in now!"

Alex led them in a zigzag pattern through parked cars, houses, and fence rows. The cacophony of the various dog breeds of Savannah began to subside.

"Alex, wait," said Madison, gasping for air. "I'm dyin' here. Let's catch our breath. Okay?"

"Okay, Mom, but just for a moment. All the dogs barking may have drawn attention to us."

The two leaned against a tall wooden privacy fence and caught their breath. Madison was bent over, holding herself up by leaning on her knees.

"You gonna be all right, Mom?"

Madison took a deep breath and replied, "Yeah. You know, who needs a fancy alarm system when all you have to do is tie a few dogs to the trees around your property."

Alex nodded. "For sure. I've gotta pee."

"What?"

"I've gotta pee. I almost wet myself when we came face-to-face with that pit bull. Now I've really gotta go."

"Go." Madison laughed. "I'll wait here and hold up the fence."

Out of habit, or modesty, Alex walked around the fence and took care of business behind some shrubs. She snapped the fanny pack in place and adjusted her holster. All of the running had discombobulated her ninja-rescuer ensemble.

She started to join her mom when a shadow caught her eye. She stopped and dropped to one knee. She glanced over at her mom, who was still leaning back against the fence.

"Mom," said Alex, barely above a whisper. "Mom, come over here. Hurry!"

Madison ran to join her and the two crouched under the limbs of a crepe myrtle tree. Alex quickly retrieved the FLIR monocular and scanned the yards and open field. She could make out two figures walking a hundred feet apart. They were heading in the direction of the loudmouth pit bull.

"Whadya see?"

"Two people walking toward the dog," said Alex. "C'mon, let's go this way."

Alex didn't hesitate and took off toward the right to put the houses between them and the approaching figures. They ran through a couple of front yards and then dashed between two homes along their joint driveway.

Now Alex had a clear view down the street and across several open spaces. She looked through the FLIR again.

"Dang it," muttered Alex.

"More?"

"Yeah," replied Alex. "I see at least three. They're all spread out, just like the other two. We can run through the yards like we have been. We should be okay."

"Let's go, then," encouraged Madison, who patted her daughter on the back.

Alex took off in a sprint toward the highway. Madison followed, but she was slower and fell behind. Alex cut through a fence opening and turned back toward the road, attempting to avoid a large open field that led to a church up ahead.

HRUMPH.

UGH.

Alex heard her mom grunt. She turned around and Madison wasn't behind her. Alex doubled back to see where her mom had gone.

Madison was on the ground and the dark figure of a man was standing over her. Alex immediately began to shake. She suppressed her fear and gathered her strength. Her mom was in trouble.

Alex carefully approached them with her gun raised—sights trained on the man's back. She resisted the urge to shoot because she didn't want to bring his friends down upon her. Alex moved slowly, walking heel to toe.

The man was leaning down to her mom. Alex closed faster. The man was grabbing for Madison's arms. Alex was almost on top of him when she stuck the barrel of the AR-15 at the base of his skull.

"You get your hands off my mother," she hissed in the man's ear.

The man slowly began to raise his arms, but it wasn't fast enough for Alex.

"Now!" she growled at him.

"Okay, okay!"

He stood and slowly backed away, the muzzle still firmly planted against his back. Alex walked backwards until she stopped, allowing the gun to press deeper into his flesh.

"Gee," the man started, "now I see why they call you Allie-Cat."

CHAPTER 36

DAY SEVENTEEN
9:00 p.m., September 25
Pickwick Street
Savannah, Tennessee

Colton studied the map and allowed the backstory of Ma Durham and her deranged son Junior to sink in. Being in the entertainment business, Colton thought this was the kind of stuff movies were made of. Unfortunately, he didn't like the fact that his family was stuck in the middle of this horror flick.

"She had a brilliant plan, all set into motion under the guise of protecting the local businesses from looters," continued Coach. "As the news stories began to break, Ma and Junior rallied their political cronies from around the community. They moved quickly to barricade the major roads in and out of town. This made sense to prevent outsiders from infiltrating the town and pillaging our homes."

"We saw that other small communities were doing the same thing on our way down here," added Colton.

"She also did something else, supposedly for the good of the community," said Coach. "She reminded everyone about what had happened to stores and businesses after Hurricane Katrina. People who claimed to be poor and downtrodden, simply looking for food, were carrying computers and televisions out of storefronts. She vowed that wouldn't happen in her town, so she dispatched newly deputized locals and issued weapons to them. They surrounded the major stores like Walmart and Lowe's first."

"In the name of security, I suppose," interjected Colton.

"Exactly, except it was really intended to commandeer the contents. She even released all of the inmates who would swear allegiance to her and Junior."

"And gave them guns?"

"Oh yeah," replied Coach.

"I gather that you aren't one of the newly deputized minions of the Durham regime?" asked Colton.

"I'm on the wrong side of the political fence," replied Coach. "I was a staunch and vocal supporter of her opponent."

"Not good," said Colton.

"Nope, not in a small town. Not only am I not deputized, I'm considered a fugitive at the top of her enemies list."

Colton shook his head in disbelief. *What kind of town is this?*

"Enemies list?"

"Yessir," Coach replied. "Within days after the power went out, Junior was given a list from his ma. People who registered their guns were approached first. Their weapons were confiscated for the good of the safety of the public. Second, she began to confiscate operating vehicles for the use of her police force."

"Let me guess, for the safety of the citizens." Colton laughed. "It sounds like she's running this town through fear and muscle."

"It's in her genes." Coach laughed. "Then she began rounding up the *disdants*, as that nitwit Junior calls us."

"*Disdants?*" asked Colton.

"The idiot means to say dissidents. The *disdants* are those who opposed Ma Durham politically or who refused to toe the line after the power grid collapsed."

"You're on the run too," said Colton.

"Sort of. We prefer to look at ourselves as the resistance."

Coach led them out of his hidden war room and secured the doors. As they reentered the kitchen, two hundred twenty pounds of muscle in the form of Jimbo Bennett came running down the stairs. Before Colton could ask Coach more details about their resistance, Jimbo made an announcement.

"Coach, we've found 'em!" he yelled before hitting the landing with a thud.

"Oh, thank God!" exclaimed Colton, spontaneously slapping Coach on the back.

"Great news, Jimbo," said Coach.

Jimbo joined them and immediately handed Coach one of the two-way radios.

"There's a problem," he started. "I guess a bunch of dawgs up there raised a ruckus and Junior's boys heard it. He's sent several men up there to check it out."

"How many, you reckon?"

"Four or five carloads," replied Jimbo. "Junior means business."

Coach began to scroll the channels of his two-way radio. "What's today's number?"

"Bill Baxter."

Colton looked puzzled.

"Twenty-three," muttered Coach. "We use a different channel to broadcast amongst our folks each day. Baxter wears number twenty-three. He's our starting tailback."

Coach found the channel and spoke into the microphone. "Tiger tails. Tiger tails. Red right. Red right. Twenty-five pull trap. Twenty-five pull trap. On go."

"What was that?" asked Colton.

"We have a code to broadcast emergency instructions in situations like these," replied Coach. "It's based upon our offensive and defensive play calling system. Heads refers to a defensive formation and tails refers to an offensive maneuver. In this case, Tiger refers to the resistance. Tails refers to an offensive plan."

"The rest sounds like French to me." Colton laughed.

"Good," said Coach. "We have the town divided into four quadrants. The north side, everything above Highway 64, is blue."

"The south side is red," surmised Colton. "And right?"

"Right is east of County Road 128, where we are now. West is everything across the street toward the river. Twenty-five refers to our secure house on Twenty-Fifth Street. The home is owned by Mark and Leslie Bryant. She's our school principal."

"They're not on the enemies list?" asked Colton.

"Nah," replied Coach. "Leslie used to be Junior's guidance counselor in high school. Despite all of his antics as a kid, she gave him a break, hoping he'd straighten out. Mark stayed out of the politics of Savannah, which has kept him off Ma's enemies list. Ironically, he's the minister at Graham Chapel, which is the rally point you'll be going to."

"What does *pull trap* mean?" asked Colton, still intrigued by the complex code utilized by Coach and the Tiger resistance.

"*Pull trap* refers to a ruse or diversion. We use it often just to aggravate Junior and the boys when we're up to something."

"Like what?" asked Colton.

"Junior has a tendency to overreact when we start an operation," replied Coach. "He'll pull guards from the businesses to respond to our diversion, and while the cat's away, the mice will play, as they say!"

Colton laughed but was anxious to get to his girls. "What do I do?"

Jimbo emerged from a bedroom with two shotguns. He handed one to Coach together with a handful of shells.

The front door opened and Clay entered with a backpack. "Sorry I'm late," said Clay. "They're all over down around the creek, looking for him." Clay handed Coach a heavy backpack, which he slung over his shoulder.

"Clay, this sure is heavy," admonished Coach.

"You didn't say how many, so I filled 'er up," said Clay.

"That's fine, son. Now listen up. You boys get Mr. Ryman safely to his family. I'll rally up with the team over at the Bryants' house. Monitor the radio for a signal, although you'll know it before I broadcast it."

"Coach, I don't know how I can thank you," started Colton. He began to shake Coach's hand and then gave him an awkward hug.

"Colton, you just take care of that family of yours. I'm sure we'll cross paths again. Boys?"

"Tigers!" exclaimed Jimbo and Clay in unison.

"Tigers!" replied Coach, who then fist bumped with his linebackers. "Let's do this!"

CHAPTER 37

DAY EIGHTEEN
Midnight, September 26
Graham Chapel Methodist Church
Clifton Road
Savannah, Tennessee

The two-way radio squawked. *"Tiger tails. Tiger tails. Red right. Red right. Twenty-five pull trap. Twenty-five pull trap. On go."*

Beau heard the call to action from his dad. He was waiting for the other two members of the team to join up with them at Graham Chapel. Beau knew things were going to get hairy as Junior's men came callin'. He really needed to get these ladies on the road, but they needed to wait on Colton. Patience, he reminded himself repeatedly.

"What did all that mean?" asked Alex.

"It means, dawlin', that we're fixin' to get you folks the heck outta Dodge." Beau laughed, trying to lighten the mood. He and Alex stood at the front of the church near a massive organ whose pipes rose to the ceiling.

Alex stared at him and crossed her arms, the dim light of one of the guy's flashlights providing just enough illumination for Beau to see her reaction.

"You think you're cute, but you're not," she lied. "And you're not funny either."

"All the other cheerleader types would disagree, ma'am," Beau shot back, deciding to tease Alex a little. He'd never forget her steely composure when she'd pointed that rifle at the back of his head. This girl was no cheerleader, at least not anymore.

"What makes you think I'm a cheerleader?" asked Alex.

Madison was standing to the side and took a step toward them. Beau smiled at her, causing her to stop.

"Well, for one thing you're a spunky one and—" started Beau, who stopped talking suddenly.

Alex closed the gap between them. She was close enough for Beau to feel her breath, and kiss her, if he dared. Alex whispered in his ear. His face went pale and Beau never repeated what Alex promised to do to his manhood if he ever called her *spunky* again. Alex turned and walked away to join her mom. Beau would never know about the big smile Alex had on her face as she put her arm around Madison.

The door swung open and the other two boys joined the group. Beau got serious and circled his team around him.

"Huddle up, guys," said Beau. He glanced to where Alex and Madison were standing, and smiled. He was smitten with Alex, despite her idle threats. "Dad's gonna raise a little ruckus on the south side to pull Junior's boys in the wrong direction. Any minute, there are gonna be cars runnin' up and down the street, lookin' for these ladies. As soon as Mr. Ryman arrives, I'm gonna take them and lead them north out of town. I need y'all to fan out east and west of here to create more diversions."

One of the boys asked, "How much of a diversion?"

"Not huge." Beau laughed. "No need to blow anything up, y'all. Besides, I think Dad'll have that covered."

All the boys gathered around Beau as he called out the plays. "Set the sirens off at the Hardee's again. They've not been guardin' it. Somebody get the dogs to barkin'. Start a brush fire over on Shell Street. That'll bring 'em runnin' out of the nursin' home. Stuff like that."

"Got it!"

"Git goin' and monitor two-three. Tigers!"

"Tigers!"

The boys grabbed their gear and hustled out the back door of the church. All wore their team colors in the form of jerseys or tee shirts. They were committed to their team and their cause.

Beau flopped into a church pew and turned up the volume on his two-way radio. He had channel twenty-three on the presets, but he wanted to monitor the other frequencies to listen for Junior's men, who were undoubtedly patrolling the streets on the north side of town.

Madison walked over to Beau and placed her hand on his shoulder. "Beau, I wanna thank you for risking so much to help us. Please tell your mom and dad thanks as well, okay."

Beau nodded and dropped his chin to his chest. "My mom passed a while back. She had breast cancer."

Alex heard this and joined them. Beau was now flanked on the pew by both of the Ryman women.

"Beau, I'm sorry to hear that. She was so young," said Madison.

"Yeah, that's what everybody says," said Beau as he looked up at the large cross with an effigy of Jesus hanging from it. "Somehow, God didn't get the memo that thirty-nine-year-old women are too young to be taken by the cancer."

The three sat quietly for a moment as Beau mindlessly scrolled through the channels. The premature death of his mom bothered him more than he usually let on. For some reason, he was comfortable talking about it with these strangers.

"God's thoughts are higher than ours, Beau," started Madison. "He has purposes we can't comprehend."

Beau nodded. "Yeah, that's what I told Jimbo and Clay when that drunk driver killed their parents on the way home from Memphis one night. I read them Isaiah 55 and everything."

"Are they your friends you referred to earlier?" asked Alex.

"Yeah, best friends. Brothers now, actually. Our dads grew up together, played ball at Hardin County and all." Beau started laughing.

"What?" asked Alex.

"Dad said Mr. and Miz Bennett left them to us in their will."

All three of them started laughing.

"We're brothers in more ways than one," added Beau.

Alex leaned into Beau and gave him a kiss on the cheek. He looked at her through sad eyes and smiled, indicating his thanks.

The back door opened and two burly young men entered with their rifles pointed into the sanctuary. They appeared to be alone.

"Beau, you here?"

"Yeah, front row," replied Beau.

"Everything cool?"

"Yeah, sure. Come on in."

For several excruciating seconds, the boys stood there. Finally, Jimbo turned and said, "Okay."

Colton emerged from the dark hallway behind the choir section.

"Daddy!" exclaimed Alex, who shot out of the front-row pew like a rocket.

"Thank God," said Madison as she covered her face and burst into tears. She was frozen to her seat, unable to move.

"C'mon, Mrs. Ryman," said Beau as he helped Madison to her feet. Colton and Alex ran to her, and the family reunited amidst tears and hugs.

Beau took the Bennett boys to the side to allow the Rymans to have their moment. He stared at Alex the entire time. He'd never met a girl like her before. Beau doubted he could talk them into staying in this tangled mess of a town. But he would make sure she knew she was welcome back anytime.

Beau queued the two-way radio and announced, "Tiger in the tank. Tiger in the tank."

He explained the plan to his brothers and they waited for the signal. The Rymans were now sitting in a pew together, exchanging the details of their day. Then it came.

"Tiger power! Tiger go!"

CHAPTER 38

DAY EIGHTEEN
3:00 a.m., September 26
Off Clifton Road
Bucktown, Tennessee

Along the south side of Highway 64, Coach and his Tigers had strategically placed fifty-five-gallon drums for operations like this one. Dropping an M-80 or cherry bomb into an open drum magnified the explosion many times over by directing the sound up and then out into the sky. The explosions, coupled with strategically placed brush fires, lent the appearance that the city was under attack.

As expected, in his typical reactionary fashion, Junior pulled his men toward the source of the explosions and corresponding fire. Coach, not allowing a great diversion to go to waste, directed his Tiger *disdants* to conduct smash-and-grab operations at any abandoned businesses. The distraction allowed Beau and the Bennett boys to escort the Rymans out of town without incident and his team restocked their supplies in the process. It was a win-win for all involved, except for Junior and Ma Durham, of course.

The barking dogs and the ruckus created by the Tigers on the north side of town served a vital purpose as well. Junior's men chased their tails, looking for the source of the commotion. They even pulled the roadblock from the Clifton Road bridge crossing over the creek. Colton was thrilled with that call, as he really didn't want to wade through the murky water at 3:00 a.m., which might be full of copperheads.

He and Madison stood to the side as Alex said good-bye to the young man who'd helped reunite the family and risked the lives of his dad and friends in the process.

"I have to be honest about something, Beau," said Alex. "You are kinda cute."

Beau crowed with laughter. Then, as young men so often do, Beau pushed his luck. "Oh really, confession is good for the soul. So, Miss Ryman, when did you first notice my good looks?"

Alex smacked the side of her AR-15. "When I had this pointed at the back of your head." She laughed. "I thought to myself—*self, it sure would be a shame to blow this pretty boy's head clean off his shoulders, but I'll sure do it if he doesn't let go of my mother.*"

"Oh," said Beau.

"Yeah, oh," said Alex.

"Does that mean I ain't got a chance with you? You know, for a date or somethin'."

Alex laughed. "That depends. Do you date cheerleaders?"

"No," he replied.

"Well, then you've got a chance 'cause I'm not a cheerleader."

"Woo hoo," shouted Beau as he raised his hand to give Alex a high five. She slapped it back and then gave him another kiss on the cheek.

"Thank you, Beau," she whispered into his ear, taking her time pulling away from his neck.

"You're welcome, Alex," said Beau, who immediately spun and exchanged fist bumps with his brothers-in-arms, Jimbo and Clay.

"Bye, boys," shouted Alex as she turned to join her parents on the bridge. She slung her rifle over her shoulder and didn't look back as they shouted to her.

"Hey, you don't have any sisters, do ya?"

"Or even a cousin. Yeah, cousins will do. Got any cousins?"

"Bye, guys," replied Alex. "Thank you!"

The family began the trek up the mountain to where the Wagoneer was stashed. It gave them a chance to talk further and plan their next move. They left the violence of the day back in Savannah and began to dream about their future.

CHAPTER 39

DAY EIGHTEEN
8:00 a.m., September 26
Off Clifton Road
Bucktown, Tennessee

They'd all slept during the night until sunrise. Colton chose to watch over the girls while they caught up on their sleep. The power nap he'd taken in Coach's cellar gave him all the rest he needed.

Colton liked mornings. Before the collapse, both Madison and Alex preferred to sleep in or *catch up on their lost sleep*. Somewhere along the line, in the handbook of how to live like a Ryman girl, they'd determined that the concept of *getting their beauty sleep* meant sleeping in too. Colton really didn't mind. Sometimes, he enjoyed the quiet time early in the morning to think or shuffle around doing *Colton things*. Even in the post-apocalyptic world, he found himself maintaining some aspects of his old routine.

Colton made sure all of the magazines for the weapons were full and he did a quick inventory of their ammunition levels. They had a little over a hundred rounds for the AR-15 and nearly two hundred rounds for the nine-millimeter handguns. He thought that would be *enough. How much is enough?*

The water supply was in critical status. He threw out the ruined bottles from the piercing arrow and gathered up the empty ones to refill.

As they'd walked back to the truck in the early hours of the morning, they'd crossed a culvert under the road, which diverted a stream down the hill. It was only a few hundred feet from where they were hidden, so Colton grabbed the empty bottles, their LifeStraw, and a bar of soap. Scruffing his seven-day stubble and a whiff of his armpits reminded Colton that he was a little gamey. He might not have time to shave, but at least he'd clean up a little bit for the girls.

As he walked toward the small creek, he thought about the ups and downs of life. One man's challenges might be greater than another's, but life presented challenges to all of us nonetheless. Colton considered himself fortunate in that he'd had a partner for most of his adult life to face the toughest of times.

Over the last few weeks, there had been a lot of conversation with his family about the concept of preparedness and what prepping entailed. He'd determined that the single most important item on any prepper's checklist was to have a partner who loved and supported you. Colton had Madison to navigate through the curves on the road of life. Each new day presented life-threatening challenges. With Madison and Alex by his side, Colton would round every bend unafraid.

Colton jogged down the road until he reached the culvert. He slid down the embankment until he reached the point where the water was flowing through the pipe, creating a shower effect. This was too good to pass up.

Using the LifeStraw, he pulled water out of a puddle and dribbled it into the water bottles. It was a slow process, but worth it. Colton considered this twenty-dollar device the single most important item Madison had purchased in the lead-up to the solar storm. Water was life. Contaminated water led to dysentery, diarrhea, vomiting, dehydration and then death. It was that simple.

Colton glanced around to make sure there were no peeping Toms, or bears, around. He stripped down and stepped under the cold mountain water pouring out of the culvert. He would never do this in the city. The many streams and creeks that dotted the mountainous landscape fed the Tennessee River from underground reservoirs. This made for a perfect hillbilly shower and Colton cleaned himself up quickly.

He began to think about the remainder of the trip. They were so close, yet their route was going to take them well out of the way. He wasn't sure if he had enough gas to make it based upon his calculations. They definitely didn't have the extra gas for any more confrontations or car chases.

He was walking up the road, still running his hands through his wet hair, when he saw the debris in the road near their campsite. An empty Ritz cracker box and the lid of a peanut butter jar lay in the middle of the street from their food supply.

Colton's heart raced. He reached for his gun and realized he'd left it in the truck. *I was only gonna be gone a few minutes.* Panicked, he dropped everything and raced back until he found the trail.

He dug in his feet and ran up the hill, slipping twice and ripping open his jeans. He scrambled past an empty water bottle, which wasn't there before. *Oh God, what have I done?* Colton's heart was beating out of his chest and his face was covered with sweat. His legs couldn't move him up the hill fast enough.

Colton burst into the clearing and shouted. "Madison! Alex!"

There was debris everywhere on the ground. They didn't respond.

"Maddie!" he yelled as he ran towards the tent tucked away by the back side of the Wagoneer.

Colton rounded the tailgate when he came face-to-face with the marauders—Mr. and Mrs. Rocky Raccoon.

"Colton, is everything okay?" asked a sleepy Madison as she emerged from the tent. Alex crawled through the opening and sat in the grass.

"Daddy, what's wrong?"

Colton turned fifty shades of embarrassment. The marauding raccoons were digging through their food supplies.

"Go on now, shooo!" he yelled at the 'coons. They moseyed out of the Wagoneer, dragging a box of cereal with them. "Hey! You've had enough. Leave that alone and tell your buddies not to come back either!"

Madison joined him to survey the mess made by the raccoon family. She hugged him around the waist and gave him a morning kiss.

"Well, aren't we smelling better." Madison laughed. "Irish Spring does clean a man up right."

Colton bent over to pick up the remains of their food. In that short period of time, several of the critters had almost cleaned them out of their non-canned goods.

"I feel so stupid," said Colton, slamming down an empty box of Fruit Loops in disgust. "I was only gone a few minutes. Were they hiding in the woods, waiting for me to leave?"

"We're in their neck of the woods, you know." Madison laughed. Colton didn't see the humor and continued to clean up the mess. Madison joined him while Alex jogged down the hill to retrieve the water bottles and the LifeStraw.

They broke camp and loaded up the truck together, but first they reviewed their route options. As the crow flies, as they say, the Rymans were only ten miles from Shiloh and the Allens' ranch. But to cross the river, they had to drive north ten miles and pick up U.S. Highway 641. Then they would work their way south via backroads to Shiloh, another thirty plus miles.

Forty miles and four gallons of gas would get them there. Colton estimated they had six gallons left. They had a good shot. Alex volunteered to navigate and ride shotgun. Madison would scour both sides of the road, looking for possible fuel to siphon out of vehicles, lawn equipment or abandoned gas cans.

Putting the excitement of Savannah and the marauding 'coons behind them, Colton navigated through the small country roads northbound on State Road 128. Everyone was on edge, fearing that the manhunt by Sheriff Junior Durham and his men would expand into other areas of the county. Luckily, they didn't encounter any other vehicles and made fairly good time as they traveled toward the bridge near Clifton.

An hour later, Colton turned toward the Tennessee River at Nance Bend. Just as the bridge came into view, Colton jammed on the brakes and forced the Wagoneer to a stop.

"Oh crap!" exclaimed Alex.

Madison leaned forward from the backseat. "We should've gone into the bridge-guarding business."

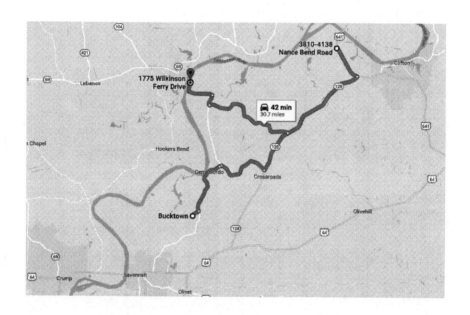

CHAPTER 40

DAY EIGHTEEN
11:00 a.m., September 26
Nance Bend Road
Clifton, Tennessee

Colton slowly eased the truck in reverse and coasted back down the slight incline in the highway. Thus far, they hadn't been noticed by the contingent of armed men who occupied the entry to the long bridge over the river. Colton didn't see any vehicles, but he was certain they were nearby.

"Daddy, now what?"

"I don't know, honey," he replied. Colton continued to ease back until they were out of view of the men. Then he backed onto Nance Bend Road a few hundred feet until the highway was out of sight, and stopped. He had to think.

Colton rubbed his temples and reached for the map. He looked at it for the tenth time that day. Their next option was to go through the town of Clifton to pick up the next river crossing. But for all he knew, Clifton might be another nightmarish version of Savannah, albeit a smaller one. They could go around the town, which involved backtracking somewhat, but the traveling distance to the next bridge crossing would consume all of their gasoline. He knew going south to the Pickwick Dam was a waste of time. He was at a loss.

Colton leaned his head back on his seat, closed his eyes, and let out a deep sigh. He said a silent prayer asking for guidance. God's answer came in the form of a tap on the driver's window, scaring the bejesus out of him.

"Howdy, mister," said a young boy, who was accompanied by an elderly man. "Y'uns all right in there?"

Alex reached for her pistol and Colton did a quick threat assessment. Neither the old man nor the boy appeared to be armed. He didn't see anyone else around, so he took a chance.

"It's okay, Alex," he whispered, holding his hand out to reassure her. Colton rolled down the window and spoke to them.

"Hi, fellas," started Colton. "I guess, yes, we're fine. I was gonna say that we're lost, but that's not exactly the truth. We know where we wanna go, but we don't know how to get there without crossing a bridge that some other folks seem to think belongs to them. Does that make any sense?"

The old man spoke up. "Oh, you talkin' about them Decatur boys. They got mad 'cause a bunch of folks left Savannah and headed into Decaturville, causin' trouble. They decided to close their borders. Nobody gets into Decatur County from thisaway unless they're Decatur folks."

"Well, that does seem to be the trend lately," muttered Colton.

"How's that?" asked the old man. "I don't hear so well."

The young boy tried to help out. "He said it's trendy, Gramps!"

"Oh yeah, I reckon so," said the old man with a shrug. "Whereabouts you goin'?"

Colton sat up in his seat and pulled the map over to show them. "Really, we just need to cross the river to get back down near Highway 64. I don't have a lot of gas and can't afford to drive all over hell's half acre looking for a safe route."

The old man pondered for a moment and pulled the young boy out of the way. He reached for the map and studied it. He nodded, smacked the map a couple of times, and then gave Colton a toothless grin.

"Well now, this might just work for y'uns," he started. "There's an old black feller down thar acrosst from Saltillo. He's got the old car ferry, but I don't reckon it's run in years. I ain't sayin' it don't, just I don't know if it can."

Colton looked back towards Madison and Alex. Madison shrugged and Alex nodded. "Let's go for it, Daddy."

"Okay, do you know how to get there?" asked Colton.

"Sure thang," said the old man. "Head back towards Crossroads and turn when you see Violet's hair cuttin' place."

"You can't miss it," interrupted the boy. "It's gawd-awful purple."

Colton remembered seeing it when they came up the highway.

The old man continued. "Turn right at Violet's and the road runs right into the old feller's place, if'n he's still alive. When the road ends, take a right. Can't miss it."

"What? Still alive?" asked Colton.

"Yeah, he was pert near ninety when I saw him last, though I can't rightly 'member when that was," the old man replied.

Colton thought about this plan again and then realized it was all they had going for them. He thanked the old man and his grandson and made his way back to the highway. Turning south towards Savannah wasn't exactly what he had in mind, so he drove quickly, looking for *Violet's Purple Hair Salon and Spa.*

"Comin' up on the right, Daddy. There's Violet's, remember?"

"Oh yeah," replied Colton. He turned down the one-lane road and wound his way through the woods. Periodically, a clearing would appear and fields of cotton, corn, and tobacco surrounded the highway. Around the last bend through the woods, the road ended abruptly at a large mound of gravel. Colton brought the truck to a stop a couple of hundred feet short of the obstruction.

"Now what? Did we miss a turn?" asked Colton.

"I don't think so," replied Alex. "The man said drive until the road ends and then turn right."

"Colton, maybe you should drive a little closer," suggested Madison.

"He might've been wrong, Daddy," started Alex. "He wasn't a hundred percent, if you know what I mean."

"Yeah, maybe," muttered Colton as he eased the truck forward. As the truck approached the gravel, he could see a driveway veer off to the right. A wooden sign hung on a single nail in an oak tree.

Colton read aloud. "Saltillo Ferry, this way, except the arrow points down toward the devil's den."

"What do ya'll think?" asked Madison.

"I say we pull in the driveway, lock the truck, and go check it out," said Alex as she gathered her fanny pack and slapped a magazine into the AR-15. "Right?"

Colton chuckled at his daughter's attitude. "Yeah, let's go see."

Everyone got their weapons ready and Madison grabbed the binoculars. Colton found a place to slide the Wagoneer into the woods, although he doubted there would be any passersby. He locked it up and they started down the tree-lined driveway, weapons at the ready.

"Do you smell the water?" asked Colton.

"Yeah, I love it!" replied Madison. "Trust me, I'm ready to get to Shiloh Ranch and stick my feet in the muddy banks of the river."

"And fish, too," said Alex. "I really liked the way Stubby breaded them. It was spicy!"

"Stop it, y'all." Colton laughed. "I'm really hungry and ready to get there. There's a clearing ahead. Fan out through the woods a little bit and let's see what we've got ahead of us."

They spread apart and walked the last hundred feet through the pine trees. They stayed in eyesight of each other and took up a position overlooking the perfectly plowed fields of wheat and cotton. A slight breeze caused the wheat spikes to sway back and forth. The only sound that could be heard was the occasional crow yammering to his buddies.

After an uneventful thirty minutes, Colton waved the girls back to the road. Alex joined him first, chewing on a wheat stalk. "Howdy, Mr. Ryman." She laughed. "You ain't from 'round these parts, er ya?"

"I see you're embracing the local culture," replied her dad, who reached out and plucked a stalk for himself. He wondered if he'd end up wearing overalls and a straw hat before it was over.

"It looks good to me," said Madison as she joined the family. "Colton, why don't you grab the truck and let's go see this gentleman about a ride."

They loaded up and slowly started across the farm, the wheels of the Wagoneer following the ruts in the soil created by decades of farm tractor and truck travel. As they cleared the tall stalks of corn on their right, an old white clapboard farmhouse came into view. The red brick fire chimney held onto the side of the house with vines and ivy.

They gradually descended the gravel drive, which was surrounded on both sides by a variety of farm implements and old vehicles. Alex was the first member of the family to see the proprietor of the Saltillo Ferry rockin' back and forth in an old white rocker, sipping iced tea from a Mason jar.

CHAPTER 41

DAY EIGHTEEN
2:00 p.m., September 26
Old Man Percy's Place
Saltillo, Tennessee

"Wait here," instructed Colton. He slowly opened the driver's door and slid off the bench seat. He didn't want to make any sudden moves. He carefully rounded the truck and held his hands away from his body.

The old man kept rockin' and finally set his tea down on the wicker table next to him. He pushed himself out of the rickety rockin' chair with a groan. He wore a plain white shirt, a pair of navy pants held up by suspenders, and a pair of work boots with the soles separating from the leather. Colton imagined that the man had been wearing the same outfit for decades.

"Hello," started Colton. "We're sorry for interrupting, but we hoped you could help us."

"Yo sho 'nuf lost," said the man as he pulled his suspenders away from his thin frame. He moved slowly toward the porch rail and leaned against the post before spitting out some of his chew.

"Well, not exactly. My name is Colton Ryman from Nashville. I was told you might be able to help us."

"Ryman, you say?" the old man replied. "I useta know da Rymans. They run dem boats up and down da river. Dat was a lotta year ago."

"Yessir, it sure was," said Colton. He liked the old guy and didn't feel threatened at all. He glanced over toward the river and could make out a large boat in the midst of some weeping willows along the bank. He decided it was time to cut to the chase.

"Mister, um," started Colton.

"Percy, young man. Ya can jus' call me Percy."

"Well, sir, Percy, we were told you might be able to take us across the river on the ferry. Do you have a ferry boat?"

"Sho 'nuf do," replied Percy. "But it's old and slow, kinda like these ole bones here."

"You look like you're movin' pretty good, Percy." Colton laughed.

"Purdy good. Now, I can take you folks across, but ya gotta help me git 'er started."

Colton's heart leapt out of his chest. Finally, someone would help them across and they'd be able to end this madness.

"Oh, yessir. My wife and daughter, they'll help too. You just tell us what to do! Thank you, Percy." Colton reached out and took the man's hand and began shaking it. It was rough and bony.

Percy smiled to Colton. "Lemme get my hat and finish off this tea. Y'uns want some tea?"

"No, sir, thank you though. I'll tell my wife and daughter the news."

Colton bounced down the steps, pumping his fists in celebration. This instantly brought the girls out of the truck, bearing smiles.

"Is he gonna help us, honey?"

"You betcha!"

The three crashed together in a hug and Colton explained the plan. Percy donned an old railroad cap and joined the three of them in the yard. After the introductions were exchanged, they walked down to get acquainted with the Saltillo Ferry.

Colton's first impression coincided with Madison's.

"Will it float?" she whispered as they walked hand in hand to the vessel. Colton glanced across the water, where he could see the small town of Saltillo. It couldn't have been more than a hundred yards.

"I don't know," replied Colton. "We don't have to go that far."

"It's about one thirty, Daddy," added the accomplished golfer in the family.

"When was the last time you took this one across?" asked Madison.

"Can't rightly 'member, Miss Madison," replied Percy. "Maybe ten year ago, or five."

Percy took them on a tour. "She ain't run regular since back in '98, best I can 'member. She don't look like much, but she can handle one truck at a time. Back before dey built dem bridges, dey was dozens like her."

"Is it coal fired?" asked Colton.

"Sho 'nuf," replied Percy. "It don't take long for her to git goin'. Grab that shovel."

For the next thirty minutes, they helped Old Man Percy fire up the Saltillo Ferry. When the engine was roarin' and black smoke was pourin', Colton drove the Wagoneer onto the back side of the boat. He made Alex and Madison stand on the bank until he was comfortable the entire rig would float. He was pleasantly surprised.

Old Man Percy, as the ferry boat began to move, sounded the usual long, single whistle to warn approaching vessels of its intent to cross the river. Percy probably hadn't noticed that boats were no longer running.

They chugged across and the unusual sound began to draw a crowd across the way. Some of the locals from Saltillo began to gather around the landing on the other side. Colton grabbed the binoculars and scanned the banks of the river. He saw a couple of men with rifles slung over their shoulders, but none appeared hostile. They appeared to be stunned by the curious spectacle of the ferry making another run after all these years.

Colton approached Percy in the wheelhouse and struck up a conversation with the old guy.

"How old are ya, Percy?" asked Colton.

"Ya know, I don't rightly know," he replied. "Last I can 'member, I started goin' to school when dem rich folks went broke in twenty-nine."

Colton quickly did the math. *Ninety plus!*

Percy continued. "Time don't rightly matter anymore. I'm at peace with da good Lord and thank him every day for the life he give me."

"How you makin' out without electricity, Percy?" asked Colton.

"I ain't got none," he replied.

"I know, nobody does. But you comin' along okay since the power went out?"

"When da power go out?" asked Percy.

"About three weeks ago, a big solar flare from the sun knocked the power out across the country. You mean, you didn't know?"

"Hmmmph. Nah, sho didn't."

The ferry arrived at the other side and a welcoming committee of about two dozen onlookers helped tie the boat off and opened the front gate.

"Percy, I don't know how to thank you, my friend," said Colton as he extended his hand to shake. Madison and Alex both rushed to give Percy a hug, which produced the biggest smile the man had probably allowed himself in years.

"Ya know sumptin', Mister Ryman? My ma always said ya lives by da sun and ya dies by da sun. She weren't never wrong."

CHAPTER 42

DAY EIGHTEEN
5:00 p.m., September 26
Saltillo, Tennessee

Colton carefully drove off the ferry onto the west bank of the Tennessee River. A sense of relief poured through his body. Crossing the river, a part of the journey that he initially had taken for granted, had become an unexpected life-threatening obstacle. In addition, for the first time since they left Nashville, he was surrounded by people who approached with smiling faces rather than rifles. It was a welcoming sight.

With their windows rolled down, Colton could hear the locals talking.

Who are they?

Why did they take the ferry?

Are they just passin' through?

Colton took a gamble, a calculated risk based upon years of studying folks at the negotiating table. He decided it would be inhospitable to drive through their town without explanation or showing his gratitude for them not shooting his family. He decided to get out of the car and speak with them.

"Colton, are you crazy?" objected Madison. "Just 'cause they're not shooting at us doesn't mean they won't."

"I know, Maddie. It'll be all right. Let me just thank our friends for letting us pass. You never know, we might cross paths again someday. I don't wanna be rude."

Alex slid across the backseat behind her dad. "I agree, Daddy. Let's be nice and then we can be on our way. Besides, it'll be getting dark. They might have a place we can stay for the night."

"Okay, Maddie?" asked Colton, although his decision was made.

"Okay, let's go for it."

Colton shut off the motor and smiled at his greeters. All of the Rymans exited the truck and spoke with the families of Saltillo who'd crowded around them. They shook hands and exchanged *oh mys* and *you poor dears*. The crowd started to grow and Colton began to realize that this might become an all-night affair, when a booming, baritone voice came from the back of the crowd.

"Well, I'll be doggone, if it isn't Colton Ryman. Look here, you son of a gun!"

The folks in the crowd parted as the most famous celebrity in the history of Saltillo, Tennessee, population three hundred and three, approached Colton. Everyone stopped talking, including Madison and Alex, who stared at Colton in a combination of surprise and apprehension.

"Russ. Russ Hilton. Are you kiddin' me? Boy, howdy, aren't you a sight for sore eyes, my friend!" The two men gave each other an embrace with some hearty backslaps.

Russ Hilton, a popular country music performer from the turn of the century, was born and raised in the tiny town of Pyburn, which was just a few miles south of Savannah in the mountains surrounding Pickwick Dam.

After bouncing around several music venues in Branson, Fort Worth, and Pigeon Forge, he'd finally returned to West Tennessee with his wife, Lisa, and their children. Over the years, older entertainers were relegated to classic country stations and secondary venues. Hilton had enjoyed the highs of his career and then gradually slipped into the twilight when they settled in Saltillo.

Even after retirement from touring, he continued to write music and had a couple of top twenties, including "Tennessee River Run" and "Shiloh," a haunting tune about the infamous Civil War battlefield.

His relationship with Colton went way back. "Folks, listen up," started Hilton, his voice booming as strong as ever. "This here is

Colton Ryman. He used to be my agent when I was playin' in Nashville at the Opry."

"As a matter of fact, Russ was one of my first clients. Do you remember that, Russ?"

Hilton started laughing, slapping Colton on the back. Russ Hilton stood six foot six and therefore towered over Colton. "Do you remember what I said when I hired you to represent me?"

"I'll never forget it," replied Colton. "They were words to live by. Russ said, 'If you ruin my career, I'll hunt you down like a dog and kill ya.'"

Everyone started laughing as Madison and Alex joined them.

"You know I was just ribbin' ya, Colton, right?" Russ laughed.

"No, Russ, actually I didn't. You scared the daylights outta me!"

Colton received another backslap from Russ, which almost knocked the wind out of him. "Well, we done good, buddy. You got me a Billboard number one, a CMA, and a spot on the stage at Vegas. I ain't complainin'."

Madison approached the hulk of a man. "Hey, Russ, do you remember me?"

"Why look at you, Madison! Dang straight I remember you. You're still purdy as a picture." Hilton wrapped her in his massive frame and gave her a hug, but it wasn't life threatening. Alex caught his attention. "No way, is this *little peanut*?"

"Alex, this is Russ Hilton," started Colton. "He was one of the first people to meet you after you were born. Russ used to refer to you as a *little peanut.*"

"Look at you, Alex, you're all grown up and a beauty queen just like your momma," said Hilton. He gave her an equally man-sized hug as he'd provided Madison.

"Hi, Mr. Hilton," said Alex. "I love your songs, especially 'I'm a Cowboy.'"

"This kid's got great taste! That was my number one the summer I met Colton."

Percy pulled away from shore and took the Saltillo Ferry across the river. A final trumpet of the horn sang so long. Russ and the

Rymans spoke for another moment with some of the locals and then the crowd began to dissipate.

Colton looked to the sky and saw darkness beginning to set in. He hated to break up the reunion, but if they were going to make the final thirty miles to Shiloh Ranch before dark, they'd need to get going.

"Look here, Colton," said Russ. "It's gonna be dark soon and y'all don't need to be runnin' these country backroads in the dark. Why don't you stay the night? We'll feed you some good down-home cookin', fix you up a comfortable bed, and maybe even sing a few songs. C'mon, whadya say?"

Colton glanced toward the girls, who both smiled and shrugged. Madison mouthed the words *why not?*

"If you don't mind," said Colton. "We could use a solid night's sleep."

"Let's do it, then," said Hilton. He motioned for a couple of young men who stood off to the side, admiring Alex. "Wilbur, look here. These folks are stayin' the night with us. Take their truck to my place and lock 'er up. Also, rustle up some gasoline for it. Top off the tanks, please, sir."

"Okay, Mr. Hilton."

"Jeremiah!" barked Russ.

"Ride with Wilbur and tell my missus that we've got three guests for the night. Then get the Hilton opened up. We're gonna have a shindig in two hours. Now, go on, boys, make it happen!"

"Yessir!"

Colton looked at his old friend inquisitively. "The Hilton?" he asked.

"C'mon, I'll show you," replied Russ.

Hilton escorted the Rymans into the center of the small town and gave them a brief history of Saltillo. It had started as a small town in the eighteen hundreds and remained a small town in the twenty-first century. It was isolated from major highways and was not an attractive destination for tourists. Hilton couldn't remember the exact reason that he and Lisa had chosen to settle in Saltillo. When they'd passed through looking for property years ago, the town, he said, just felt like a good fit. Now, Hilton stood larger than life in the middle of nineteenth-century farmhouses and Greek Revival buildings.

"Wait, hold up," said Colton, bringing the entourage to a halt as they emerged in the center of town. "This street sign reads Russ Hilton Way. Really?"

"Why sure." Russ laughed. "Dolly Parton has her own road in Pigeon Forge. The town decided I should have my own road too."

"Is this the main drag?" asked Alex.

"It sure is, Alex," replied Russ. "Now, Rymans, of the infamous Ryman Auditorium, may I present to you, drumroll please, the Hillbilly Hilton."

Hilton put his arms around the Rymans and turned them toward a building in the center of town. It looked like a rustic lodge out of the mountains. Built of logs and river rock, the structure towered over the street. At the peak of the roof line was a sand-blasted wood sign that read Hillbilly Hilton.

"Wow!" exclaimed Colton. "Russ, I had no idea. This is incredible!"

"Thank you, Colton."

"It looks like the Country Bear Jamboree at Disney," added Alex.

"Good eye, little lady," said Russ. "It's a pretty close replica. Lisa and I would take the kids to see that mouse, but all they wanted to do was hear the bears sing."

"It's wonderful, Russ," said Madison, glancing up and down the street. "But, I mean, is there enough population around to support it?"

"You know, we built it for ourselves. Colton knows what it's like at the end of a musician's career. You play the grand venues for a while, then you start to taper off into Branson or the Stockyards or the Dew Drop Inn. We decided to find a good place to raise our family and build our own Music City. Tell ya the truth, we don't charge admission. We don't sell beer or drinks. We don't even open on a regular basis. We've got a BBQ pit in the back, and every once in a while, we open up and I play a few sets—like tonight."

"You're gonna open tonight?" asked Alex.

"Yes, ma'am," replied Russ. "Me and your daddy are gonna play a few sets together, aren't we, Colton?"

Colton turned pale. "I don't know, Russ."

"C'mon, Colt," encouraged Madison. "It'll be fun."

"Oh, gawd," groaned Alex.

CHAPTER 43

DAY EIGHTEEN
8:00 p.m., September 26
The Hillbilly Hilton
Saltillo, Tennessee

Madison and Alex sat with Lisa after filling their bellies with pork barbeque, baked beans, peanut slaw, and fried hush puppies. They were introduced to the newest addition to the Hilton family, young Wyatt Thomas Hilton. Lisa lamented about how Russ had tricked her into naming their baby boy with the initials W-T-H—*what the hell,* which were the first words out of her husband's mouth when she told him she was pregnant. They once thought five kids was plenty. God gave them Wyatt, and now they loved their half dozen more than life.

The house was packed with the citizens of Saltillo. They all came by to say hello to the Rymans during dinner. Some told stories passed down from generation to generation of how Captain Tom Ryman's riverboats used to pass by Saltillo, moving commodities produced in the south from East Tennessee, Alabama, and Georgia to the Mississippi River.

"Good evening, folks!" shouted Hilton over the noisy crowd. His voice boomed without the need of a microphone. Everyone gradually settled in and turned their chairs toward the stage, where Hilton sat on a stool with his banjo, accompanied by a large man who wielded a big bass cello like it was a violin. Colton joined them on a stool and was meticulously tuning a guitar.

"Most of y'all have met my friend Colton Ryman and his family. Let's give 'em a big round of applause to welcome them proper."

The room burst into applause and everyone smiled at the big round table containing the Ryman girls and the Hilton family, which was located at the front of the stage.

"I was one of Colton's early clients, way back when, but we quickly became pretty good friends. But one thing he and I never did together was play a few tunes. So he agreed to join me and Big Willie on the bass, if that's okay with you folks."

"Yeah!"

"Let's hear it!"

"It's time for a happy hoedown!"

The crowd laughed at this last suggestion. The boys in the band whispered among themselves and they got ready. Russ got it started by clapping his hands.

CLAP—CLAP—CLAP!

CLAP—CLAP—CLAP!

Everyone in the crowd started clapping in unison and then Russ started stomping one foot in unison with the rhythmic clapping. He nodded to Big Willie, who began to slap the big bass.

THUMP –THUMP—THUMP!

THUMP—THUMP—THUMP!

The house was rockin', and the boys began singin'.

We're born in the mountains, but it ain't the place we call home.

Lord knows, good times were there, don't 'member why we roamed.

On the Tennessee River, we're good ole boys, we get together, singin' this song.

My Tennessee River, why did you call, now we play together all night long.

Russ took the lead as the crowd continued to stomp their feet.

Me and my woman's done made our plans, walkin' with the good Lord, hand in Hand.

Gonna raise a family, Lord, settle down, with six young'uns in this sleepy town.

The boys in the band sang the chorus.

On the Tennessee River, we're good ole boys, we get together, singin' this song.

My Tennessee River, why did you call, now we play together all night long.

Now it was Colton's turn.

My name is Ryman, I'm a Texas boy, but Nashville called, 'cause music runs in my veins.

Been on the road runnin', done been shot at, plumb wore out, lookin' for a place to rest my brain.

The crowd joined in the chorus.

THUMP—THUMP—THUMP!

On the Tennessee River, we're good ole boys, we get together, singin' this song.

My Tennessee River, why did you call, now we play together all night long.

CHAPTER 44

DAY NINETEEN
8:00 a.m., September 27
The Hilton Residence
Saltillo, Tennessee

Colton and Madison enjoyed an intimate night together for the first time in weeks. The relief provided by crossing the river and the stress-free environment of Saltillo allowed them to wash away the cares of the world for one night.

They came down the wide, sweeping stairs of the Hilton home to the smell of sausage cooking on the cast-iron stove. Alex was already there, playing with the Hilton kids.

"Good mornin', honored guests!" greeted Russ. "Have you enjoyed your stay at the Hillbilly Hilton so far?"

Colton gave his friend a firm handshake and then a bro-hug. He'd had a great time last night, and for about ten hours, they'd forgotten about the post-apocalyptic world that had chased them to the quiet town. Reality set in when he glanced out the bedroom window and saw the Wagoneer backed in front of the house, pointing south toward Shiloh.

Lisa Hilton finished feeding the children and then sent them on their way to take care of the baby and other chores. The adults and Alex settled around the kitchen table and enjoyed the hearty breakfast of sausage and grits, with fresh milk from the Hiltons' cows out back.

"Look, Colton, I'll cut right to the chase," started Russ. "We'd like y'all to consider staying here in Saltillo. I know our little town doesn't seem like much, but it's safe. We grow our own food, we've not had any trouble, and the folks in town like y'all."

"Man, thank you, Russ," said Colton, looking at Madison and Alex to gauge their reaction. "We sure feel welcome and I think we could get along well with everyone. I mean, of course, we'll talk about it after breakfast." The sound of thunder rolled off in the distance.

"Please do," said Lisa. "We've got a house picked out for you guys. It isn't big, you know, like what you all are used to, but we'll help you make it into a nice home."

"Thank you, Lisa," said Madison, glancing at Colton as she finished up her meal. "We'll definitely talk about this some more after breakfast."

"Fair enough." Lisa smiled as she stood up and cleared the plates. Alex and Madison immediately joined them and approached their sink, half of which was already full with soapy water. Lisa provided instructions on the dishwashing method they employed to conserve water.

"Okay, seriously, Colton," started Russ. "I know we talked about Savannah. Ma and Junior should not be messed with. Those two are nuts and administer revenge without hesitating."

"I think we've already crossed them," said Colton. "We kicked an angry hornet's nest down there. It'll take a while for them to settle down."

"I know. I saw the lead stuck in your fenders." Russ sat back in his chair and crossed his arms across his chest. "She'll find you."

"I know, Russ, which is why we have to leave. We can't endanger this many people by staying here. I couldn't live with that."

Russ smiled and leaned forward to pat his friend on the back. "You're a big boy and I respect what you're sayin'. We can handle ourselves too, you know. Besides, we're tucked way up here in the corner of the county. Saltillo is one of those, you know, *you can't there from here* places."

Colton laughed. "You've got that right. Any more, you can't get anywhere unless you have a horse and a canoe."

"So where are y'all headed?" asked Russ.

Colton thought for a moment. He'd put his friend, and the beautiful little town, at enough risk. The last burden they needed to shoulder was the Rymans' whereabouts.

"It's safer if you don't know, Russ. But I'll say this. We'll be close enough for me to have another go at that guitar on stage with you someday."

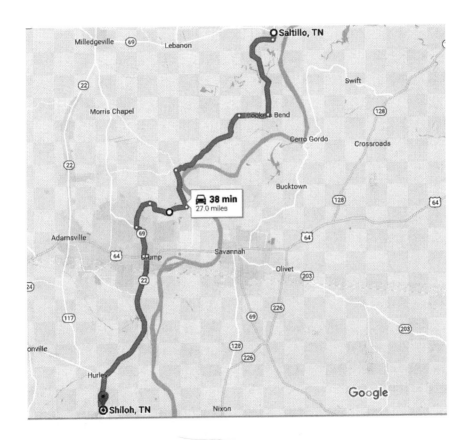

CHAPTER 45

DAY NINETEEN
9:00 a.m., September 27
Hooker's Bend, Tennessee

Madison admonished Colton for not discussing the decision with her and Alex first, although she wholeheartedly agreed with him. Saltillo was a beautiful town and the residents had come together as a family. Madison had seen enough of the evil that lurked within Ma Durham and her offspring Junior. She didn't want their trail to lead to Saltillo, resulting in harm to any of those nice people. In addition, there was the sense within the Ryman family that they were on a mission. They wanted to see their journey to the end—come hell or high water.

The Rymans followed the route that took them south along the Tennessee River until they could cross Highway 64, their next big challenge. Their fuel levels were no longer an issue, thanks to the generosity of the good people of Saltillo. It was only thirty miles from the outskirts of town to Shiloh.

Just fifteen minutes into the countryside, the Rymans were reminded of the benefit of The Weather Channel on DirecTV or the Internet to provide them today's travel forecast. They began to experience raindrops falling on the windshield, and dark storm clouds began to form to their south and west. Colton picked up speed the best he could, but the Wagoneer and the approaching storm were destined to collide.

By the time they arrived in Hooker's Bend, where the Tennessee River took a pronounced turn, the rain was pouring down on top of them, and the wind began to bring visibility to near zero. The loss of the windshield wipers to the lady marauder on the Trace was now coming back to bite them in the butt.

"Guys, this is not good," muttered Colton as he pressed his face to the windshield to follow the road. "I'm afraid I might get two wheels off the shoulder and land us in a ditch."

"Daddy, even if we go ten miles per hour, we'll be there in a couple of hours."

They'd experienced a number of roadblocks since they'd left Nashville—all man-made. Now, they faced a more common method of impeding progress on the roads, natural obstructions like fallen trees, floodwaters, boulders and mud slides.

Colton continued on the road as the storm worsened. Low-lying areas began to fill the road with water, causing them to hydroplane slightly despite their slow speed. The inside of the windshield began to fog up from the increased anxiety within the car. Madison diligently wiped the window with a cloth, silently cursing the old Wagoneer's ventilation system for not doing its job.

BOOM!

A lightning strike hit on the hill just ahead of them and to their right, causing everyone to jump and scream. Colton reacted by turning the steering wheel hard to the left, and then as the rear of the truck began to skid on the slick road, he whipped it hard back to the right, overcorrecting the truck's course. It was too much and they spun around, finally resting in the middle of the road, pointing in the opposite direction towards Saltillo—just as a large oak tree split in half by a lightning strike came crashing across the road, blocking their path.

"Enough," said Colton dryly. "Let's find a place to park and ride out the storm. When it clears later, we'll get going again."

"No arguments here," said Madison.

"I totally agree," added Alex. "Besides, I think I need to check my pants."

CHAPTER 46

DAY NINETEEN
3:00 p.m., September 27
Glendale Road
Coffee Landing, Tennessee

"Being on the road makes us an easy target," started Colton. "Let's pull in here and wait for the weather to clear." Colton navigated the Wagoneer up the clearing created by the utility company for the massive overhead power lines that crossed the road. They bounced along the makeshift road until they reached a point where the trees provided some cover. Colton steered into the woods and then the wheels started to spin.

He had unknowingly crossed a dry creek, which was rapidly filling with rainwater. The soft, silty bottom sucked the rear wheels of the Wagoneer deeper into the quicksand-like earth. Colton put the truck into reverse, attempting to back out of the trees. The rear tires spun in place as the rear end of the Wagoneer dug in deeper. He attempted to swap between forward and reverse, creating a rocking motion to get them out. It didn't help. They were stuck.

"Great," muttered Colton as he slammed the steering wheel with both hands out of frustration. "God, we're so close. Please."

Everyone remained silent while Colton allowed his anger with himself to subside. They'd been through so much, and now this. He began to second-guess everything—leaving Nashville, not stopping in a secluded spot elsewhere, and turning down the offer to remain in Saltillo.

Finally, he let out a deep breath and laughed nervously. "Let me go take a look. Y'all wait here."

Alex looked out at the pouring rain and answered, "No prob."

"Honey," started Madison, "I'll help you. What can I do?"

"Give me a kiss for starters," replied Colton, who was determined not to let this get them down. Madison happily obliged and reassuringly touched her husband's face. The rain had slowed somewhat and the tree canopy helped catch a lot of the rainfall.

Colton exited the truck and found that he'd gotten the Wagoneer stuck in a big way. He considered building up rocks, gravel and logs in front of as well as behind the tires to give them some traction. But his repeated spinning of the tires had created a perfect mold of mud around the rear wheels. He began to wonder if they'd ever be able to get the truck out.

"Congrats to me." Colton laughed as he returned to the front seat and shut the door, bringing a spray of misty rain with him. "I did a great job of putting us out of business."

"What's the plan, Daddy?"

Colton leaned back against the driver's door and allowed his head to smack the window as self-inflicted punishment. "I don't know, Allie-Cat. I guess we'll have to hoof it."

"Fine by me," said Alex.

"What about our stuff?" asked Madison.

Colton hadn't thought about this. If anyone came across the Jeep, they'd take everything. He immediately began to look around the woods. He envisioned several hiding places, including across the clearing and away from the embedded Wagoneer.

"We can do this, y'all," started Colton. "We'll pack the absolute necessities to get us these last fifteen miles to Shiloh Ranch. We'll keep our backpacks as light as possible. Everything else, I'll hide in the woods around us. We'll have to write down where our stuff is in case I forget."

"Are we gonna walk in the rain?" asked Madison.

"We can wait," replied Colton. "As hard as this wind is blowing, I suspect this is a fast-moving storm system. It'll blow through soon and we can leave then. I think it will be safer and easier to cross Highway 64 at night with the assistance of the FLIR monocular."

Alex crawled up on her knees and rummaged around in the back of the Wagoneer, which was taking on rain through its broken window. She pulled the backpacks forward and they immediately assessed their contents.

Madison took the lead on determining what to take. "I read in those survival guides that your bug-out bag should be one part Swiss Army knife, one part grocery store, and one part wilderness outfitter. When we packed these before we left, I kept that in mind. They should be lightweight as it is, but we could lessen the load by leaving some food behind except for the high-calorie MRE bars."

"Okay," said Colton. "Let's start there."

They all began to unpack and repack their backpacks. Each of them put on a fanny pack and distributed their ammunition load. One thing they agreed upon was that they would not leave any of their weapons or ammo behind. They brought one change of clothes except for their additional socks, considering the wet conditions. Colton added a tarp to his load, as well as rope to create a makeshift tent if necessary.

After exchanging ideas, they agreed this was all they needed to walk the four or five hours to Shiloh Ranch. If something unforeseen happened along the way, they could always return here and regroup.

The rain finally began to subside and Colton set about hiding their valuables throughout the woods. With the assistance of Alex, his expert in determining distances, he cataloged everything's location so they could locate it later, even if it was several weeks.

The last thing Colton did was reach back in his memory banks to his days as a boy when he was around his friends who enjoyed working on cars. He planned on leaving the truck unlocked so anyone finding it wouldn't break out any more of the windows to gain access. The keys, however, were stored away in his backpack, together with the plug wires and distributor cap, which he easily removed. This disabled the old truck so that it couldn't be hot-wired. Finding the replacement parts should be difficult for any potential thief. Finally, he siphoned out as much gas from the Wagoneer as he could and filled the remaining empty gas cans, which he hid in the woods as well.

The rain ended and occasional glimpses of blue sky could be seen through the storm clouds as they roared off towards Nashville and Clarksville. Everyone double-checked their packs and were satisfied with the hidden locations of their survival gear. It was time to go.

As they made their way through the woods on the slippery mixture of fallen leaves and wet pine needles, Colton reflected upon the last stretch of the journey toward their new home. He firmly believed that one of two things would happen when the Rymans finally reached Shiloh Ranch.

They'd either step foot on something solid and good, or they'd learn to fly.

CHAPTER 47

DAY NINETEEN
9:00 p.m., September 27
Federal Road
Shiloh, Tennessee

Colton was confident the events of the last five days on the road, and the two weeks preceding their decision to leave home for Shiloh Ranch, would be looked upon as a turning point in their lives that insured their survival. Their experiences were part of a process for the Ryman family that helped them discover the core of their strength and proved their will to survive.

Hiking the last fifteen miles to Shiloh was fraught with deadly risks. In addition to the threat of stormy weather and any unforeseen calamities like twisted ankles, they could face local residents who might overtake them along the way.

Although they hadn't faced the dangers posed by the desperation of their fellow man since they crossed the Tennessee River, Colton was cognizant of the fact that the mere act of traveling through or near someone's property in this dystopian landscape could expose his family to a violent confrontation with someone who was in fear for their own safety.

They were cautious as they approached Highway 64 and the small town of Crump, which was the gateway to the Harrison-McGarity Bridge into Savannah. They had walked an extra distance to avoid the crossing near the river. Colton was sure a similar roadblock might have been established although he considered the possibility Ma Durham left the west side open for travelers to be lured into a false sense of security until they arrived on the Savannah side. In either case, he had no desire to get close enough to see.

The town of Crump didn't consist of much more than a couple of small businesses lining the road and a handful of homes. His earlier concerns about crossing the five-lane highway dissipated as soon as he arrived at the road's edge. The town was deserted. There were absolutely no signs of life except for a dog barking in the distance.

Pleased with their good fortune, Colton led them across the road to the safety of a stand of trees next to a bait and tackle shop. The plate-glass windows of the fishing store had been broken and the interior was relieved of its contents. Apparently Ma Durham's protection racket had not yet extended to this side of the Tennessee River.

Very little was said between the weary travelers, who were wet from a spontaneous, two-minute shower ten minutes after they'd left the Wagoneer behind. Nobody was interested in changing clothes for fear of another pop-up shower, so they continued in their damp attire.

Laughing, Alex broke the silence as they found their way back onto State Road 22, which led them into the Shiloh National Military Park.

"What's so funny?" asked Madison, who was the fussiest about being wet.

"I was just doing the math," replied Alex. "We've come a hundred and sixty miles in slightly less than five days. We could've walked that distance in the same time and avoided a lot of aggravation."

Colton laughed with his daughter. "Yeah, but think about all of the interesting people we wouldn't have met!"

"Ha-ha," said Madison, perking up as the maroon sign indicating their left turn toward Pittsburg Landing came into view. "Walking would've been boring. Excitement is where it's at."

"Yup, excitement keeps the heart pounding," added Colton.

They made their way onto Federal Road and once again took in the smells emanating from the Tennessee River. The sounds of overflowing, rain-swollen creeks became deafening as they entered the canopy of the trees that enclosed the quickly narrowing road that ended at Shiloh Ranch.

Excited, yet nervous, Colton could sense Madison and Alex picking up the pace. Madison giggled a little as she broke out into a slight jog. Alex laughed as she began to run and pass her mother.

Not wanting to be left behind, Colton joined them and grabbed his girls' hands as they rounded the bend to the entrance of Shiloh Ranch, giddy with excitement—until they stared down the barrels of half a dozen rifles.

THANK YOU FOR READING TURNING POINT!

If you enjoyed it, I'd be grateful if you'd take a moment to write a short review (just a few words are needed) and post it on Amazon. Amazon uses complicated algorithms to determine what books are recommended to readers. Sales are, of course, a factor, but so are the quantities of reviews my books get. By taking a few seconds to leave a review, you help me out, and also help new readers learn about my work.

And before you go…

SIGN UP for Bobby Akart's mailing list to receive special offers, bonus content, and you'll be the first to receive news about new releases.

eepurl.com/bYqq3L

VISIT Amazon.com/BobbyAkart for more information on his next project, as well as his completed words: the Doomsday series, the Yellowstone series, the Lone Star series, the Pandemic series, the Blackout series, the Boston Brahmin series and the Prepping for Tomorrow series totaling nearly forty novels, including over thirty Amazon #1 Bestsellers in forty-plus fiction and nonfiction genres.

Visit Bobby Akart's website for informative blog entries on preparedness, writing, and a behind-the-scenes look into his novels.

BobbyAkart.com

READ ON FOR A BONUS EXCERPT from

SHILOH RANCH
Book Four of The Blackout Series

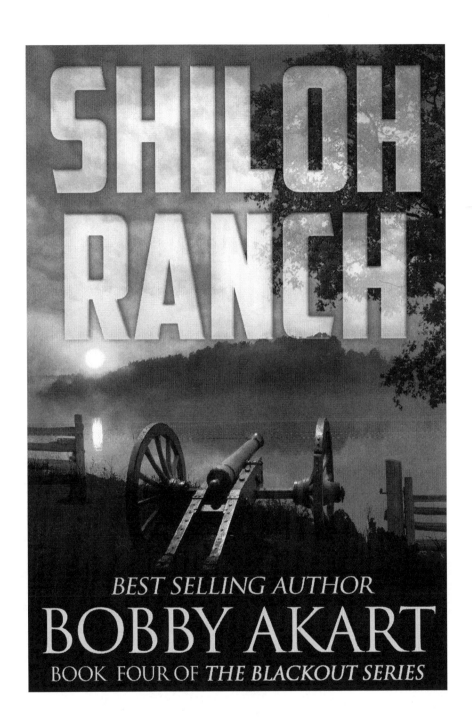

BEST SELLING AUTHOR
BOBBY AKART
BOOK FOUR OF *THE BLACKOUT SERIES*

PROLOGUE

Early Morning Hours
April 6, 1862
Headquarters of Confederate General Albert Sidney Johnston
Shiloh, Tennessee

During the latter part of 1861 and into early 1862, the Civil War reached levels of violence that shocked the North and South alike. For months, the Union Army had worked its way up the Tennessee and Cumberland rivers. By February 1862, Kentucky was firmly in Union hands and the fight came to Nashville, Tennessee's capital. Major General William Harvey Lamb Wallace, an Illinois attorney, commanded the second brigade against the confederate stronghold of Fort Donelson. The southerners attacked Wallace's brigade with a vengeance, killing over five hundred Union soldiers. Wallace prevailed nonetheless, but the battle had a profound effect upon him.

A collision was coming between the mighty armies of Major General Ulysses S. Grant and the confederate forces led by Generals Albert Johnston and Pierre Beauregard. On the morning of April 6, 1862, General Grant was having coffee at the home of William and Annie Cherry — Cherry Mansion, located on the east bank of the Tennessee River in Savannah. Grant was joined by General Wallace and General Prentiss, as well as Mr. and Mrs. Cherry.

Mrs. Cherry, a southern sympathizer, had been irritated with her husband, a pro-Union partisan, for allowing the Union generals to occupy their home. Cherry had assured her that the stay was temporary while they awaited their troops in Nashville to join them.

Nonetheless, this was an opportunity for her to voice her displeasure to her guests about the war between the states.

"My family has never owned slaves," said Mrs. Cherry. "This is only one aspect of why this confrontation with the government was necessary. Every state, north and south alike, was granted the power to govern its people by the Constitution. As Washington continues to force it's will upon us, our hand was forced."

"Madame, I am a guest in your home and as such, I will respect your opinion," started General Grant. "But I must remind you that it was the Confederacy which fired the first shot upon our Nation at Fort Sumter almost one year ago. President Lincoln did not wish to pursue a war, he merely wants to preserve our Union."

Mrs. Cherry persisted. "But is it not true that President Lincoln is using slavery as an excuse to spread his brand of federalism across the South. In fact, the issue of slavery is a means to an end. He wishes to force our state governments to stop exercising our sovereign powers."

Mr. Cherry stepped in. "Now, Annie, please. General Grant is a guest in our home. He is not here for political discussions nor will he change his plans based upon ..."

The pounding on the front door startled the group and a soldier abruptly entered the foyer.

"General, a courier has arrived sir," announced Grant's aide-de-camp.

"Read the message," said General Grant.

"Sir, from the south, elements of the armies of the Confederacy, *Crew's Battalion*, have advanced across Pittsburg Landing. A larger advance has been observed from the armies of Generals Johnston and Beauregard."

Grant stood and slammed his coffee onto the table. This development complicated his strategy of awaiting General Don Carlos Buell, Commander of the Army of Ohio to march to Savannah along the Natchez Trace from Nashville. Once the two armies were merged, Grant intended to engage the forty-four thousand troops of the Confederacy gathered at Corinth, Mississippi. His goal was to cut off their supply lines by destroying the Confederate railroad center there.

210

"A surprise attack, sir?" asked General Wallace.

"Indeed, William," replied Grant. "This is Johnston's doing. He's the finest general in the south and he deserves our respect. We have to move quickly to slow his advance until General Buell arrives."

Grant pulled out a map of the area which identified Shiloh, Pittsburg Landing, and Savannah along the Tennessee river. He began to trace his fingers across the map.

"Johnston will move along the banks of the river, using the landing at Pittsburg to resupply," he began. "That places the strength of their forces within two miles of our main army. They've got to be slowed until General Buell arrives."

General Wallace joined his side. "General, I learned at Fort Donelson that these southerners have a will to fight like no other. There passionate about their cause as opposed to being hired soldiers like the majority of our troops. From my experience, they will fight night and day to advance through our foothold."

"If we don't stop the advance, they'll drive my army into the Tennessee River."

Wallace made a suggestion. "General, allow me to reinforce our lines here, at the church located at Shiloh — meaning *place of peace*. My men know the enemy. They have gained the fighting spirit from their opponents. We will do our duty for you General, and the Union. We will fight fire with fire."

General Wallace's troops quickly advanced to the white-washed Shiloh Church where the Union's resistance stiffened. For nearly eight hours, Wallace's men fought in a thick area of woods near the church. General Wallace himself led the defense of a sunken road which ran past Shiloh Church. They held their position for hours until they were overrun late in the afternoon.

They valiantly sacrificed their lives to buy precious time to allow General Buell's Army of reinforcements to arrive. They ultimately perished but the exhausted Confederates chose to wait until the break of dawn on April 7th to continue the Battle of Shiloh.

As the lines broke, Wallace was wounded by a piece of fragmented shell which struck him in the head. He lay there as the battle raged around him, unable to move or communicate. He watched his men die and the Confederate soldiers advance.

Throughout the night, he waited. He listened. The war quieted and the aura surrounding Shiloh Church settled in. The sun rose and the battle ensued. He began to see the uniforms of the Army of the Ohio — dark blue jackets with shoulder straps, adorned with nine brass buttons down the front.

General Buell had arrived in the night!

General William Wallace was removed to Cherry Mansion where he died with his wife by his side. He was hailed as a hero for turning the tide on the bloodiest battle between north and south of the time. This small area of woods at the Shiloh Church where Wallace's men took a stand became known as the *Hornet's Nest*, and is considered one of the major turning points in the Civil War.

CHAPTER 1

12:12 a.m., September 28
Front Gate
Shiloh Ranch

Colton tried to shield his eyes from the blinding light. A low-lying fog began to settle in, causing the ground to disappear within an eerie, dramatic glow. His mind raced, but not toward a solution.

He thought of his daughter, Alex, as a newborn. She was lying in her crib—crying. He couldn't discern whether the grating sound of her cries were on some level from a distant memory or in the present.

His memories shifted to the moment when she was born—the moment his beloved wife, Madison, gathered the strength for one last push. He remembered Alex's head appearing. *I saw her first!*

We all know about life's forks in the road—those seminal events that create a turning point on our respective journeys. One door closes, and then another door opens. Each of us has cycles like the changes in seasons. But the moment his child was born, the moment was beyond surreal. He'd transformed from a free-wheeling, high-flying talent agent to a dad charged with the responsibility of keeping this tiny baby alive.

Everything became different for Colton when Alex was born. His world was gone, but a new one had opened up. It was much smaller, shrunk down to the dimensions of a six-and-a-half-pound squallin' mass of baby girl. In that moment, he promised God, and his newborn's mother, that he'd always protect their daughter.

Now, as threatening guns held by faceless men behind blinding spotlights placed the Rymans in danger, he felt utterly helpless and trapped with no way out.

Clippity-clop. Clippity-clop. Clippity-clop.

A familiar sound, yet he couldn't place it. The fog consumed his brain and the surroundings.

A horse—approaching at a steady pace.

"Whoa!" shouted the rider. "What do we have here, boys?" The creaking sound of metal accompanied the rider as the gates to Shiloh Ranch opened. Boots crunched onto gravel as the horse whinnied.

Colton tried to speak, but couldn't. He was back in the present but still frozen in time.

"*Un hombre, dos mujeres,*" replied a Hispanic voice. *One man, two women.*

The silhouette of a large man approached, causing Colton to instinctively step between the approaching figure and the Ryman women.

"Daddy," whispered Alex, "what do we—"

"Lower your arms so I can see your faces," instructed the man.

The reflection of light upon a nickel-plated sidearm caught Colton's attention as it was pulled from the man's holster. Colton hesitated and then lowered his arms slowly. He contemplated pulling his own weapon to defend his family but knew it would result in certain death.

The man laughed, deep-throated and genuine. "Well, slap my head and call me silly!" he roared. "If it ain't Colton Ryman. Why you little cotton-picker! What the heck are you folks doin' out here in the middle of the night?"

"Jake, is that you?" asked Colton, exhaling a sigh of relief so big that it could've knocked down the doors of all three little pigs' homes at once.

Jake Allen holstered his weapon and stepped into the light, all six feet six inches of him. He was grinning ear to ear.

"Of course it's me, Colton!"

Colton stepped forward to shake hands and bro-hug his old friend. "Sorry to show up unannounced. We tried to call but got your voicemail. Then my email server was having trouble and, well, you know."

"Verizon, right?" Jake laughed. The men shared an embrace of two old friends who were both dang glad to see each other. "Ladies? Madison and Alex?"

"Hey, Jake," replied Madison, still trembling as she received a bear hug of her own. Tears of joy and relief began to stream down her face.

"Now, c'mon, darlin'," started Jake. "Why the tears? Did Chevy stop makin' trucks?"

The jokes spurred the Rymans and the onlookers into laughter. It eased the tension of the earlier standoff and allowed everyone to relax. Colton said a quick prayer to God, thanking Him for restraining nervous trigger fingers on this night.

"Listen up, boys," yelled Jake. "These folks are the Rymans from Nashville. They are pert near family. A couple of y'all grab their things and take them up to the main house." Three of the ranch hands immediately shouldered their rifles and hopped the four-rail fencing that surrounded the Allens' property.

"I'll keep this, thanks," said Alex politely as one of the men offered to take her AR-15. Colton touched his daughter on the shoulders, attempting to reassure her.

"Honey, we're safe now."

"I'm not giving up the rifle, Daddy."

Colton put his arm around his daughter, who had grown up a lot in the last four weeks. "Jake, you remember Alex, don't you?"

"Well, look at you!" exclaimed Jake. "You're all grown up and pretty as a peach. Taller than your momma already!"

"Hey, Mr. Allen," said Alex as she gave him a hug. Alex seemed reserved, anxious about the whole situation. Colton hoped she could find a way to relax.

"Are y'all up for a short walk?" asked Jake. "From the looks of those backpacks, it appears you've been hoofin' it for a ways at least. I can have the boys run to the stables and rustle up a wagon if you'd like?"

Colton looked to the girls and then responded, "I think we can walk another half mile, if my memory serves me correctly."

"It does," said Jake. "This fog has been settling in along the Tennessee River for the last several days as the nights have gotten cooler. Tomorrow, we'll walk around the place after it burns off in the morning. We've added some things since y'all were here last. Plus, it's a little more crowded around Shiloh Ranch, you know, under the circumstances."

Madison spoke up. "I hope we're not imposing."

"Oh no, Madison. I didn't mean it that way. It's just that we've added quite a few ranch hands. Life is a lot different now and more dangerous."

Colton laughed. "That's an understatement."

It took the group about ten minutes to reach the main house, where candlelit lanterns swayed slightly on the ropes that held them to the wraparound porch. They talked about the last time the Rymans had visited and a little bit about the extraordinary event that led them to the front steps of the Allens' magnificent log home.

"These solar flares happen all the time," started Jake. "But I had no idea they could knock out all the power."

"I did," said Alex. "I learned about it in school and then I was able to convince Mom that the threat was real."

"It's hard to imagine the power of the sun until you've experienced it firsthand," said Jake. "I told Emily it was kinda like a gas buildup in your belly. If it's just a little gas, you might politely let out a little toot."

Madison and Alex giggled. Colton simply shook his head. He could only imagine where the rest of *Professor Jake Allen's science lesson* was headed.

Unfortunately, he was about to find out as Jake continued. "But let's say you've got a lot of gas. You know, after eating a plate of burritos or something. This gas, you see, has to escape your belly. So it does, but still isn't massive, right?"

The girls were in stitches. Madison was pleading for Jake to stop. "No more, Jake," she said with tears of laughter streaming down her face.

Jake was relentless. "But, back in the day, when we were kids, sometimes you'd like to really drop one on your friends. You know, let it build up and time it just right so as to blast them real good. So you let it build up and set your internal stopwatch."

Colton joined in the laughter. "Jake, *no mas! No mas!*"

"When the time is right," Jake continued, ignoring the pleas for mercy. "You drop your F-bomb. Boom! The room is cleared out, or in the case of this solar flare—boom-boom, out go the lights!"

Now, all three of the Rymans were bent over in laughter, holding their knees. Jake hopped up the steps and opened the front door. He turned to them and proudly announced, "Welcome back to Shiloh Ranch, my friends. *Mi casa, su casa!*"

Chapter 2

8:00 a.m., September 28
Main House
Shiloh Ranch

Colton sopped up the red-eye gravy with a biscuit. He and Madison had woken up at sunrise in the guest bedroom facing the east. They were exhausted the night before and had forgotten to draw the curtains, creating a natural alarm clock. Not that it mattered, however, as the main house was bustling with activity before dawn.

A plate of ham and grits coupled with what was commonly referred to as poor man's gravy made for a filling country breakfast. The Allens had a smokehouse filled with cured country ham, and when it was pan-fried over their wood-burning stove, the drippings made for a tasty sauce to add to the meal.

"The smokehouse is one of the things we've added since y'all were here a few years ago," said Jake. "We built it old-school, if you know what I mean. There are no windows and only a single entrance. We've got a fire pit in the center, where we burn hardwoods to dry the meat. First we cure the meat with a salt rub, then we smoke it."

"That explains it," said Alex as she took another sip of water. "I've never tasted anything so salty."

"The smokehouse was Stubby's idea," interjected Emily Allen, Jake's wife. At thirty-nine, Emily was slightly younger than her husband of twenty years. They'd married when he was still a country crooner on Printer's Alley in Nashville. The two had been through some trying times in their marriage, as Jake had enjoyed his fame, and alcohol, a little too much. But the bond they shared over their son, Chase, and Jake's subsequent maturation kept the family together.

218

"Where is Stubby?" asked Madison. "I haven't seen Bessie either."

"Oh, they get a real early start." Emily chuckled. "They get goin' way before the crack of dawn. They feed the hands and then the livestock. Jake and I try to stay out of the way during this process."

"The hands?" queried Alex.

"Yeah, the farmhands," replied Jake. "We have eight now, plus our gardener and landscaper. You'll meet them all later. Trust me, we're one big extended family now."

Colton removed Madison's plate and took it to the sink, where Emily was scrubbing the dishes with a soapy sponge. His mind replayed breakfast at the Hiltons' just a couple of days prior. He wondered if Russ and Jake knew each other.

"Do you know Russ Hilton?" asked Colton, leaning against the kitchen cabinets. Jake finished up his plate and pushed away from the table.

"We've met. He played a few weeks in Branson just before I opened up my place. Good man. He had a great career."

"Like you, Russ was one of my first clients," said Colton. "You guys are practically neighbors."

"You're kiddin'?"

"Nope. They bought a place up north of here in Saltillo. Russ built his own honky-tonk in the middle of town called the Hillbilly Hilton."

"Wow, who knew?" quipped Jake. "We'll have to check it out. By the way, are you still pickin'?"

"Great, here we go," groaned Alex.

Colton ignored his daughter's protestations and answered, "Yeah, now and again. Russ and I belted out a couple of tunes while we stayed the night with them. I remember our nights around the campfire from our last visit. I suppose we could pick up where we left off."

"Heck yeah!" said Jake. "I've actually got a couple of new songs rollin' around in my head. When we find the time, I'll run 'em by ya."

Suddenly, the door flung open and in walked Stubby Crump, who at five feet eight inches tall and nearly two hundred pounds was the textbook definition of a man built like a fireplug. In his late sixties, a lifetime of athletic endeavors maintained a muscular build with thick arms and legs and a neck that wasn't readily visible.

Born as Darren Wayne Crump, Stubby's family had owned all of the land on the west side of the Tennessee River near the original Milo Lemert Bridge, which crossed into Savannah. The bridge was taken down by explosives in 1980 and replaced with a more stable one. During the expansion efforts, the Crump family was paid handsomely by the government for their property and ultimately sold off their remaining acreage located south of the bridge to several Hardin County ranchers and farmers. This two-hundred-acre tract was purchased by Jake and Emily fifteen years ago and the Crumps, despite having enough wealth of their own, chose to work for the Allens as caretakers of the place. Money didn't mean much to the Crumps. They gauged their worth and success by a good day's work.

"Well, lookie here what the cat's drug in." Stubby laughed. He was followed into the large open living space by his wife of nearly fifty years, Bessie.

Alex sprang out of her chair to greet them. She'd taken a liking to Bessie in the past when they spent a lot of time in the kitchen, whipping up Southern delicacies designed to harden the arteries of any human being.

"Hi, Bessie!" she exclaimed as she ran to give the older woman a hug. They say old married couples begin to look alike and the Crumps were no exception. Bessie was as round as she was tall but a perfect match for her stocky husband.

Bessie gave Alex a hug and then stood back to survey the budding young woman. "Aren't you somethin', Alex. And so tall, too! You Ryman women got all the good genes up in the big city."

Alex gave her another hug and then hugged Stubby as well. Colton noticed the transformation in her demeanor. He must've missed the connection that his daughter had made with the Crumps before, but he was glad to see the relationship rekindled.

Colton and Madison exchanged pleasantries with the Crumps as the group moved into the living area to recap the events of the last month. Jake relayed the string of coincidences that had led to their unexpected stay at the ranch.

On the Sunday before the solar flare hit, a drunk driver had careened out of control in his pickup and crashed into the gas pumps at a local convenience store in Branson. The truck burst into flames and instantly ignited the fuel, which spread across the parking lot and into the adjacent fireworks store.

"It was straight out of a Stephen King novel," explained Jake. "The local fire department quickly became overwhelmed, and the whole block began to burn."

"Did your place catch on fire too?" asked Colton. "I don't remember seeing anything about that in the news."

"No, we were okay, but the extent of the damage caused the buildings to crumble, and the street where many of the venues were located was closed. The local officials announced that it would be unsafe to operate any large-scale music events for a week or so until the cleanup could be completed and the fire department could get back on its feet."

Colton leaned back on the leather couch and contemplated the ramifications of shutting down Branson for a week. Millions of dollars were lost by the merchants, hotels, and the performance halls.

"That sounds drastic," Colton added.

"Yeah, we thought so as well, but you can't fight city hall," said Jake. "Stubby had just finished another project, and we needed a quick vacation. We loaded up and headed down. It worked out, obviously."

Alex edged up in her seat. "I feel terrible, but I haven't asked you about Chase. Did he not come with you?"

"Oh no, he's around," replied Emily. "He went huntin' with the Wyatt boy from the adjacent farm. They love to explore and look for food. I really think it's because he gets bored around here."

"He wouldn't get bored if he'd pitch in with the chores, right, Stubby?" asked Jake.

Stubby shifted uneasily from one leg to another and didn't respond. Colton surmised the older teen was not interested in the day-to-day activities of running a ranch and would prefer to play in the woods.

The awkward moment lingered, so Colton decided to change the subject. "Last night you said something about a grand tour. I'd love to see what you and Stubby have done with the place."

"Let's do it," declared Stubby, also appearing anxious to move on from the subject of Chase's contributions. "Bessie, you wanna bring Madison and Alex up to speed on what you've got goin' on?"

"Yes, sir, I do. C'mon, ladies. We'll tidy up the kitchen and I'll show you what keeps this place hummin' along."

"Okay, Colton, time for the nickel tour," said Jake as he led the men out into the bright morning sun.

CHAPTER 3

10:00 a.m., September 28
The Grounds
Shiloh Ranch

"We're up to a hundred Holsteins now," said Stubby as Jake and Colton followed along. "When I convinced Jake to add the dairy operation to the ranch, his first question was who's gonna milk 'em?" Stubby paused the tour as one of the Mexican farmhands ran up to him with a bottle of warm milk. He took a sip and smiled.

He offered the bottle to Colton, who hesitated.

"It's safe," said Stubby. "A lot of folks think that drinking milk straight from the cow isn't healthy because of *E. coli*. That may be true on those big corporate farms, but we take care of our dairy operation and the cows. They're all grass fed and monitored for sickness."

"Well, I hadn't thought about that," started Colton apologetically. "It's just that I've never drunk warm milk before, especially straight out of the cow." Colton took a sip and then another.

"Whadya think?" asked Jake.

"Not bad. Does it come in chocolate?"

Stubby laughed. "Give me that!" He took the bottle and finished it off before handing it back to the young man.

"I was hesitant when Stubby recommended the dairy cows," said Jake. "The Wyatts offered to set us up with their beef cattle, but Stubby had an overall plan."

Stubby motioned them toward the barn. "I felt like the Wyatts had enough beef cattle, so I decided to go in a different direction. The Holsteins are one of the best milk producers in the country. Most of cated in Middle and East Tennessee. That set us

...d this as a commercial operation?" asked Colton.

...ith other possibilities in mind," replied Stubby. "The ...stein cow produces about nine gallons of milk per day wh... y're lactating."

"That's a ton of milk!" exclaimed Colton.

"Well, more like ten tons over the course of a year," added Jake. "They lactate for around three hundred days."

"You can't possibly drink that much," said Colton.

The men approached a pair of the doe-eyed black and white dairy cows and rubbed their soft muzzles.

"That's true, but we have a lot of uses for the milk produced," said Stubby. "We lop off the cream, which is great for desserts and fruit. Bessie has a number of yogurt recipes, and Maria, whom you haven't met yet, is an expert cheese maker."

"I'm impressed, guys," said Colton.

Stubby pulled a block of cheese wrapped in red wax out of his pocket. He handed it to Colton. "Try this later," he said. "After they make the cheese, it's dipped in hot wax to seal it. Some is stored in the root cellar around fifty degrees. It'll last for nearly twenty years that way. We leave some at room temperature, which accelerates the aging process and creates sharper flavors. That's what you have there."

"How much do you have?" asked Colton.

"A day's milk production of roughly nine gallons will produce a one-pound block of cheese. Since the power went out, we've accumulated several hundred pounds."

"Good grief," said Colton. "Now I see why you have all the help."

The three men walked through the barn, where a couple of cows were isolated in pens. Stubby stopped to check on them.

"They're ready to calve," said Stubby.

"How do you know?" asked Colton. "They look just as fat as the others."

"Without getting too technical with a description of cow parts, you can first tell by their behavior," replied Stubby. "Initially, they separate themselves from the herd during calving season. But once they're really ready to calve, they'll pace a lot and paw at the turf. They become restless, constantly getting up and down. That's when I bring them in here."

"Are you nervous about birthing a calf without a vet around?" asked Colton.

"Yeah, a little," replied Stubby. "The Wyatts offered to help. Emily went to nursing school and trained in an emergency room, so we told them we'd trade her doctorin' for their vet experience courtesy of Lucinda Wyatt, who grew up on a cattle farm."

Jake led the group from the barn and turned to Colton. "The world has gone to crap, Colton. I don't think I need to tell you that. We all have to rely upon each other to survive. Stubby had some excellent foresight and led me into a direction of self-sustainability without me knowing it."

Stubby protested. "Now listen up, Jake. There wasn't any trickery here. Everything had a valid business purpose too."

"Oh, don't get your hackles up, old man, or I'll whoop ya." Jake, who towered over Stubby by a foot, laughed. "The decisions you made the last couple of years will save all of our lives. All I'm sayin' is if you'd come to me two years ago and said we need a hundred dairy cows in case the world comes to an end, I would have probably run ya off!"

"But Bessie could stay, right?" asked Colton, laughing.

"You betcha!" replied Jake. "Her cookin' skills allow for being opinionated."

Two men rode by on horses at a pretty quick pace. They were headed out towards the northern part of Shiloh Ranch, where the cows grazed.

"Do you think everything is okay?" asked Colton.

Jake led them to three cut tree stumps where they could sit and talk some more. "I'm sure it is. I would've been told if there was a problem."

"This was a pretty big operation before the grid collapsed," said

Stubby. "Now, we have our regular chores in addition to securing two hundred acres. Jake and I've been very concerned about people wandering onto the ranch by accident, or intentionally. I want to believe the best in our fellow man, but you never know."

Colton uttered a nervous laugh and then shook his head. He spent the next twenty minutes recapping the trip to Shiloh Ranch in detail. It was the kind of frank discussion men had without unnecessarily frightening everyone.

"Memphis has the largest population of any city in the state, and it has the highest crime rate," said Jake. "It's a matter of time before refugees spill out of Shelby County in our direction."

"Or tribes will form," interjected Stubby.

"What do you mean by that?" asked Jake.

"Well, look at it from our point of view first," replied Stubby. "Around Shiloh, Pittsburg Landing and throughout West Hardin County, landowners are binding together to protect their farms, exchange services, and trade goods. The same type of arrangement will be taking place in the cities."

"We came together in our neighborhood eventually," added Colton. "Then everyone got scared or weary of the effort and turned to the FEMA camps for protection."

Stubby walked over to the barn and grabbed a rake. He began to push the dirt and rocks around and created several piles. He continued to doodle in the dirt while he spoke. "It won't take long for the city dwellers to realize there's strength in numbers. Tribes will be formed for the purposes of looting, murder, and creating criminal gangs to survive. As is the case here, like-minded people will flock to one another, which is where things will become incredibly dangerous."

Stubby began to drag a pile of rocks away from the other piles to the edge of some fescue grass. He continued. "The smart looters will parlay their early successes in the first couple of days into employing junior mercenaries or pirates to expand their operations. Career criminals will turn into career post-collapse pirates, pouncing on the weak and taking their supplies. It's just a matter of time before they take their show on the road, leading them right to our neck of the woods."

Stubby caused the rake to scatter the pebbles into the tall grass by fanning out the rocks until they became hidden from sight.

"If they come in large enough numbers, we'd have a heckuva time turnin' them away," said Jake, who stood to take a turn with the rake. "Here's our problem."

He drew a line with the end of the handle through the dirt. Then he crossed the dirt and drew a line all the way to Stubby's piles of debris. Using the end of the rake handle as a pointer, he expressed his concerns. "Our problem is that we have our backs to the Tennessee River," started Jake, pointing to the first long line. Then, referencing the many piles of debris in the area Stubby identified as Memphis, he continued. "When these piles of human debris venture out in our direction, we'll be trapped with only one exit, the bridge into Savannah."

"I can assure you that we won't be welcome there," said Colton.

Stubby spoke up as Jake continued to push the small stones through the rich river-bottom soil. "I've known the Durhams and the Pussers my entire life. None of us will be welcome there, and Savannah will never be an option for us unless things change drastically. This leads me to my next point. While the threat from these pebbles is a potential future problem, the immediate concern I have is Ma and her son."

CHAPTER 4

11:00 a.m., September 28
The Grounds
Shiloh Ranch

Madison was in awe at the extent that Shiloh Ranch had changed from a weekend getaway into a fully operational farm complete with dairy cows. She no longer looked at Bessie as an older woman who was an expert in Southern cooking. This lady had skills learned through years of practice that would be critical to their survival.

"This is the garden," said Bessie. "It doesn't look like much now because we've harvested all of the spring and summer crops. We've just finished planting spinach, lettuce and radishes to produce a little somethin' during the early winter months."

"There are some things growing over there," said Madison, pointing toward three plots of the garden adjacent to the horse stalls.

"That'll be next week's project," said Bessie. "Our ground crops like potatoes, carrots and onions will be ready to harvest then."

"You seem very well organized," added Madison. "None of this was here before."

"Well, we did have the container gardens behind the house, but they were used primarily for flowers. Now, they are part of the overall growing program. Each one contains a variety of foods like tomatoes, peppers, and cucumbers. We use companion gardening so they all play well together."

A covered pavilion was in full use by some of the Allens' employees. Fires were burning, and a full-blown canning operation was underway.

"Come on," urged Bessie. "There's someone I'd like you to meet."

Madison followed along and watched in amazement as the vegetables were prepared and the fires were stoked. A woman wiped her hands on her apron and approached the group.

"*Hola!*"

"Hey, Maria, please meet our friends from Nashville," said Emily. The woman shook Madison's hand.

"I'm Maria Garcia," she said. "It is my pleasure to meet you." Madison noticed that Maria enunciated her words very deliberately. Although she had a heavy Spanish accent, she spoke slowly to use proper English.

"It's nice to meet you, Maria. I'm Madison Ryman."

"*Oh, bueno!* Your husband is a country star too, like Mr. Jake?"

Madison and Emily laughed. "Oh, no. Colton, my husband, only sings around the campfire. We'll leave the good singing to Mr. Jake. Goodness, it's very hot in here." The heat from the fires was staying within the pavilion, as there was very little breeze.

Maria smiled and nodded before walking back to a long concrete countertop covered with canning supplies. Ball jars, Tattler lids, and other tools were all in use, as Maria had a very organized crew performing the difficult task of canning without electricity.

"We have to keep the fires hot and at a fairly even temperature to keep the water at a rolling boil," said Bessie. "Before the lights went out, we could use the propane gas grills or even the kitchen stove to heat the pressure cookers. Propane is in short supply and we use the solar power primarily for refrigeration. Burning a fire makes more sense."

"There's no shortage of trees," said Madison as she looked around the perimeter of Shiloh Ranch.

"That's true, but we didn't cut enough wood in the spring to anticipate this," said Bessie. "Seasoned firewood may become a problem if we have a harsh winter."

"Can't you just cut more?" asked Madison.

"We can, but pine takes about six months to season and hardwoods like oak take as much as a year. Plus, there's the problem of fuel for the chainsaws. We don't have the manpower to send the ranch hands out foraging for gasoline. Stubby has plenty of diesel for the farm equipment, but gas is a scarce resource."

Madison shook her head as she looked around the ranch. "We had four extra cans of gasoline, but those fools shot holes in the cans and most of it drained onto the highway."

"You were shot at?" asked Emily, unaware of the details of the Rymans' journey to Shiloh Ranch.

"Emily, you've no idea what it's like out there. We've been shot at and we had to shoot back." Madison looked at the ground and became teary-eyed. Only the sight of Alex riding on the back of a beautiful spotted Appaloosa in the horse pen prevented her from becoming more emotional.

"Really?" asked Emily, appearing to be shocked at this revelation.

"Unfortunately, yes. It's a different world out there, Emily. It's a different world just across the river too."

The three women stood silently for a moment until Bessie suggested they walk over toward the horse pen. Madison regained her composure as Bessie, who sensed what Madison was feeling, comforted her and led her by the arm.

The guys approached from the other side and eventually all of them were watching Alex take the distinctive leopard-spotted horse by the lead as she walked her around the circular structure.

"Hey, Allie-Cat," shouted Colton. "Who's your new friend?"

"Hi, Daddy! This is Snowflake. She's an Appaloosa!"

"Javy, come on over," instructed Stubby. A Mexican man not much taller than Stubby removed his straw hat and joined the group. Stubby explained that Javier Garcia had joined the Shiloh Ranch a couple of years ago as a general ranch hand and ultimately brought his wife Maria to America to work as the Allens' housekeeper.

As the dairy operation grew, Javier, who preferred to be called Javy, added some friends from the mountain cattle ranches near the Mexican border of West Texas, who were most likely in the country illegally. Stubby didn't ask and didn't care. The men worked hard, were loyal, and asked that virtually all of their earnings be sent to their families in Mexico via Western Union. That proved to Stubby they were honorable and loyal.

"I gave up trying to understand the politics of immigration a long time ago," said Stubby as Javy returned to help Alex with Snowflake. "All I know is this. If I had to be in a foxhole again, any of these men would have my back."

Alex joined the group as they started back toward the house when a gust of wind shifted the breeze and a horrific odor into their nostrils.

"Whoa!" exclaimed Colton. "What the heck is that?"

"Ha-ha." Jake laughed. "We showed y'all the good stuff first, but we've saved the best for last."

"Ladies and gentleman," started Jake, removing his signature charcoal black snapback cowboy hat and using his best circus ringmaster gestures, "presenting the Shiloh Ranch latrine and composting facility. Take a whiff, friends!"

"Ugh," groaned Alex.

Stubby stepped forward and took over the presentation. "Jake can be a little dramatic at times. I think he'll be a mighty fine entertainer when he grows up. We have indoor plumbing in the main house, as you all know. Our water wells are scattered around the property and each of the pumps is outfitted with a small solar array providing it power. This keeps water running to the toilets."

"Is this the sewage treatment plant?" asked Madison as she burrowed her nose in her sleeve.

"Sort of, Madison," replied Stubby. "A septic tank and sewer system has been in place since the home was built. But this summer I added a manure compost pit to create manure tea."

"No way!" lamented Alex. "You guys are out of your minds."

"Take it easy, Alex." Stubby laughed. "It's not to drink. It is, however, simply the best organic concentrated fertilizer you can make. What you have here is a self-contained sewage facility for both human and animal waste designed to create liquid compost made from manure steeped in water, just like you'd steep a cup of tea."

"I used to like tea," murmured Madison under her breath.

"It's high in nutrients, especially nitrogen," added Bessie. "We put it on all our vegetables, especially the green leafy ones. The liquid manure really soaks into the soil and hits the roots."

"Gross," said Alex. "Will it make the vegetables taste like, um, poop?"

"No, honey," replied Bessie. "If anything, manure tea brings out the natural colors and flavors of organic vegetables. It's easy to make and we can create a fresh batch in about two weeks."

"Fresh?"

"Well, you know, a new batch."

Stubby led the entourage back towards the main house and away from the ripe stench of the compost.

"Well, I wouldn't want that job," said Alex, who quickly broke away from the pack to avoid the smell.

The covered porch of the main house wrapped the entire perimeter of the home. The group pulled seven rocking chairs onto the east deck. A cool breeze emanated from the Tennessee River, which could be seen in the distance through the now leafless oaks.

Emily and Bessie went inside and retrieved a pitcher of sweet tea and glasses for all. They tinkled with the sound of ice. The scene was reminiscent of any Southern home's porch in normal times.

"If my memory serves me correctly, I think you'll like this," said Bessie as she handed Colton his glass. "Do you still like an Arnold Palmer?"

Arnold Palmer, the golfing legend from the sixties and seventies, created his own Southern concoction consisting of sweet tea and roughly half lemonade. Palmer and his wife experimented with the mix at their home until it became his signature drink. In his memoirs, Palmer recalled how he ordered his favorite drink while in a Palm Springs restaurant and a woman overheard him place the order. She told her server that she wanted an Arnold Palmer and the simple drink became legendary.

Colton took a sip and smiled. "Sweet nectar of the South. Let's raise our glasses to the recently departed Arnold Palmer. God rest your soul, my friend."

As everyone raised their glasses, Colton continued. "I wasn't sure if I'd ever see an ice cube again. I have to say that you guys are very well prepared for the apocalypse."

Jake responded, "We owe it all to Stubby and Bessie. They had a homesteader mindset, which has translated into one heck of an operation, as you've seen. But, as you may recall, Stubby is a former Army Ranger. He understands weaponry and defensive measures that, frankly, never crossed my mind until the compost hit the fan."

Stubby laughed and then stood to sit on the rail, where he could face everyone. "Folks, all of the things that we have goin' for us here won't make a hill of beans' difference if we can't defend it. Simply said, *if you can't defend it, it isn't yours.*"

Madison nodded her head in agreement. The Rymans had experienced firsthand what desperate people would do to survive. They had defended their neighborhood and their home from depraved human beings who were willing to kill to take what they needed or wanted.

Madison set aside her glass of sweet tea and spoke up. "Listen, we've come here uninvited, but we can help. We want to be a part of your family and pull our weight. None of us knows anything about gardening or milking cows or composting, but we're willing to learn."

Alex chimed in, "Speak for yourself on that composting part, Mom."

"Maddie is right about that," added Colton, ignoring Alex's comment. He turned his attention to Jake but then looked directly at Stubby. "There is one thing we've experienced that only you've seen in your lifetime—the depravity of man. We'd appreciate some training in the use of firearms. We'll help defend Shiloh Ranch as well as make it a place where we can all live together without fearing for our lives. We'd like to make this our home too."

CHAPTER 5

Sunset, September 29
Cherry Mansion
Savannah

The Brumby Rocker was far from being in bad condition despite being one of the oldest pieces of furniture remaining in the historic Cherry Mansion. The white paint looked a little faded from its exposure to the setting sun, an event the Brumby had experienced since it arrived on the porch in 1933. Like its present occupant, the bones of the Brumby were pretty old, but they were still sturdy. Both the chair and Ma Durham had a steely resolve—hardened by years of weathering storms.

Creak, creak, creak.

The Brumby Rocker continued its back and forth motion as Ma slowly pushed it on the old wooden floorboards of the covered porch. She sat alone with her thoughts. Her boyfriend, Bill Cherry, the former president of the Hardin County Chamber of Commerce, was the owner of Cherry Mansion and a direct descendant of the original owners. Wild Bill, as he'd become known around Hardin County, had a penchant for partying, which Ma tolerated to an extent. Like so many other men in her life, Wild Bill Cherry was nothing more than a tool to advance her goals. She didn't care for alcohol but allowed Wild Bill his fun as long as he obeyed. It was a relationship that suited both parties.

Creak, creak, creak.

Ma, like the Brumby Rocker, was showing telltale signs of aging, including crow's feet, gray hair, and older looking hands. She stared down at her bony, wrinkled digits that resembled those of a much older woman than Ma's mid-fifties. She realized long ago that she was not a looker like many of the hussies she'd grown up around. Ma knew, however, that she had feminine wiles, a woman's power, which she covertly used to influence the men who needed it.

Men were weak in Ma's mind. For the most part, their minds were focused on one thing. Her ability to manipulate men when she was younger brought her into a position of power in Hardin County. After the solar flare brought the power down, she created a brilliant plan to control the horny fools of the county, including Wild Bill and her son the sheriff, Junior, to do her bidding.

She provided them sex but not from her, of course. There were plenty of others around to do the dirty work of servicing the menfolk within her charge. Initially, it was designed as a barter system of sorts.

"Everyone must pull their weight," she'd told the townspeople in those early days after the grid collapsed.

The young women of the town were told that they could either work at the Vulcan Quarry or they could do other, less strenuous work. Initially, many of the women were appalled at the suggestion. They would not sacrifice their morals by having sex with Ma's crew. But after several days of pounding rock at the quarry, the façade of chastity came crashing down. Brothels controlled by Ma sprang up around Savannah to service the men.

Not unexpectedly, the men would get out of hand from time to time, usually as a result of too much alcohol. They would abuse the women, and soon the brothels began to empty of able-bodied employees. The women of Savannah simply ran away.

This was bad for morale, in Ma's opinion, so a solution had to be reached. She needed new recruits, and she quickly developed a new plan of attack. She was proud of two major decisions she'd made related to the collapse of the power grid.

First, Ma considered herself brilliant for having armed men ready to secure all of the major retail stores around the town. She had a hunch the solar flare might cause more damage than the media let on. She was right. When it came crashing down, she instantly became the power broker she'd always dreamt of being. Controlling the government as mayor was one thing. But there were restrictions, rules, and *watchers*—prying eyes making sure she *did the right thing*. But after the collapse, she could run things the way she saw fit. Uninhibited. Lawless.

As this newfound unrestricted power took hold, Ma solved several problems with one brilliant plan. She used the Emergency Broadcast Network and the local radio station to invite folks from all over to join them in Savannah. The new residents needed to meet certain criteria. She was looking for working automobiles, muscle, medical personnel, and more girls for the boys.

Her invitations via the radio broadcasts worked. Cars began to arrive from far and wide, and they were greeted by Wild Bill. He would prescreen the occupants of the vehicles to determine if they helped fill the town's needs, and if they did, they were taken to the county jail for additional screening.

Their cars and belongings were confiscated. The men were told harm would come to their women if they didn't go to work in the quarry. The women were then placed into sexual slavery.

The newcomers didn't always cooperate and the result was the execution of the men in front of the women. The women were then turned over to Junior and Wild Bill, who *trained* them.

Creak. Creak. Creak.

Ma didn't care. She had a town to run and expansion plans in mind.

Nooooooo. Pleeeeeease. Nooooooo.

The screams could barely be heard over the creaking of the Brumby Rocker. If a stranger walked onto the front porch of the Cherry Mansion, they might have heard the muffled sounds emanating from the basement cells, which had been built during the Civil War. However, those strangers would be focused on the aging woman slowly rocking on the porch of this magnificent antebellum home as she watched the sun set on another day.

THANK YOU FOR READING THIS EXCERPT OF
SHILOH RANCH, book four of The Blackout series.

The entire six book series is available on Amazon.com.

You may purchase signed copies, paperback and hardcover editions of Bobby Akart's books on www.BobbyAkart.com.

Made in the USA
Columbia, SC
21 January 2021